Acclaim for Ellen Gilchrist's

The Cabal
and Other Stories

"Gilchrist's deft gift for dialogue, coupled with wise and humorous insights into characters that seem pulled straight out of life, make *The Cabal and Other Stories* sparkle."
—*St. Louis Post-Dispatch*

"The charm and eccentricity of Southern Womanhood and her kissin' cousin, Southern Kinfolk, are revisited by Ellen Gilchrist in her newest batch of kudzu-covered short stories. . . . With her long line of books on southern life and love, Gilchrist has made the list of fine storytellers of that particular reality."
—Ann Prichard, *USA Today*

"Ellen Gilchrist is a writer to be reckoned with. Dazzling, talkative, some might even say chatty, her narrators and characters have kept up their jaunty, funny, and occasionally heartbreaking side of the conversation for years. . . . As is so often the case with Gilchrist, the story is not about a single, isolated protagonist but a larger ensemble. She likes to have one rambunctious character get everyone else all riled up and then sit back and see what happens. Mostly what happens is lots more talking, and this is the charm of Gilchrist's writing."
—Diana Abu-Jaber, *Portland Oregonian*

"Full of Gilchrist's elegant wit and personality. . . . Each story is taut and forceful."
—Brian Baise, *San Francisco Chronicle*

"Gilchrist demonstrates in her latest collection of short fiction not only that she is a remarkably adept storyteller but also that the novella, particularly in her hands, is a highly effective literary form—one that offers a more involved and involving plot and more complete character development than one finds in short fiction, while at the same time more tightly structured than most full-length novels. . . . In 'The Cabal,' and in the short stories that follow, Gilchrist is southern to the core. . . . She glimpses colorful but very realistic people's lives and isolates their search for a degree of inner peace." —Brad Hooper, *Booklist*

"Ellen Gilchrist has long been revered by critics and fiction enthusiasts as a voice of the South that has no parallel when she lights on characters like Rhoda in *Victory Over Japan*. And like that indomitable pair, Miss Crystal and Traceleen, who strike out across the pages of her stories in their own gaits, speaking their own brand of southernese and twisting their worlds to their own particular views. . . . Memories flow, and delicious intrigues follow." —Annette Sanford, *Dallas Morning News*

"Readers will recognize Gilchrist's signature narrative style, one that is (implausibly) dispassionate and boisterous at the same time—as if nothing about human nature could shock her even as she relishes the spectacle of her characters colliding, blundering, and negotiating their lives." —Jane Kollias, *Washington Post Book World*

"The world Ellen Gilchrist unfolds in her vivid new story collection is rich with intimate exchanges between finely etched characters. The stories here—particularly in the title novella—are convincingly chaotic. Characters' lives and interests intersect and bump against one another in ways that are at once random and entirely natural."

—Jim Gladstone, *New York Times Book Review*

THE CABAL

AND OTHER STORIES

THE CABAL

AND OTHER STORIES

ELLEN GILCHRIST

BACK BAY BOOKS

LITTLE, BROWN AND COMPANY

BOSTON   NEW YORK   LONDON

Originally published in hardcover by Little, Brown and Company, April 2000
First Back Bay paperback edition, June 2002

The characters in this book are imaginary.
Any similarity to real persons, either living or dead,
is purely coincidental and not intended by the author.

Library of Congress Cataloging-in-Publication Data

Gilchrist, Ellen.
  The cabal and other stories / by Ellen Gilchrist. — 1st ed.
    p.   cm.
  Contents: The cabal — The sanguine blood of men — Hearts of
Dixie — The survival of the fittest — Bare ruined choirs, where
late the sweet birds sang — The big cleanup.
  ISBN 0-316-31491-9 (hc)/0-316-16922-6 (pb)
  1. Southern States — Social life and customs Fiction. I. Title.
PS3557.I34258C34 2000
813'.54 — dc21   99-36893

10 9 8 7 6 5 4 3 2 1

Q-MART

Printed in the United States of America

For
Marshall, Ellen, Aurora, Zachary, Cameron,
Felicia, Augustus, Noelle, Abigail, Juliet, William,
and for their beautiful and steadfast mothers

"He longed for the mirth
Of the populous earth
And the sanguine blood of men."

J. R. R. TOLKIEN

CONTENTS

THE CABAL

A SHORT NOVEL

PREFACE

THIS IS THE STORY of a group of people who had a bizarre and unexpected thing happen to them. Their psychiatrist went crazy and started injecting himself with drugs. The most useful and dependable man in their lives became a maniac in the true sense of the word. He was the glue that held their group together. He was the one who had taught them to trust one another. He had told each one of them the best things he knew about the others. One by one he had planted seeds of kindness and empathy in their hearts. For example, if the members of the group thought of Celia Montgomery, they didn't instantly think, She's the richest woman in the South. Instead they thought, She truly loves the arts, she loves the theater, she loved my performance, she loved my book, she has overcome terrible health problems, she never complains, she can be depended upon.

If they thought of Augustus Hailey, they didn't think, He's *queer*. They thought, How could anyone be that helpful and polite twenty-four hours a day? I have never known a man as full of goodwill toward the world. His uncle worked with Jonas Salk. We might all be dead of polio if it weren't for his family and their four-generation support of scientific research.

These were ideas Jim Jaspers planted in their heads. Later, when he went mad, they didn't know what to do. It tore the fabric of their common reality. A brilliant, useful man who had spent his days solving other people's problems became the cause of them. Much harm was done, many sleepless nights were spent by the twenty-two people who had put their lives in his hands. This is the story of some of them. It is not a warning or a proscription. It is an attempt to keep an account.

∾ 1 ∾

CAROLINE JONES was driving her Cabriolet to Mississippi as fast as she dared, watching ahead for cops and passing on the left side. It was Thursday and she had to be there Monday morning. She was going to Millsaps College to fill in for a poet who had died the week before. The poet had been a black woman with an attitude so big no one was surprised when she died and only a few people were sorry. Still, her death had left the English department in a mess.

This was lucky for Caroline as it had given her a chance to regain her status in academia. She had ruined her reputation by quitting a job at Yale to go whore for the movies. It was not entirely Caroline's fault that she had been seduced by Hollywood. Her parents had given her bad advice. They had taught her to worship money over all other things. It would be years before Caroline began to recover from the greed they had placed in her heart, but that is another story. For now she was driving to Jackson, and she was in a hurry. When the movie scam fell through, she had been forced to go back to Nashville and live with her parents. She had lived there for seven months while she searched for a job. She had almost given up hope when the call came from an old friend at Millsaps.

"There's a job teaching Shakespeare and poetry," her friend said. "You'd have to be here in a week. I'll find you a place to live and in the meantime you can stay with me. I told them you were the best young poet in the South. So the job is yours if you'll take it."

"How much?"

"You won't like it. Thirty thousand. A third of what they were paying Topeka. They see this as a chance to recoup those losses. But the job is here, if you'll take it."

"I'll be there. Anything to get away from here. What do I have to do?"

"Start packing. I'm excited. It will be marvelous to have you here. A dream come true." He giggled, then laughed out loud. His name was Augustus Hailey. He was a good-looking, tall blond man who had been her closest friend at Vanderbilt. He had been her confidant and running buddy. He had kept her grounded and made her laugh. He had gone shopping with her and talked her into cutting her hair. Also, he had believed in her poetry, even when she stopped believing in it herself.

"If we're both there, something will happen," she said. "I've never been in Mississippi, Augustus. I don't think I've ever crossed the border."

"I'll take care of you. You know that. Is there anything you need?"

"Start finding me a boyfriend. A house, a boyfriend, a health food store. I've decided that's all anybody needs."

"Well, I don't know about the health food store but there's a theater group I think you'll like. Actually, it's a cabal. The people who run this town are in it. They all go to the same psychiatrist. Isn't that a kick? On Monday morning he gets to hear six different versions of the cast party from the weekend before." Augustus was in high gear, his imagination and good humor taking flight at the thought of having his old friend for a colleague.

"I didn't know psychiatrists practiced on Mondays. The two I saw never went to the office on Monday."

"Well, whatever day they go in. What were you doing at a psychiatrist's office? You're the sanest person I know."

"Quitting Yale? Going to Los Angeles? By the time I got home I was a basket case. I was down to size-four Gap jeans."

"You must have looked fabulous."

"I looked like a refugee. Also, I haven't written a poem in fourteen months. Maybe I'll never write again."

"We'll see about that. Well, get off the phone. Start packing. I'll tell the board the good news. The head of the department will call you later. Her name's Gay Wileman. You'll like her. She's a good person, one of us."

Now Caroline was on her way. She had crossed the state line into Mississippi and was coming down the Natchez Trace Parkway, "the old buffalo trail," Eudora Welty called it. Caroline was peopling the woods with Miss Welty's characters as she drove. I'll do a good job for these people, she was thinking. I'll teach as hard as I can. I'll teach the dumb ones and the smart ones. I'll give something to every student if it kills me. Then I'll start writing again. If I'm teaching poetry, it will make me write. Well, who cares if I write or not? Who gives a damn about publishing some crappy little poems in magazines that don't pay? Where did I get the idea that I'm a poet? There're only one or two poets in any generation. That confessional dribble I've been writing isn't poetry. I should be writing plays. Maybe this theater needs a play. If they're rich

there would be backing. Well, forget about that. I have a job teaching
school and I've got to take that seriously this time. She hunkered down
over the wheel of her little green Cabriolet. It had been her graduation
present from Vanderbilt. It had two hundred thousand miles on it but it
would last until she could afford another.

Outside of Tupelo, Mississippi, it began to rain. It was raining so
hard the windshield wipers could barely move. The small car began to
weave from side to side. Caroline stopped underneath an overpass and
watched the rain come down on the kudzu-covered hills. She reached in
the backseat and found a sandwich her mother had put in the car. She
ate the sandwich. She opened a bag of cookies and ate one. Then she
did an unexpected thing. She pulled a notebook out of a side pocket of
the car and began to write a poem. It was the first one she had written in
more than a year.

THE MUSE OF CHOCOLATE CHIP COOKIES

Sugar makes me know the rain
As if I were rain and it were me
Here at the top of the food chain
Burning dinosaurs and trees
In my Cabriolet, punching holes
In the ozone
Ready to rape and pillage
Or be pillaged, we shall see. . . .

"Oh, God, that's so stupid," she said and kissed the page she had written. She pressed the notepad against her chest. I will write a play, she
decided. If Tennessee can make plays out of his family, so can I. I'll
write about Granddaddy bossing Daddy around and Momma sweeping

the porch three times a day and the money they won't spend and their twin beds and Aunt Lannie across the street smoking herself to death in that decaying house and DeDe and me up in the attic drinking crème de menthe in July. My family's as dysfunctional as anyone else's. Just because they're attractive and don't abuse their children doesn't mean they didn't harm us in other ways. I'll start the play with Mother sweeping the porch. Then Daddy comes out with a water cannon to try to get the squirrels off the roof. Then Teddy comes across the porch with his Boy Scout hatchet to break down the door because I locked him out of the house. Audiences are mine for the taking. They'll be riveted. They'll believe anything I show them.

Caroline ate a second cookie, spilling half the crumbs on the lap of her white pants. The rain was slacking now. She pulled back out onto the highway and drove on into Jackson.

She called Augustus from the car phone when she was on the outskirts of town. He was standing in the driveway when she arrived. The house was perfect, as she had known it would be, a two-story stucco house painted off-white with a lavender door. There was a line of crepe myrtle trees in full bloom beside a brick wall. It was a jewel of a house as he was a jewel of a man. I don't need a boyfriend, Caroline decided. Augustus will be enough for me.

"You're just in time, Puss," he said. "There's a funeral this afternoon that you must attend. It's Jean Andry Lyles, the most powerful woman who ever lived on the planet, I'm sure. She founded the theater and ran it for years. Now she's died suddenly at sixty and her family is fighting over the funeral with her twenty-nine-year-old lover. There will be two funerals actually, one on each side of the cathedral. Thank God you're here. I won't have to sit with either faction. We'll sit up in the balcony and watch the fireworks. Oh, it's going to be wonderful. Jean would have loved it. They were fighting over her Rolodex, last I heard. God knows what's transpired by now."

"Her Rolodex?"

"To get the numbers to call about the death. She knew everyone, of course. Peter Brook, Uta Hagen, the president, senators, scads of movie stars."

"How did she die?"

"Suddenly. That's how they're dying here this summer. It's so ironic. First Topeka, now Jean. They hated each other. Topeka bowed to no one and Jean had to be queen. Well, now you will meet the cabal. Most of them will be on Jean's family's side. But since she was a civil rights worker in the sixties, that faction will be split."

"How much time do I have?"

"Several hours. They had to change the time of the funeral because the minister they wanted had another one at two. The lover wanted her cremated because she told him that's what she wanted but he's been overruled by the family. It will be an old-fashioned burial."

"How big is her family?"

"Five sons and a dozen nieces and nephews. It will be the event of the year. I'm so glad you're here."

"Grab some suitcases. I came to stay, as you will notice."

She picked up a cosmetic kit and a suit bag and Augustus followed with two large suitcases. He was so agile and strong, besides being handsome, that it made Caroline sick to think he was gay. Goddamn all the good-looking men being gay, she decided. It isn't fair. It proves there is no God. There might be a Mad Hatter but no God would do this to women.

She followed him through the lavender door and down a marble hall, which opened into a long narrow dining room that looked as if it belonged in the Cloisters. Then across a green and white kitchen and up a wide staircase to a tower. "I designed and built this," he said, turning on the stairs. "It's a place to watch stars. What do you think?"

The stairs ended in a round room with skylights and a curved wall of windows that looked out upon a garden. In a corner was a bed covered with a dark blue satin comforter. There were roomy dressers. A hall led to a sitting room with a telescope pointing through another skylight.

"It's heaven, Augustus. I get to live here?"

"As long as you like. I've found you an apartment to look at but it won't be available for a month. I'd adore to have you here if you're comfortable with this."

He stood in the doorway smiling. She went to him and put her arms around his waist and held him there. They had met their first day at Vanderbilt, standing in line to sign up to work for the student newspaper. He had been skinnier then but just as handsome, just as self-assured. She had been burning up in a new sweater set. "I love a woman who will wear a sweater set when it's ninety degrees in the shade," he had said. "I'm Augustus Hailey from Oxford, Mississippi. Let's go get a cup of coffee when we finish here." He had smiled a fabulous wide smile, and Caroline had made her first gay friend. There hadn't been any gay men at her prep school and there were none who admitted it in the boys' schools that came to the dances. But Caroline was a reader. She knew about gay men and she guessed Augustus was one before he told her. He told her as soon as they sat down at a table in the student union. "I can't decide what to do about rush," he began. "I don't know if I can get anything done in a house full of wild boys. I'm gay, you know. I'm in love with an older man, the son of a music executive. He's an SAE but he never goes over there unless he's really bored. He wants me to pledge SAE but my uncles were Kappa Alphas here. I'm only going through rush to please my mother. Do you think we should give in to that sort of pressure, or not?"

"I don't know. Do they care if you're gay? I mean, the fraternity boys?"

"Are you kidding? With my looks and grades, not to mention my family's money, they wouldn't care if I had two heads. They have to have people who study and make good grades. They're always in trouble over their grade point average. My lover, Sam Cook, is practically the king at SAE."

"Well, I guess it depends on what you want to do." Caroline was completely entranced. As she continued to be for the four years of their friendship. As she was now, looking around the gorgeous, perfect house Augustus had built and decorated in his spare time. Caroline had lots of interesting and intelligent men in her own family. But she had never met one who could decorate a house.

"The funeral starts at four," Augustus said. "You're doing me a vast favor by going with me. Besides, it will be a wonderful way to see the cabal. They'll be at their best and worst, on common and alien ground, with the body of a queen at stake. It will be interesting to see who talks to whom, who consoles whom, who goes afterward to the son's house and who goes to the lover's. He shared it with Jean and I heard it now belongs to the sons. Jean didn't know she was going to die, of course, but even if she had I wouldn't put it past her to have left the house to her sons, just to make sure there were fireworks."

"The sons and the lover hate each other?"

"They wouldn't even come to the theater on the same nights, even when Jean was acting or directing. Oh, it's marvelously juicy. You will go with me, won't you?"

"I wouldn't miss it. Let me put on a suit."

Augustus went back down the stairs and Caroline tore open a suitcase and began to get dressed. She had a new beige suit she had been meaning to save for the first faculty meeting, but she put it on with her new Donna Karan hose and a string of pearls she had borrowed from her mother. She started to add a colored scarf, but already she was under Augustus's spell and decided to stay minimal and chic. She even gave up rolling up the waistband of her skirt and compromised by wearing high-heeled sandals instead of pumps.

"What are you doing?" Augustus yelled up the stairs. "Do you need any help?"

"I'm almost finished. I'm trying to be perfect so you won't complain." She moved down the stairs holding in her stomach and with her head held regally and high.

"Fabulous suit," he said. He was standing at the landing wearing a suit he had ordered from a tailor in London. An off-white shirt, a pale peach-and-orchid-colored tie. He smiled his best smile. "But I'd lose the sandals. Don't you have some pumps?"

"I'm wearing these shoes. I've got to find a boyfriend, after all."

"One that wants a lady, I would hope."

"That won't work. Let's go. I'm wearing the sandals. They're Cole Haan. I spent my last paycheck on them before I quit."

"I'm rethinking them. After all, it is hot still."

They went out through the garage and got into Augustus's convertible and drove through Jackson to the Episcopal cathedral. It was downtown on the main street across from the governor's mansion. People were coming from every direction. Dressed-up, elegant-looking men and women converging on the church from north, east, south, and west. A young man in a pinstriped suit was standing at the top of the stairs to the cathedral. Beside him was a coffee-colored nun in her habit. On the other side was a tall woman in a mauve dress. The men and women going up the stairs either stopped and talked to these three or passed them by without turning their heads. "It's started," Augustus exclaimed. "Oh, my God, it's happening before they get inside. See the young man on the stairs? That's Mack Stanford, Jean's lover. Isn't he gorgeous? He puts out so much heat it's unbelievable. He worshiped her. Now he's going to be kicked out of his own house by the sons. He had the Rolodex this morning, but I heard they were going to make him turn it over."

"He's twenty-nine?"

"Just right for you, you're thinking. Well, he was completely fascinated by her. He won't be ripe for picking this semester."

"Who's the nun?"

"The mother superior of an order down in Madison County. They come to the plays. They turned out in force for *Tiny Alice.* We revived it last year. They brought a bus to *The Skin of Our Teeth.* Jean cultivated them, and I think I heard somewhere Mack was a Roman Catholic. The tall woman is Cindy Milligan. She's a power in the arts, one of the cabal. Her husband owns an outdoor advertising business. They're rolling in dough."

They had parked the car and were walking toward the cathedral. They were saved speaking to Mack because he and his coterie went into the church before Augustus and Caroline reached the top of the stairs.

The church was packed. There were only a few seats left in the back, so Augustus got his wish and they went up the stairs to the balcony. In old times it had been the place where the slaves sat.

An usher led them to seats in the second row. He handed them a small printed sheet. It was an outline of the service and the music, mostly Bach. There was one surprise. A soprano from the Delta was going to sing "Ave Maria" and "The Great Speckled Bird."

"Who thought that up?" Augustus whispered, pointing to the paper. "Jean would die."

"Well, she did." Caroline giggled, smothered the giggle, and squeezed Augustus's hand. It was already the best funeral she had ever attended. Augustus was the most fun of anyone she had ever known. It was too good to be true that they were in this town together.

Everyone was seated and the organ was playing but no minister approached the pulpit. Mack was talking excitedly with a man seated next to him. The man got up and walked up the aisle and around the coffin and went off into the part of the church from which the minister usually entered. The crowd stirred and whispered, then was quiet.

"Oh, God," Augustus said. "You know there were supposed to be people speaking, but at the last minute that was canceled. Mack had asked me to say something. Well, maybe that's going back in. The man who got up is William Harbison, a lawyer who's integral to the theater. He's a friend of Mack's. He's coming back. He's sitting down." The man had returned to Mack's pew. There was much whispering. The organist had finished all the Bach on the program and was playing Pachelbel.

Mack and the woman in mauve stood up and moved out into the aisle and went down and around the coffin and over to where Jean's family was sitting. Mack began talking to one of the sons and pointing to the program. The choir director left the organ loft and came down the stairs and joined the group. Two of the sons stood up. One of them took Mack by the arm. Mack pulled his arm away. A tall man wearing a black suit and a black shirt came running down the aisle, tearing down the aisle, sprinting down the aisle. When he got to the men he began to talk and they all listened.

"That's Jim Jaspers," Augustus whispered. "The shrink I told you about. What do you think they're doing? I think Mack wants to say something and they won't let him."

"Jesus Christ," Caroline whispered back. "In an Episcopal cathedral."

Jim Jaspers had his arm around Mack Stanford. There was much nodding of heads. A baby began to cry, louder and louder. The organist began to play Handel. The people gathered in the aisle went back around the coffin and across the left transept and disappeared through a door.

The choir director returned first. He walked to the back of the nave and talked to a woman wearing a green tweed suit. She followed him down the aisle and up onto the sanctuary and across it to the choir.

In a few minutes everyone else reappeared and returned to their seats, except for Jim Jaspers. He walked down the aisle to the back of the nave and stood behind the last pew.

The baby was crying louder and louder. He was screaming. The mother and father stood up and hurried down the aisle carrying the baby. It was twenty-four minutes after four.

The crowd had been completely quiet for the first fifteen minutes. Now they were beginning to talk among themselves. The coffin stood in a sea of whispering voices. A slant of light from a rose window fell upon the lilies that adorned it. "Just like the mummies," Caroline whispered. "Maybe we had to wait for that light."

The minister came back into the church. He bowed his head to the altar, then walked down to the side of the coffin. "Our soprano has developed a problem with her voice," he announced. "We are sorry for this delay but we were waiting to see if she might recover. In her absence, Miss Carlene Hunt from Yazoo City will be singing the 'Ave Maria,' accompanied by our organist, John Zavier Semmes."

"Mack got rid of 'The Great Speckled Bird,'" Augustus whispered. "What a coup! I didn't know he had it in him. Oh, this is truly fabulous."

The minister bowed again to the altar, then climbed briskly up to the pulpit and began the Service for the Burial of the Dead. "I am the resurrection and the life, saith the Lord: he that believeth in me, though he were dead, yet shall he live. . . ."

Two women came hurrying down the aisle and squeezed into seats next to Mack and his entourage. "The lesbian food editor of the paper and her girlfriend," Augustus whispered. "She worshiped Jean. She waited on her hand and foot. She's always late everywhere she goes. This time she lucked in."

In an effort to pull the funeral back together the minister was reading every prayer in the burial service. With only the "Ave Maria" and two hymns he was worried it would not last long enough to be effective. He was an old friend of Jean Lyles and had played the Cardinal opposite Jean's Alice in the theater's original production of *Tiny Alice* and also in the revival, which Jean had directed. He had approved of not having people speak at the service, since obviously Jean wouldn't be able to control what they said, but all this changing music at the last minute was upsetting, not to mention all the public displays of animosity. Plus, the young woman from the Delta had left the cathedral in tears. "The days of our age are threescore years and ten," he read. "And though men be so strong that they come to fourscore years, yet is their strength then but labor and sorrow; so soon passeth it away and we are gone."

He finished the *Domine refugium* and started in on the *Domine illuminatio*. The food editor was weeping uncontrollably into a handkerchief. "The Lord is my light and my salvation," he read. "Whom then shall I fear? The Lord is the strength of my life; of whom shall I be afraid?"

The air conditioning hummed. The smell of expensive perfume was everywhere. Mack and his entourage faced the front without looking at the family. The family faced the front without looking toward Mack. The minister read on. "Oh, hide not thy face from me," he read. "Nor cast thou servant away in displeasure."

Among her children Jean Lyles had a favorite daughter-in-law. Her name was Lauren Gail and she was the mother of Jean's oldest grandson and granddaughter. Both of them were children who were attractive and kind and did well in school. Jean adored them and adored Lauren Gail for having them and for putting up with their father. Lauren Gail was a true Yankee, raised in New England and educated in experimental schools. She was a sculptor and a painter and the kindest person Jean had ever known. Lauren Gail was completely without guile, having never been given any reason to lie or be on her guard when she was a child. She was an enigma in Jackson, Mississippi, where she wore old clothes, gained weight after her children were born, joined every effort to advance public education or protect the environment, and always had time to talk to Jean on the phone as long as Jean wanted to talk. With Jean's death she had lost her main support in an alien world. She was devastated by the loss. On the family's side of the cathedral she was the only person weeping.

It would be late Monday afternoon before she learned that Jean's death had made her wealthy in her own right, so wealthy that she would be able to divorce Jean's adulterous son if she liked, so wealthy she could go anywhere she wanted and live any life she wanted to live.

On the cathedral steps Lauren Gail had been the only member of the family to speak to Mack. She had stopped and embraced him and asked him to come and visit her when he was able.

Everyone noted the embrace. Everyone watched as the oldest son, Charles, shepherded his children into the cathedral without waiting on his wife. Everyone knew about his mistresses, his weekends in New Orleans and Oxford and on the coast, his almost total neglect of his family, his arguments with his mother, his murderous hatred of Mack.

During the service the five brothers sat with their wives and children wondering about how Jean had divided the estate. Her lawyer was not a close friend of theirs. They knew the estate was left to the family, but they didn't know in what portions.

The oldest son was thinking, There are five million dollars. If she left me my share it will cover my losses last year in the market. If she tried any funny business I'll contest it. Of course I will.

The second oldest son was thinking he should have gone to see her more often and been nicer about Mack. The third son was getting mean. She was undependable. She might not have taken into account all his alimony and child support. She might not have counted in that he had twice as many children as his brothers. The fourth son was spending his. He knew exactly the kind of J series sailboat he would buy as soon as the money was in the bank. The youngest son was simply grieving. Like Lauren Gail, he had lost a mainstay. He had been very young when his mother got rid of his father and the father left Mississippi never to return. He could barely care that the money would pay his gambling debts. He didn't care about the money. He wanted his mother back.

The daughters-in-law didn't know what to think. They had loved her too. She had always been kind to them even if she did like Lauren Gail the most and everybody knew it.

The service wore on. The soprano from Yazoo City did an adequate but not brilliant job on the "Ave Maria" but only moved a few people to tears.

"Unto God's mercy and protection we commit you," the minister said at last, really meaning it, barely able to hold back his own tears at the memory of Jean's wonderful, powerful face. "The Lord bless you and keep you. The Lord make his face to shine upon you, and be gracious unto you. The Lord lift up his countenance upon you, and give you peace, both now and evermore, Amen."

The organist began to play "A Mighty Fortress Is Our God." The coffin left the church, followed by the sons and daughters-in-law and the grandchildren and nieces and nephews. Mack Stanford and his group stood up but did not follow the procession. They kept on standing while the people around them nervously made their way out into the aisle.

"Let's be late getting outside," Augustus said. "I don't want to get rooked into going to the son's house first. I want you to see Jean's house.

She collected primitive and early American art. I heard the sons had already been by to make an inventory. They sent the youngest son and two of the wives. It may all be dismantled by the end of the week."

"Aren't we going to the cemetery?"

"No one is going but the immediate family. It's a private cemetery lot in Woodland Hills where only three families are buried. Mack isn't going. They arranged this so they could shut him out. Which is another reason to visit them last. They won't be there for another hour."

They took their time leaving the cathedral, but it was not time enough. The coffin was loaded on the hearse, but there had been some trouble with the other limousines, and the family was still there waiting.

Both factions had gathered followers. Mack's entourage had grown by three actresses, an actor, and the head of the theater department at Tougaloo, a burly black man who looked like a wrestler.

The head of the theater department at Millsaps was in the crowd around the sons, but when he saw Augustus coming down the stairs he walked up to them. "Let's go talk to Mack," he suggested. "He's having a rough time of it. Jean was his life, you know."

"This is Caroline Jones," Augustus said. "The poet I told you about. She's taking Topeka's place this fall. I expect you to take care of her. Caroline, this is Darley Hitt."

"Oh, Caroline," Darley said. "Augustus lent me your book. It's lovely, such sensual poems. I'm delighted to know you. Delighted you're here." He took her hand. He was a darling-looking man. Dark curly hair with gray streaks at the crown. Wearing an old-fashioned seersucker suit and a blue and green patterned tie. If he's gay too, I quit, Caroline decided. Enough is enough. And what about that Mack? What about that action?

The three of them proceeded down the remaining stairs, going in the direction of Mack Stanford. Had Augustus said heat, Caroline was thinking. It was heat all right and to the tenth power. Even in his bereavement he exuded sexuality and charisma. "Jean found him playing Stanley in *Streetcar*," Augustus whispered. "She brought him here and starred with him in *Sweet Bird of Youth*. Then she took him home and kept him. But I'm first in line, remember that."

"No, you're not," she whispered back. "No dibs on this, old buddy."

"Caroline," Mack said, when they were introduced. "Jean was so excited about your coming here. She was on the committee at Millsaps that brought you here." He was interrupted by Jean's oldest son, Charlie.

"I think the cathedral would rather we all just cleared out now," the son said. "They have a wedding tonight and Father Archer asked that we not stay in the way. You can take your friends somewhere else, can't you?"

"What in the hell are you up to now, Charlie?" The Tougaloo theater director stepped in the way. "Leave Mack alone, do you hear me? This has gone far enough. This whole thing has been disgraceful."

Charlie took the theater director by the arm and pulled him up on the steps and then the theater director hit Charlie in the face and then the fight began. Augustus pushed Caroline out of the way and stepped in to help separate the men. The man in all black, the psychiatrist Jim Jaspers, came racing over. He was very tall, very powerfully built. He pulled the theater director away from the son, and Augustus and two other men held the son.

"Get this rabble away from my mother's funeral," the son was yelling. "Get your goddamn queer buddies out of here, Mack. I can't take looking at you anymore today. I can't believe you'd show up here. You killed her, you son of a bitch. You're the one who did it."

The middle sons joined the crowd and managed to get their older brother in tow. Augustus and Jim Jaspers had the theater director and were pulling him toward his automobile. A pair of black teenagers on the other side of the street were politely smothering their giggles. Two policemen pulled up in a car and got out and walked up on the steps. Order was restored, but just barely.

"Well, that was wild," Caroline said, when they were in the car and leaving the scene. "I thought that guy from Tougaloo was going to kill Jean's son."

"Charlie Lyles is a pain in the butt," Augustus said. "Someone needs to kill him. Well, at least you got to see Jim Jaspers in action. What did you think of him?"

"I don't know. He turned me off somehow. What's with all the black clothes? Does he always dress like that or just for funerals?"

"He wears black a lot. He was Jean's psychiatrist for many years. She's the one who brought him all his patients. She made his career in Jackson."

"Well, it was something to watch. The best was when he came sprinting down the aisle to talk to the sons. I mean, this was a funeral."

"He's intense. He's an unusual man. I went to him a few times. Listen, we're lucky to have a real psychotherapist in Jackson, one who's a medical doctor. They are rare. The good ones are rare."

"Maybe I was wrong about him. Maybe he's just sad."

"He'll be at Mack's. Talk to him there. So you want to take over Jean's lover, do you?" Augustus giggled, the old cruising laugh they had shared so many times, at Vandy, in Florida, in New York City, in San Francisco.

"Dibs, dibs, dibs."

"I thought there were no dibs."

"Well, I take it back. I think he liked me. He was looking me over. Thank God I wore these shoes."

"He treats everyone that way. That's the seduction, that's the heat. He makes everyone think they're the most important person in the world."

"He should run for president."

"He studies Clinton. Jean said he's fascinated by the man."

"Where's he from?"

"Texas, of course. Irish German probably. It's a common mix down there. God, I'd love to fuck him."

"You and me. He'd make up for that lousy thirty thousand if I could snag him. So how much were they paying Topeka? Whose poetry I despise in case I haven't told you."

"I don't know exactly."

"Yes, you do. Tell me. I may want to ask for a raise. So what did they do with the money? They didn't give it back. I never knew a department to give money back to the administration."

"I'm not talking about it. I shouldn't have told you what I did."

They argued about Augustus's telling her Topeka's salary until they turned off a wide highway into a gated subdivision with contemporary houses set on two-acre lots. At the end of a dead-end street was the long, low glass and stone house Jean Lyles had shared with her lover. The entrance was a stone creek that went under wrought iron gates. Ferns grew beside it in a stone wall. Water ran slowly over the stones. Huge golden carp swam lazily among water lilies. The creek continued under windows beside wide double doors. A uniformed butler opened the door and they went past a collection of Native American pottery and down steps into a sunken living room with a wide stone porch on the back. Everywhere there were paintings of great elegance and beauty.

On a long table were Native American pots, some large enough to hold a gallon of water, made of pottery so thin it might be from the Ming Dynasty.

"Are those real?" Caroline asked.

"Yes."

"I can't believe they're just sitting there. They could break."

"They haven't. They won't."

They went down the stairs and into the living room and were served champagne. People came up and were introduced. Mack came across the room and took her arm. "I'm so embarrassed about that scene on the steps," he began. "I seem to keep apologizing to you."

"Oh, please don't do that. People are sad. People do strange things when they are grieving."

"I have something I want to show you. When I saw you at the funeral I thought, How perfect, as though Jean planned it."

"What is it?"

"Come with me. It's something you should see."

"Of course." He took her hand and led her back across the living room and up the stairs and down a hall into a small, spare bedroom. "This was her reading room," he said. "Your book of poems is on the bedside table. It might be the last thing that she read."

"She died in here?"

"Yes. I'd gone out to run. It was early in the morning. She'd complained of feeling ill the night before. There's no understanding it. No understanding death. We all pretend we don't know it's coming. Then it's here. Doing this to us, tearing us apart, taking us back to nature. I don't want to stay in this house. It doesn't matter to me to leave it. I couldn't be here without her."

Caroline moved to the bedside table and picked up her book of poems. A red ribbon with a medal on the end was in the book. It was between a poem called "Mirage" and one called "Morning."

"I forget I can do this," she said. "I have no faith in it anymore. There was Shakespeare and Cervantes and Dante and Wordsworth. Now there are the rest of us. I think we are here too late. I think it's all been said. Still, I learned a lot writing this book. About love at least. I don't know about death. No wonder I can't write worth a damn."

"I think you're too hard on yourself."

Augustus came hurrying into the room. "I need you, Mack. Jim's gone crazy. He's taking off his clothes."

They hurried from the room and down the hall and into the living room and out onto a porch where Jim Jaspers was standing on a stone wall in his boxer shorts with his black shirt tied around his head. "You're all in cages," he was yelling. "You're locked up in cages with bars made of your mother's bones. You can't get out. You can't see where you are. You're in a space–time continuum. You're made of carbon and you're going to die. You're going to die before you ever taste of freedom. You don't have the slightest idea of freedom. You've never been free a day in your lives. I could tell you where you are but you won't listen. You refuse to listen to me."

The food editor and her friend were standing beside the wall begging him to come down. Darley Hitt was beside them. Jim Jaspers kept on orating. "I have tried to save your hides. I can't go on telling you forever. You have to take some responsibility. Jean took responsibility. Now she's gone into the red-hot business of the atoms and you're still walking around your cages. You won't learn a goddamn thing from this. I'm sick of the lot of you. Sick and tired of the whole damn thing."

"Come down off the wall," Augustus asked. "Come and have a drink, Jim. Come down off the wall."

"Where were you when I needed you?" Jim yelled at him. "Off chasing young boys around the bars. Get your hands off me, Augustus. You don't want to make me mad."

"Come on, Jim," Mack said. "It's Jean's funeral, for God's sake. Don't do this to us now."

"You brought all this on yourself, Mack," Jim said. "This is your karma. You must have been a real shit in your last life to end up being a houseboy for Jean. She was the meanest bitch I ever met and that is why I loved her. At least she was mean, at least she was free."

An older man who ran an insurance firm and a middle-aged lawyer both came to help. The older man climbed up on the wall and took Jim's arm. "Come on, Jim," he said. "We'll call your partner if you want. Call Donna," he said to the lawyer. "Go call Donna, for God's sake. Someone call his partner, Donna Divers, and get her over here."

"Fuck you, William," Jim yelled. "Did I call the Internal Revenue Service when you were making tax shelters out of nursing homes in Pearl? Did I call your wife when you screwed her in the divorce? Get your hands off me. I am enlightened and you are a speck of dust. This is freedom I am showing you. It did no good to tell you about it, so I'm showing you."

They managed finally to get him off the wall and out of the house to the front yard. On his way through the living room he knocked a thousand-year-old Pueblo vase off the table and broke it into pieces.

When they were in the front yard the lawyer pulled a cell phone out of his pocket and called Jim Jaspers's partner, a child psychologist named Donna Divers whom Jim had trained to help out with his practice. She was not a physician but she was an intelligent woman who took up the slack when Jim's patients wanted help with their small children or grandchildren. Jim did not treat children. He believed the best way to help children was to cure their parents. His patients had kept insisting, however, so he had found Donna and trained her. The lawyer had sent his sons to her to make them stop fighting on car trips and driving his wife crazy. So he knew Donna's phone number and he called it. "Jim's having some sort of problem, Donna," he said when she answered. "Could you come over to Mack Stanford's house and help us out with this? Jean Lyles's house, on Meadowbrook Lane, off Meadowbrook Boulevard. . . . You'd better come see for yourself. . . . He took off his clothes. Okay, thanks. We'll take care of him until you get here."

"Donna's coming to help you, Jim," he said. "Joe has your suit. Let's get your clothes back on."

"You son of a bitch," Jim said. "One time in my life I do something you don't understand and you call my partner? You call the cops on me? You think you have the right to judge or control me?"

He grabbed his suit from the insurance man's hands and stood defiantly in the driveway holding it. His car was on the street and was not blocked in. He backed up in its direction. "Did I call the special prosecutor when you were subpoenaed in the Espy case? Did I, William? All I did was help you and help you and help you. Who's going to help old Jim? That's what I'm asking now. Who's going to help me?"

He began searching in the pockets of his pants for his car keys. "Don't lay another hand on me, any of you. I'm leaving. Go back in the house. Go back to your so-called lives."

He got into his car and started it. Augustus and Mack started toward the car to stop him but the other two men held them back. "Let him go," William said. "Leave him alone. I'll call Donna and tell her not to come.

"I don't know if this is an aberration or some real illness," William said. "But we have to do something about it. We can't have him going around Jackson saying those kinds of things. My God, what do you think is wrong with him?"

"It looks like mania to me," Augustus said. "I don't think that was just whiskey."

"We aren't competent to know what's wrong with him," Mack put in. "He's our psychiatrist, for God's sake. I can't believe he said those things to all of you."

"A psychiatrist doesn't get drunk and yell at his patients," Augustus said. "This doesn't happen."

"It just happened," William said. "Maybe we should call the medical board."

"We better send him somewhere to get well," the insurance man suggested. "I'll lend him our plane. He can use our plane to go anywhere he needs to go."

"Let's all talk in the morning," Augustus said. "Jean was his oldest patient. He might be, God knows, overcome by grief. He might be feeling guilty. How much had he had to drink, Mack?"

"Only one drink that I gave him. He was acting funny at the funeral. He was acting funny before he got here."

"It couldn't be drugs," William said. "He hated drugs. He'd go crazy if I took Robaxin for a toothache. I never knew anyone who hated drugs as much as he does."

"That's right," Mack added. "He used to rail about coffee."

They went back into the house. People came up to them and asked for explanations. The men told them what they knew.

Caroline had been helping pick up the pieces of the broken Pueblo vase. The food editor and her companion and Caroline carefully picked up each piece they could find and lined them up on a space on the table. It was very strange to touch pottery that was a thousand years old. "We are very strange," Caroline told the editor. "People are the strangest things in all creation. Two days ago I was in Nashville, Tennessee, about to die of boredom. Now I'm in the middle of all of this."

"This is nothing," the editor answered. "You haven't even skimmed the surface of this city. This town has got more secrets and art and talented and troubled people and mystical stuff going on than you could ever imagine in a thousand years. Before you even get to the racial problems."

"The mystery rose from the racial problems," her companion said.

Augustus came and found Caroline and helped them pick up the remaining fragments of the vase. Then he and Caroline went out and got into his car and started off toward the home of Jean Lyles's oldest son.

"The second wake," Augustus said. "Well, they'll never top the entertainment at the first one."

"How did you meet all these people?" Caroline asked. "How did you get involved in all of this?"

"I tried out for a role in a Tom Stoppard play. I figured any group that was doing Stoppard would be interesting. I just went down to the theater one evening and there they were. Well, they really are a powerful and interesting bunch of people and fun to know. Maybe this wasn't a good introduction. I sure hadn't planned on Jim Jaspers going crazy while we watched."

"How many of these people see him?"

"Everyone. I didn't know William, the lawyer who was helping get him off the wall, the one in the corduroy jacket. I didn't know he saw him."

"I don't want to stay too long at this second place," Caroline said. "I want to get some sleep tonight and go over to Millsaps tomorrow and meet the people who hired me. I'm starting to get worried about that."

"You're meeting the people who hired you. Monday's only registration. There's plenty of time for everything, Caroline. The students here are nice. You'll like them. Besides, you'll be teaching the gifted ones. It's our only real creative writing class. A girl who's the daughter of one of the mainstays of the theater will be in it. She's a wild thing. I want you to take an interest in her, if you can. Well, we'll see."

"Who's the girl?"

"Her name's Camilia but we call her CeCe. Her mother is Celia Montgomery, who's married to the richest man in the Delta. Celia's one of our actresses. The father used to act too but he's out of it now. He had heart surgery last year."

"Are they part of the cabal?"

"Founding fathers."

"Do they go to Jim Jaspers?"

"Celia did and CeCe does. I don't know about Donald. One reason I want you to take an interest in CeCe is this thing with him. This is going to be hard on people who are in the midst of a transference."

"What is going to be hard? You don't think getting drunk at one party and taking off your clothes is the end of his seeing his patients, do you?"

"He wasn't drunk, Caroline. There are bruises all up and down his arm. Needle tracks, I imagine. I've seen that before."

"Jesus Christ. That's always been hard for me to imagine. I can hardly get a shot without going into cardiac arrest. I can't imagine anyone injecting themselves with something."

"That's what I love about you, Caroline. I adore the way you can shut out anything you disapprove of. It's a gift. A real blessed gift."

They had come to a narrow curving street with huge old pine trees on either side. It was fragrant and dark and still. The road turned into a circle. At the end was a driveway going up a hill to a white house with columns. "It's a copy of Dunleith," Augustus said. "Not a perfect copy, but close enough. Jean used to joke about it."

He stopped the car in front of the steps and a servant came out and took the car to park it. They walked inside. There were drawing rooms on either side of a wide hall. Subdued conversation and subdued-looking people were everywhere. This was not a party. This was a funeral, and the sons and daughters-in-law and grandchildren were acting like it was one.

A waiter came by and took their orders for drinks. Servants were passing small trays of sandwiches and pastries. Men were in groups on the porches. Women were sitting on the sofas. Augustus took Caroline from group to group and introduced her.

A frail-looking woman in a billowing blue and white silk dress came up to them and held on to Augustus's arm. "Celia," he said, and introduced her to Caroline and left them to talk.

"I have a favor to ask of you," Celia said. "Augustus knows. He said it was all right to ask. Could we find someplace where we can talk?"

"I really need to get something to eat first," Caroline began. "I'm starving. I drove all day, then as soon as I arrived we came to the funeral. I really need something to eat and I need to speak to our hosts."

"Don't worry about them. You can do that later and we can certainly get you something to eat." Celia commandeered a waiter and ordered him to bring food to the library, then she took Caroline's arm and led her to a book-lined room with huge leather chairs facing a fireplace. Sitting in one of the chairs, she seemed as small and frail as a child. As soon as they were seated, two waiters appeared carrying tray tables and practically bowing. "These are my caterers," she explained. "I lent them to Charles and Lauren Gail. This had to be hastily thrown together, as you can imagine. Is that something you can eat? Is there anything else you need?"

There was sliced turkey and ham and little sandwiches on a tray and a second tray of fruits, cheese, and desserts. It was enough food for four people. "It's perfect," Caroline said. "More than I need." She began to eat the sandwiches. Celia watched for a second, then dismissed the waiters and began.

"I'm on the board at Millsaps," she said. "So I know all about your wonderful book. We had a special meeting to bring you here to take Topeka's place. We are all thrilled you are here." She paused, then went on. "I have a favor to ask of you. I have a daughter, my only child, who's had a bad time the last few years. It's the times, of course. Everyone is suffering versions of this. Now I have her back in school and I'm hoping you will find time to make friends with her. She dreams of being a writer, so it would mean so much if you would talk to her, be a role model for her. I'm having a house party in the Delta next weekend. I was hoping you might come. You could fly down with us or I'll send a car to get you. It's a two-hour drive. You could see a working plantation. We're going to the blues festival in Greenwood. I think you'd enjoy that. People are coming from Memphis and maybe an actor from New York. He got his training here at Paine Theater. Anyway, please think it over. We would treat you as our honored guest."

"I don't know. I can't promise anything. I haven't been to the college yet. I may have to work." Caroline was drawing back. Baby-sitting a recalcitrant girl was not what she had in mind for Jackson.

"Please think it over. Come for one night if two is too many. Or stay until Monday afternoon. We will fly you down. There are extra cars at Oak Grove if you need them. It was my grandfather's place." They were joined by a tall, dark-haired man with a handsome, sanguine face. "Jake Rivers," Celia said. "He writes for the *Clarion Ledger*. He's a sports-writer but he sometimes acts for us. We want him to review the plays but he won't. Jake, this is Caroline Jones. Tell her she can't know Missis-sippi until she knows the Delta."

"I liked your book of poems," he said. "Augustus gave me a copy of it. It's beautiful work. I hope you'll go on doing it."

Caroline had not been admired in many months. It was a heady drug and she gave in to it.

"I'll come if I can." She laughed. "Tell me what you all know about this psychiatrist, Jim Jaspers."

"Why do you ask?" Celia moved in, looking worried.

"He took off his clothes and started dancing on top of a wall at Mack Stanford's house. I mean, what a shrink. I might go and see him."

"Oh, no." Celia looked completely dismayed. Jake stood back and listened. "Tell me what he did."

"He took off his clothes and started dancing on a wall and talking about existential freedom. It was hilarious, to tell the truth. I'm sorry, maybe I shouldn't have told you about it."

"Oh, yes. I mean you should. Jim's diabetic. He may have been taking medication and it didn't mix with alcohol. He's a wonderful man, the best psychiatrist in the South. People come from all over to talk to him." She turned to the reporter. A look passed between them. The reporter took up the refrain.

"He's the best psychiatrist around here. I went to him when I was having problems with being paid fairly at the paper. He was so smart, so incisive. He told me exactly what to do and I did it and I won. What happened at Mack's must have been a mistake of some sort. Jim Jaspers wouldn't do anything like that."

Augustus came into the room with one of Jean's younger sons and Celia got up and moved to him. "What happened with Jim?" she asked. "Caroline said he was acting strangely. Was he ill?"

"I think he must have been. I'll talk to you about it later, Celia. It's nothing. Don't worry about it now."

"I would have been there but Lauren Gail asked me to help with this. He didn't actually take off his clothes, of course. Not Jim."

"Don't think about it, Celia. It was a mistake, that's all. Call me tomorrow and we'll talk about it then."

"I should have gone to Mack's but how could I? Well, I'll go now."

"Stay here and help Lauren Gail. That's what Jean would have wanted. You don't want to go over there now. Just stay here."

"He took off his clothes?"

"Not exactly. He was trying to make a point and people were drinking too much. Please don't make me talk about it now. I want to finish introducing Caroline to people." Augustus made his escape. He was not in the mood to talk about what he had just seen because he hadn't decided what it meant or what he could do to help.

Augustus took Caroline to speak to the sons. The oldest son, Charlie, was acting as though nothing had happened at the funeral. The other sons were being pleasant. The wives were kind and very well dressed, with the exception of Lauren Gail, who was wearing a long baggy dress and flat shoes and was doing most of the work. "They seem like nice people," Caroline whispered to Augustus.

"It's hard to be mean when you're anticipating being left a million dollars apiece," he answered. "Well, the younger ones are nice enough, but boring. She was a great director and actor but she bred badly. I've seen it before. You can breed out charm in one generation if you aren't careful. You can breed out real intelligence, the thing that can't be measured, so easily it's scary. Ephemeral, like all wonderful matter. Oh, well."

"You're really grieving for this woman, aren't you?"

"Yes, my love, I am." He put his arm around her and held her close to him. "So the universe has sent me you."

The governor arrived with his wife. "We'll go home as soon as we speak to the governor," Augustus said. "I don't support him and he knows it. He's bad on gay issues but we need state money for the theater so I have to be nice." He took Caroline to be introduced to the cool, wary man and his entourage. Then they said goodbye to their hosts and went down the long marble stairs. Their car appeared and they got into it and left. They drove through the residential districts of old Jackson. There were pine trees as tall as skyscrapers and sheltering and fragrant. The stars were very bright in a clear, moonless sky. It was a lot like Nashville,

Caroline decided. Except for the marvelous talk, the sultry, sweet accents, the long vowel sounds, the melody of the speech. Seductive, she decided. I'm being seduced.

"Celia asked me to come to the Delta and counsel her daughter," she said. "So is this all a big put-on? The reason I'm here is to take care of the patroness's wayward child? I'm beginning to wish you hadn't given all these people my poetry to read. How many books did you buy?"

"I ordered ten, but I haven't given all of them away."

"The largest order ever received by Star Arrow Publications of Atlanta, Georgia," Caroline sighed.

"As for CeCe," Augustus said. "She's an interesting girl. You might like her. It's not her fault she was raised by idiots."

∾ 2 ∾

AUGUSTUS WAS UP AND DRESSED when Caroline came down at nine the next morning. "The phone's been ringing since eight," he reported. "People are really upset about Jim. I was thinking of calling his receptionist, but she doesn't come in until nine. I thought maybe I could just ask for him and pick her brain."

"So what do they say? The people who are calling?"

"They want to know what's going on. Peggy Dillan, the food editor you met last night, said she saw him Tuesday and all he did was tell her he was enlightened and that she was lucky to know him at this stage in his life. She said it scared her to death. Then she decided it was some psychiatrist's trick to make her think."

"That's what he said last night. That he was enlightened and we are specks of dust. He shouldn't be practicing psychiatry if he's doing drugs. You saw needle tracks on his arm?"

"I surely did." Augustus handed Caroline a glass of orange juice. He giggled. "I was going to offer you a few sessions with him if you're really blocked. I was going to give them to you for a present." He shook his head and poured coffee for her. "So maybe I'll hit you on the head instead."

"As a matter of fact I wrote a poem driving down here." She took the juice and drank part of it. "It was so stupid it cheered me up. Maybe I wasn't blocked. Maybe I was bored. Well, go on and call the receptionist. Let's see what she says."

She sat down at the breakfast table and began to spread cream cheese on a toasted bagel. Augustus dialed the phone.

"Is Jim coming in today?" he asked, when the receptionist answered the phone. "No, it's Augustus Hailey. I just wanted to chat with him. It's not important. Okay, I'm glad . . . That's good then. Thank you, Cherry. Thanks a lot.

"She says he's gone out of town. His appointments are canceled for the week. What do you think that's about?"

The phone rang. He answered it. "He did what? At Java Two? Are you sure? What time was this, Mack? Who told you?"

He hung up and turned back to Caroline. "He's sitting outside a coffee shop near the Millsaps campus. Sitting in zazen, chanting. A friend of Mack's called him and reported it. I'd better go and look for him. There are eggs waiting to be scrambled. Can you take care of yourself?"

"I want to go with you. All I need are some shoes." She stood up and ran upstairs. When she came back down they went out and got into the convertible and drove to the Millsaps campus and across it. "Here's your new home," Augustus said, as they went through the front gates. "I didn't mean for this to be your introduction."

They crossed the pretty little campus and went out the back gates and down the street to a small shopping area with cars parked all around.

"The coffee shop is the one in the middle," Augustus said. "I don't see his car, or him, do you? Well, I know the owner. Let's go in and see what she says."

They parked the convertible and went into the coffee shop. No one was there but a couple of students reading newspapers. The owner was stacking cups.

"Lisa, have you seen Jim Jaspers this morning? He's a tall dark-haired man, probably wearing a black shirt. He's very tall. He's been in here with me. I think you know him."

The woman shook her head, then motioned to them to come to the back with her. She led them into the kitchen before she spoke. "He was sitting by the front door when I got here at six," she said. "I have a lot to do this week. The students are returning this weekend. So he was just sitting there on the ground. He's some kind of doctor, isn't he?"

"Yes."

"I think he's nuts. He asked me if he could pray for me to become enlightened. I was opening the door. It scared me so I went back to the car and called the police. When they came they talked to him and he got up and sat at a table. So I opened the place and one of the policemen stayed until he decided it was all right.

"He sat there for two hours chanting. Then he came in and thanked me and then he left. I don't want that guy back over here. If he comes again, I'm going to have him arrested."

"If he comes back, call me," Augustus said. He wrote down some telephone numbers and handed them to her. "If you can't get me, call the second number. It's a lawyer. He'll know what to do."

"Who is he? What's wrong with him?"

"We don't know yet. He's sick, that's all, but he's not dangerous. He's a pacifist, a really peaceful man."

The owner followed them out of the shop. She stood waving while they drove away.

"Now what will we do?" Caroline asked.

"Finish breakfast. Wait for the phones to ring."

When they got back to the house there were three messages from William Harbison. "We have to do something right away," he said, when Augustus returned the calls. Caroline was leaning toward the phone. Augustus flipped it to speaker mode so she could hear. "You don't know what's been going on with this Espy thing, Augustus. I've been called back to testify again. Jim's been strange about it. He was helpful in January but lately he keeps saying strange things. He acts like he thinks I'm guilty of withholding information, or God knows what. It's all a witch-hunt, of course, but Jim keeps giving me these looks and saying, 'Tell the truth,' as if I wasn't telling the truth. It's taking two years out of my life to mess with this shit, not to mention the travel costs and the lawyers. I postponed testifying last month by telling them I was in psychotherapy caused by Mother's death. Jim backed me up on that. They have his name on a medical excuse. Now what if they call him as a witness and he starts all that staring off into space and talking about carbon atoms. I'm a decent man with a good reputation in the world. I don't know how Celia ever talked me into going to him in the first place. . . ."

"Well, he writes prescriptions for great sleeping pills," Augustus put in.

"Don't make a joke of this, Augustus. I just talked to Mack. He said he'd called you and you'd gone to get him off the ground in front of a coffee shop."

"William, calm down. They don't call in someone's psychiatrist in a federal case about bribery in high places. They don't investigate the witnesses, do they?"

"That's all they do. They're trying to scare people into lying for them. Well, what do you suggest? Do you have any ideas?"

"Let a few days go by. Let him settle down. If you hear from him, offer him help. That's all we can do, and don't worry, William, he isn't going to tell lies about us."

"He might not know the truth from lies at this point. I think he's gone completely nuts. I think he's cracked, and I want him off the streets and into a hospital."

"Okay. We'll do that. One day at a time."

"That's easy for you to say. You don't have Donald Smaltz on your heels. You haven't been caught in that web, but lots of people around here have been. Everyone who supported Espy when he ran for Congress. Lives are being ruined by the dozens, perfectly nice people. The Espy family have spent generations bringing themselves into prominence. Mike might have been our greatest Mississippi senator if they hadn't decided to kill him."

"Okay, William. You keep in touch with me. I'll be right here. Call if you hear from him, and if I hear anything I'll call you. And don't worry. This might not be as bad as it looks."

Augustus hung up the phone. "But it is as bad," he told Caroline. "Now I'm lying for him. I couldn't bring myself to tell William about the needle tracks, not in the mood he's in. Someone has to keep his head while all about them wheel shadows of the ancient desert birds, wouldn't you say?"

"You'll be the one. You always are."

"Thank you. I pride myself on that and I'm glad you noticed." He sat down at the table with her and began to eat the cold scrambled eggs he'd been trying to eat for three phone calls.

The rest of the weekend was quiet. Augustus drove her around town so she could get her bearings. Then they went out to the reservoir to watch a regatta.

On Sunday they read newspapers and went for a two-hour walk. Every few hours the phone would ring and someone would want to talk about Jim but no one had seen or heard from him since the coffee shop chanting. Everyone was praying he had left town.

"For his own sake he should get some help," they kept saying.

"It wouldn't be good for him to keep on working," others said.

"Did he say anything about me?" everyone kept asking.

William Harbison was a good man. He deserved the good reputation he had in the world and he was right in thinking he had been unfairly targeted in the Espy investigation. All he had ever done for Mike Espy was write wills and read contracts for small business deals in the Delta. William believed the Espy investigation was the meanest of all the special prosecutor's attempts to harm the Clinton administration and certainly the most racially motivated. The Espy family were good people who had striven hard for many years and now were being murdered.

Murder was on the mind of the business tycoon who called William Harbison right after Harbison hung up from talking to Augustus on the morning after Jean Lyles's funeral, the morning of the coffee shop chanting as it would forever be known in the memories of Jim Jaspers's friends and former patients.

"I'll kill somebody if that son of a bitch starts talking about me," the owner of the largest heavy equipment dealership in the Delta said to William Harbison. "My wife got me into his office, and I told him things I don't want brought up. I want this guy sent to the loony bin, William, before we all end up spending another year in D.C. Are you listening?"

William was listening. The powerful old man on the other end of the phone was his main source of income. He was also an old man with plenty to hide and the money and moxie to make sure it stayed hidden. The thought of D. B. Duval in Jim Jaspers's office talking about his sins was so hilarious that William almost felt like laughing. The thought of what he could and would do to protect himself was not, however, humorous.

"What did you hear?" William asked.

"Everything that's been going on. How that Jaspers guy was spouting off about his patients and how he was down at Bill Hoxie's coffee shop chanting Communist chants and scaring Lisa Hoxie to death. I want him out of this town, William. You get that done."

"Who told you all of that?"

"What the hell difference would it make? Get on this, William. Get on it today."

"I will, D.B. You can calm down. He was chanting Buddhist sutras. They're prayers. The people who chant them are enemies of the Chinese Communists. It's not what it seems. He doesn't know anything that would affect the Espy investigation. He's just a doctor who's having some problems. He may be all right by next week. Let's all try to keep this in perspective. I know what you've been through, D.B. I've been through it too. You know I'll always protect you any way I can."

"Get back to me, William. Get that guy in the loony bin. We've got three airplanes you can use to take him anyplace you can think of to take him, but get him out of this town. That's a threat."

"Okay, D.B. I hear you. I'll do what I can."

"Why on earth would Jim be stupid enough to try to treat D. B. Duval?" William asked Augustus, when he got him on the phone a second time. "That's the question I can't answer."

"Because he thinks he's God," Augustus said. "He's decided he can do miracles. We have all gone into that office and told him he was a genius and now he's decided to prove it and believe it. Everyone's involved in this, not just Jim."

"You get D. B. Duval mad at you and you'll need a god to save you," William said. "He's capable of murder, Augustus. He is not playing by the rules the rest of us understand."

"Don't overreact. This is all being blown out of proportion."

"No, it's not. It's a big thing and it affects big people. Call me back the minute you hear any news."

"Okay, William. Just hang on. If you can."

"If he harms D.B., he'll never practice medicine in the South again. That's for starters."

"I know, William. Comprendo. I understand."

∾ 3 ∾

MONDAY WAS AN EXCITING DAY on the Millsaps campus and Caroline was excited by being there. The office they had given her was small but lined with oak bookshelves. The desk was adequate. There was a steel table with a computer better than the one she had at Yale. "Was this Topeka's office?" she asked. The head of the English department, a gray-haired lady named Gay Wileman, was showing her around.

"Alas, no. That was snatched up by the Faulkner scholar. This was his office. Is it large enough? We have other storage space, a room with locked cabinets and shelves. We can get you anything else you need."

"This is fine. I'm teaching Shakespeare. He doesn't take up much room."

"Well, the creative writing seminar."

"That takes patience, not equipment. I don't believe in workshops, by the way. I think they do more harm than good. I'm going to work with tutorials and use the workshop time to study other literature."

"That's how Eudora taught when she was here." Gay smiled. "I was

in her class, you know. It was the only time she ever taug[h]
Two semesters. It was an idyll. She let us read our storie[s]
each other if we wanted to but no one was required to do it."

"I hope I get to meet her."

"Oh, I'm sure you will. The cabal all know her. I heard Augustus
saw to it that you met everyone at the funeral."

"You call it a cabal?"

"It's a joke. But they are the people who fund the arts in the state.
They are powerful. Take Celia Montgomery."

"What about her?"

"She and her husband gave five hundred thousand dollars to endow
a chair in women's literature." Gay smiled. She sat down in a leather
chair and Caroline took a seat behind the desk. "Nice chairs," she said.
"Very, very nice."

"We would appreciate it if you would find time to talk to CeCe,
Celia's daughter. I know she is hoping you will find time to counsel with
her."

A squeeze play, Caroline decided. I'll be damned. My old man
couldn't have done it better. "I don't know," she answered. "I'm not sure
I want to get involved in that."

"Let me tell you about her. She was a rising ballet star in the best
school here. Then she quit. When she was about twelve she just quit.
Wouldn't have anything else to do with it. She dyed her hair blue with
stuff she bought at the drugstore. By the seventh grade she was in complete retreat from all she had been offered. She's an only child. Celia
wanted a career in the arts, but she wasn't strong enough to really pursue
it. CeCe is very strong. She graduated from Jackson Academy by the
skin of her teeth and now she's here. She is excessively bright and her

ɔoetry is really quite good. She published three poems last year in the literary magazine of her high school. Let me show them to you." The woman got up, walked to a shelf, and took down a magazine that was waiting there. She opened it to a poem and handed it to Caroline.

Caroline took the magazine but didn't read the poem. "I'll read it," she said. "And I'll help if I can. I'd really like to see the classrooms now if I could. Could you show me how to get there?" She stood up.

"Of course. It isn't far from here. It's just across from the student union. I'll walk you there."

They walked out of the office building and down a set of stairs to the wide sidewalks of the campus. It was a beautiful, soothing place, with old brick buildings and huge trees shading them. "I heard Jim Jaspers put on quite a show at the funeral," Gay said. "Were you there for that?"

"Does everyone in Jackson know about it?"

"So many people depend on Jim. He takes care of my husband's old aunt, who's in a nursing home. Dementia. He's been caring for her without charging us. He's a good man, a good and useful man. I hope he's all right. I hope this was just a blip on the screen."

"Maybe he's just tired," Caroline lied. "It would wear one out to listen to other people's problems all day."

"It's what I do," Gay laughed. "And you'll be doing it too now that the semester's started. I don't envy you having the writing seminar. They are interesting, exciting students but sometimes they have the most problems."

"Creative people cultivate madness," Caroline said. "I'll be glad to be back with William Shakespeare. Harold Bloom says he was the most normal and sane of our geniuses. We don't know much about his life but what we know tells us he was a genial man who was nice to people. Bloom says he saved his creativity for the plays and didn't waste it on his life."

"Tell that to CeCe, would you. That's what CeCe Montgomery needs to hear."

CLASSES BEGAN on Thursday. They would meet Thursday and Friday and then recess for a long weekend. Celia Montgomery had written a note to Caroline formally inviting her to the Delta for the weekend. "Mack Stanford will be there," the note said. "He liked you so much. We are all dedicated to helping him get through this. Please call if you can join us at Oak Grove. We hope so much that you will."

Caroline called and said she would go, but only for two nights. "I have to come back to prepare for classes," she explained. "Until I meet the students I can't really know how to teach them."

"We're flying down Friday afternoon. Mack and CeCe and myself. Will you go down with us?"

"I'd better drive my car. I'll feel better if I have my own car."

"Then I'll fax you a map."

"Fine, and thanks for asking me. I'm looking forward to it."

It would have been hard to miss CeCe Montgomery. Even in a group of students with the moxie to think they could be writers she stood out.

She was wearing a pair of army surplus fatigues and a white T-shirt with a picture of the Blues Brothers. *ON A MISSION FROM GOD*, it said on the shirt. Her hair was cut off as short as a boy's. She was fifteen pounds overweight. She had three earrings in one ear and another one in her nose. The thought of counseling CeCe about anything seemed impossible. She was as hard-looking as an iron cube. With her were two boys her age. One was tall and looked like an athlete. The other was short and blond and looked like he was stoned or drunk.

They came into the classroom and found seats on the side near the windows. They waited.

"I'm Caroline Jones from Nashville, Tennessee," Caroline began. "Like you I dream of becoming a writer. I have published a book of poems and perhaps a dozen articles in respectable magazines. I taught at Yale for two years. I used to be a distance runner and I'm thinking of taking it up again. I hate elective surgery, including face-lifts and breast implants. I studied philosophy as an undergraduate but don't believe in much except perhaps the perfectibility of some men and women, the lucky ones. I've printed for you a list of books I think are important for a young writer to have read. The starred ones are books that were meaningful to me. I'll want you to have read at least five of these books and written reports on them by semester's end. Please try to spread them out if you expect your grades to arrive on time.

"I'm going to begin today by telling you what I know or think I know about point of view. This will hold true for poems, stories, or certain kinds of nonfiction pieces.

"What else? I am not going to have a workshop where you all read and criticize each other's work. If there are some of you who desperately want to do this I'll arrange extra sessions and moderate them for you. I prefer to work with you in tutorials. You give me the stories or poems and we'll have private discussions about them. If you think I don't understand your work you can quit at any time up to midterm. There will be no exams. Okay, any questions?"

Caroline had been avoiding looking at CeCe and her friends. Now she looked that way and was surprised to see CeCe's hand in the air. Also, she was smiling.

"That will make a lot of extra work for you," CeCe said. "If we want to work in a workshop and have tutorials, can we do both?"

"There are only fifteen of you. We'll have time to make arrangements that suit each of you. I haven't taught for two years. I'm eager to work." Caroline laughed and found CeCe laughing with her. She had a dazzling smile. A good, happy laugh.

"What did you do when you didn't teach?" CeCe asked.

"I whored for the movies. They told me they would pay me two hundred thousand dollars to write a screenplay about the life of Edna Millay and I fell for it. All I ever got were a couple of small checks, a huge rejection complex, allergies from living in California, and I lost my trust in my fellowmen. Plus I quit my job at Yale. I need you people. I've got to put my life back together. So use me. I'm easy."

The whole class was laughing now. They seemed to draw nearer and Caroline took up a piece of chalk and told them everything she knew about point of view.

An hour passed like a minute. They took a break and went out into the hall and bought coffee from a machine and leaned against the walls. CeCe and her male friends had gone outside to smoke. When the class reconvened they sat in the front row. Caroline continued the lecture on point of view, asking different students to suggest sentences that illustrated the different possibilities.

At five to five Caroline put down the chalk and thanked them for the afternoon. "You now know about a tenth of what I know about writing," she said. "We may be able to quit by Thanksgiving."

CeCe stood up and stretched. She shook her short curls from side to side. "That was great," she said. "I'm really glad you came here."

That night Augustus cooked pasta and Caroline made a salad and they sat out on the patio with mosquito candles burning and talked about their day at school.

"I've got an introductory poetry class," Augustus said. "I volunteered to teach it because I was fighting to keep it in the curriculum. We're losing so much. I've got about twenty students. There are a couple of football players who obviously think it's going to be an easy course. One of them seemed quite bright. I think I might inject him with some Yeats or Auden or maybe even Dylan Thomas before it's over."

"How did you begin?"

"With Auden, Eliot, then a poem by Seamus Heaney. I read them that. Then had them read *Howl*. Then I read part of it out loud. The problem is texts."

"Try Rilke. I've had success with that. Also, Edna Millay. Shakespeare was such a teacher for her. If you know Shakespeare and you read Millay closely, you find the influences everywhere. Subtle, I doubt she knew they were there. Anyway, I know we've had this argument before but Millay holds up and young people understand the poems. Not just women either. The young men like her too."

"Are you going to the Delta tomorrow afternoon?"

"Yes. I'm curious, and besides, Mack Stanford will be there. He's the sexiest man I've ever seen in my life. I just want to warm my hands at that fire."

"I'll come up Sunday and spend the day. I can't get away until then. I might fly to Greenville and drive back with you."

"I didn't mean to stay that long. I was coming back Sunday morning."

"But the blues festival is going on. You won't want to leave when you start hearing that music."

"When do we work around here? I thought we were supposed to be teaching school."

The phone began ringing while they were eating dessert, a charlotte russe Augustus had made for her.

He answered the phone and talked for a minute to someone. As soon as he hung it up it rang again.

"Jim's been arrested," he said to Caroline after the second call. "He was picked up after running into a tree. The police found drug paraphernalia in the car. This is going to be a shit storm. It happened last night. He was just released from the hospital. He broke his nose on the steering wheel."

The phone rang again. This time it was someone who really knew what had happened. Augustus listened for a long time. Then he found his address book and came back to the phone and gave the caller a telephone number.

"What did they say?" Caroline asked.

"He's in a manic-depressive break precipitated by injecting himself with an anesthetic used as a pre-op for surgery. He was in a coma all night. No one knows how to treat it because anyone who ever used the drug recreationally died."

"Why did he do it? Was he in pain? Maybe he went crazy from listening to everyone's troubles."

"He is a Zen Buddhist. He sits in zazen. That was Cane Healy,

Celia's brother, who's an internist. He said Jim found a chat room on the internet and read that the anesthetic, I can't pronounce the name, brought enlightenment. He took it to find enlightenment. And to think we went to him for advice."

"Enlightenment doesn't exist. All there is is the present moment, nothing else is real. We can't know first causes. We don't know why we're here or how we got here or how long the human race is going to last, much less the planet or the solar system or the universe. We don't know how big the universe is and we can't find out. Our scale is too small. We have no idea what we know. Didn't he know that?"

"He was brilliant when he was sane. Now he's insane."

The phone rang again. This time it was Celia. "God knows what he's saying," she said. "I want to worry about *him*, but my God, Augustus, he could be saying anything. People believe what they hear, especially if it's about wealthy people. We have to get him out of Jackson."

"What did Cane say he said?"

"Well, mostly more stuff about he was enlightened and they should leave him alone. I called his partner, Donna Divers, and she told me all she knew. I guess she's terrified she's going to be sued. This has been going on for some time, you know. This isn't just something that started last weekend. Donna said they knew last winter he was in some sort of trouble but that he went to Dallas to a clinic for a week and they thought it was over."

"Have you seen him this spring?"

"Yes. I knew something was wrong but he told me he had blood sugar problems. He knows everything about my life, Augustus. If he starts telling lies about people, they will be based on enough truth to ruin us all."

"Where is he now?"

"He's here, wandering around town with a broken nose. What can we do?"

"I don't know. Joe Biggs offered him a plane the other night to fly him anywhere he wants to go. Also, William said the Duval planes are there if he needs them."

"D. B. Duval?"

"It seems he was talking to him too."

"That's unimaginable. I don't want D. B. Duval involved in this. We could all end up in grocery store tabloids if that got out."

"William said you told Sally Duval to send D.B. to see him."

"I might have done it. Well, that makes things worse. Not that they could get much worse. I have paid him sixteen thousand dollars to treat CeCe so she won't end up doing drugs and now she's going to find out he is a dope addict. He's been giving her B-twelve shots, in the office. He could have injected her with this stuff."

"It's very sad," Augustus said.

"It is sad but it's also very scary. Come down to the Delta with us this weekend. We'll have a meeting and decide what to do."

"I'm coming but it won't be until Sunday. I have to prepare lectures for next week."

"We couldn't even claim insurance for CeCe's therapy. I was paying two hundred dollars a visit for her to talk to a dope addict."

"Calm down, Celia. CeCe's fine. Caroline Jones liked her very much, by the way. She was raving about CeCe. Here, talk to her." He handed the phone to Caroline. She shook her head, but he insisted. "I liked your daughter," she said. "And I'm looking forward to the weekend with all of you."

"I wish you'd fly down with us. You could see the Delta from the air. There are cars at Oak Grove. You can have a car all to yourself if you like. Augustus is coming Sunday. You could go home with him."

"Then I will. When are you leaving?"

"Friday afternoon. We'll wait for you. When can you get away?"

"I can be ready by five, I think."

"I'll send a car for you at five. Oh, this is good. This is perfect."

"I'll meet you at the airport," Caroline said, hanging on to some power. "Just tell me how to get there."

"It's beside the main airport. There's an entrance marked Jackson Air Services. Our hangar is the second one in a row of four. It's painted sky blue and says Montgomery in white letters over the door. Are you sure you don't want me to send a car?"

"I'll find it. I'll be there as soon as I can get away."

"Well, don't hurry. Anyway, I'm delighted you can join us. We'll be waiting for you. You'll see us there."

Friday was a hectic day at school. Students were lined up trying to change classes. Caroline's poetry class had to be split into two sections. "I'll need to be paid more to teach two sections," she told the head of the English department. "I know how much Topeka made for the same work, you know. I was making forty thousand at Yale the year I began there. I don't mind doing extra work as long as I'm paid for it."

Gay Wileman was smiling. "Good for you," she said. "I'll put in a request with the dean. It will go through. Now that we've met you everyone is excited that you're here. I'm sorry about the pay. That wasn't my idea. Next year we'll do better."

"Did you hear what happened with Jim Jaspers?" Caroline asked.

"I've heard it all."

"The reason I brought it up is I know a woman psychiatrist in

Nashville who might talk to some of his patients if they need her. She helped my mother a lot. I talked to her once or twice when she was seeing Mother. She's very consoling. Augustus is worried about what the patients will do."

"I saw him myself a few times," Gay admitted. "I should have told you that the other day. I'm not really surprised by all of this. The last few times I saw him, in the spring, I was upset, well, uncomfortable, with how it went."

"In what way?"

"I don't know. He talked about himself the whole time. I don't think psychiatrists are supposed to do that. I deal with crazy people all the time around here. I know insanity when I see it. I don't know. He would say things that seemed so strange. He gave me poems he'd been writing. None of them made sense. I don't think psychiatrists are supposed to ask their patients to criticize their poems. I should have known."

"No, you shouldn't," Caroline answered. "You didn't have enough information. We all go around doing the best we can with the information that's available to us. It wasn't up to you to evaluate the shrink."

"I guess you're right. Thanks for saying that." She paused, then went on. "I heard you were going to the Delta with Celia. Also, that you had met CeCe and liked her."

"Does everyone know everything everyone does around here?"

"Well, everyone's interested in you, because you're new."

"Will everyone know if I get a salary raise?"

"If the dean denied the request they would know." She smiled. "Don't worry. He'll sign on."

∾ 5 ∾

THE GOVERNOR'S DAUGHTER understood what was happening. She was a manic-depressive who had learned to control the disease by taking her drugs and hating the mania. She had been the first to know there was something wrong with Jim. She had been monitoring it for months, since the day when he stopped in the middle of a session and began to write a Zen koan. She had noted it in her diary. Unfortunately for the other patients, she left in May to lead a trade delegation to Europe. Although she did not forget Jim's strange behavior, she had been lulled into believing it was a projection.

"What's wrong with you?" she had asked him several times. "Something's wrong, Jim. You don't seem like yourself. Is it your back? You shouldn't be sitting for these long hours if your back is bothering you. You need a better chair, or else lie down and I'll sit."

"My blood sugar's doing crazy things," he answered. "I'm on a strict diet, no sugar, not even potatoes, so I'm hungry, to tell the truth." He laughed, letting her in on his humanity. "And, of course, it's been a busy two months. What with the indictments all over town in the Espy investigation."

"Are you having to take insulin?"

"No. It's not classic diabetes. It's a genetic thing. My brother has migraine headaches. Thank God I've been spared that most of my life."

"You don't seem like yourself."

"Don't worry. I'm taking care of myself. I won't let you down." He had smiled at her out of his deep blue eyes and she had allowed him to overcome her better judgment. Then she had gone off to take the business leaders of the state to Europe to open markets and arrange art exhibits for the state of Mississippi. Still, she did not forget the way Jim had jumped up from his chair and gone to his desk and written a jumble of words he called a Zen koan and thrust it upon her. It seemed like mania, but she supposed it could be explained by blood sugar levels. So she was not surprised when the phone call came at four in the morning to her hotel room in Italy. She answered in Italian, but the voice on the other end of the line was her father's.

"Something's happened here," he said. "The psychiatrist you and your buddies at the ballet guild go to has gone crazy. He's running around town telling people he knows you. He called my secretary three times today trying to get your phone number over there. He told her you were his best friend and that he had to talk to you. I did a check. First he went crazy at a funeral, a buddy of you-all's died. Then he had a wreck. When the police got there he was in a coma. They found drug paraphernalia all over the car. I heard he was going to lose his license to practice medicine."

"Slow down, Daddy. Is this a secure phone?"

"How the hell would I know? Your mother's been awake all night. She wants to know what you told him about her."

"Nothing. I don't talk to him about you-all. Now just slow down. Who died?"

"Your friend, that actress who owns the theater. She had a heart attack. It looks like this psychiatrist got drunk at the funeral and made a scene. Then he had this wreck last night. He made all these calls to my office yesterday and the day before."

"He was going to tell me Jean died."

"No. He told my secretary he had to have some money you had promised to invest in some book publishing business he wants to start."

"Mania. Well, hold on, Daddy. As soon as I get up I'll call his secretary and find out what's happening. Where is he now?"

"One of his patients sent lawyers. He's out of jail."

"Well, that's a relief."

"What did you tell him about us, about your mother and me?"

"Nothing. I talked to him about myself. About my condition and what drugs I can take safely. I used him for a medical doctor, Daddy. It's your genes that gave this to me. It's your mother and aunts that went crazy."

"You told him that? You told him my mother went crazy? Aunt Betty? You told him about her? I can't believe you'd do that, Sister. Do you know what would happen if that got out?"

"You can't run again anyway, Daddy. What do you care? Everyone in Arden, Mississippi, knows your mother and her sisters went crazy. They were manic-depressives and we can treat that now. I live a normal life if I take care of myself."

"How is Howie? Is Howie there?" Howie was the husband of Margaret, which was the governor's daughter's name. He was a good man who had been a star quarterback at Ole Miss. He was smart and he was good and he loved his wife. He had taken a six-month leave of absence from his job at a tractor company to accompany her to Europe on the state's business. He was planning on running for governor himself one day and knew what side political bread is buttered on.

"He's right here, Daddy. In the bed with me. Do you want me to wake him up too or could it wait until morning?"

"What time is it there?"

"It's four fifteen."

"Oh, well. You call me back in the morning. We have to do something about this."

"Call Dr. Jaspers's office and offer to help send him somewhere for treatment. He's sick, Daddy. He needs help."

"What about all the drugs they found in his car?"

"He's a medical doctor. He was trying to medicate himself. Don't go crazy, Daddy. This will not affect you. If you want to worry, worry about all the people involved in the Espy case he had in treatment. That's the big problem."

It was six in the afternoon before the governor stopped worrying and started making effective calls about the matter. He called the head of the county board of health and the chairman of the state medical board and then he called Celia.

"There are hospitals for doctors," he told her. "Jay Epstein said he'd escort him to Nashville to that place up there. It might help if some of you would call and tell him you think that's a good idea."

"I barely know the man," Celia lied. "I went to him when I was distraught over my husband's health. We are all telling him to go somewhere, Warren. I don't think calling in the medical board is going to do anything but make him mad. I wouldn't make him mad if I were you. He's been treating everyone in town who's been called before special prosecutors. We don't want to make trouble for any of those people, do we?"

"Well, we'd better do something about this. You know my daughter had contact with this man. He could start any kind of rumors. You have to stop this kind of thing before it gets out of hand, Celia."

"William Harbison has put a plane at his disposal to fly anywhere he wants to go to get help. What else can we do?"

"Well, hell, Celia. This isn't helping. We've got to do better than this."

"Let the weekend go by. If he hasn't called William by Monday, well, that's Labor Day, by Tuesday, then you call me back and we'll decide on a course of action. I'm as worried about this as you are, Warren. We're all worried about it. People at the theater told him their troubles. We have enough bad publicity over there without this."

"You ought to put on plays that don't stir folks up so much, Celia. I don't know why you always have to be so controversial."

"That's what Paine Theater was for, Warren. Art is controversial."

"Okay, okay, I don't want to argue with you about that today, Celia. You call me Tuesday then and let's decide what we can do."

6

THERE ARE ALWAYS FORMS to be filled out in modern universities. When she was at Yale, Caroline had hated and resented them, but this year she had decided to just go on and fill them out.

When she finished her classes on Friday afternoon she went into her office and filled out forms at lightning speed. She pretended she was in a tennis match, playing fast to throw her opponent off balance.

At five o'clock she shoved the unfinished work into a desk drawer and walked out of the English department, feeling important and mature. She could do it. She could be a grown person who wasn't annoyed by the insane complexities and overkill of the modern world. Working's wonderful, she decided. Teaching's an ancient and honored skill. Honest work among people who mean what they say and keep their promises. It's my heritage to be an academic. My grandfather taught Latin at Sewanee. Why did I ever think there was anything in Hollywood Trash Money Dreams and How Stupid Can You Make a Film and What's the Price of Your Honor and Pride that could ever compete with the beginning of a school year in a good and honest college? Nothing.

She got into her Cabriolet and drove to the Jackson airport believing she had money and power figured out and in their place. The brand-new Learjet didn't change her mind about that. She felt no envy for Celia's money or her airplane. All she felt was curiosity about these new people who were making their way into her life. Of course, there was Mack Stanford. What he had was way past money or the trashy power it buys. He had the real thing. Real sexuality and kindness and charisma. Probably had it when he was born, Caroline decided. Probably got held more than any baby in the nursery. Well, I'll be his friend. I will. That's not a joke. Why do I always have to make fun of myself? I could take myself seriously if I wanted to. She giggled at the thought. Well, not while I live with Augustus, of course.

The ride to the Delta was smooth, luxurious, and fast. Mack was sitting up front with the pilots because he was taking flying lessons and wanted to watch. The women sat in the back. CeCe and Caroline were on seats that turned into beds and Celia was on the backseat with CeCe's Australian shepherds. CeCe was reading *Go Down, Moses*, one of the books that had been starred on Caroline's list. Celia was reading the September *Vogue*. Caroline looked out the window at the clouds. Then she put the seat back into its full reclining position and went to sleep. She didn't wake up until they had landed in Greenville and were taxiing down the runway.

They were met at the airport by a pair of matched silver Lincoln Continentals. The cars had drivers dressed in matching black suits. "You go in the car with Mack," Celia said. "I don't want anyone to have to put up with these dogs."

"Then you go with us too."

"No, I don't want you to be distracted. I want you to see the land at sundown." Celia smiled and placed her hand on Caroline's hand. "Go on. Before it gets any darker."

It was seven o'clock when Mack and Caroline got into the Lincoln and were driven down into the flat, darkening beauty of the Delta. "The richest land in the world," Mack said. "It's the delta of three rivers. The Yazoo, the Sunflower, and the Mississippi. Technically, it's a flood plain but everyone has always called it the Delta."

"Are you doing all right?" Caroline was sitting beside him on the backseat. He seemed so needy. She forgot all her jokes about wanting to fuck him and felt real pity for his loss and his sadness.

"I think so," he said. He paused, then looked at her and smiled. It took him a while to get the next words out, as though he wasn't sure he should say them. "There really isn't a good time to have your psychoanalyst go crazy, is there?"

"I know a woman in Nashville you can talk to. She's the most motherly person I've ever met. If you really needed someone to talk to you could go up there. You can stay with my parents. They'd be glad to have you."

"That's very kind of you. But I'll be all right. I have a lot to do. I have to move on, you know. But let me tell you about the Delta. Look out there, behind the trees, that's the levee. Wait a minute." He leaned up into the front seat and asked the driver to find a road up to the top of the levee.

"To understand the Delta you must start with the rivers and the bayous," he went on. "Think of what it took to build these levees. There is the main one going all the way down the river from above

Cairo to New Orleans and many smaller ones protecting houses and fields. Long ago they were built by mule teams pulling slip wagons. Flat wagons made of two-by-fours. They would tie all the boards together and pile dirt on top of them, then when the mules had pulled them to the top they would loosen the boards and the dirt would fall out. It was the late 1920s before there were any tractors here. Celia has photographs from the early days. Before that the Indians built them by hand, huge mounds, some as big as football fields. We'll get out and look. Celia told me to give you a tour." The driver turned off the pavement and went up a gravel road to the top of the levee. They got out and walked to the edge. Below lay a long, sloping fall and a smaller levee and then the wide expanse of the big brown river. It was very still.

"A levee is much wider than it looks from below," Mack said. "It is sometimes as wide as a two-lane road and sometimes even wider. Its width varies as it goes along the river. I had a book about levees when I was a child. I used to study it and try to build them in the yard." He smiled. It was the second time Caroline had seen him smile. The sadness he was enduring had crossed his face completely until now.

"It's like the stars," Caroline answered. "It makes you feel small to be near a river this big. I can't imagine them building this with mule teams."

"Many people died from typhus and yellow fever, or drowned. Luckily there was plenty of dirt to build with. The topsoil along the river is very deep and so thick it sticks to your shoes like glue."

"It doesn't seem that it could break, but it has, hasn't it?"

"The bad one was in nineteen twenty-seven. It broke about twenty miles from here, at Mount Bayou. The water moved out across the land at about fifteen miles a day, just a sheet of water moving across the land. It had rained so much that year it had filled all the tributaries and made the Ohio River run backward. My great-uncle was General Paxton, who was in charge of flood control. I heard stories of the flood every day of my life."

"It may help explain the culture," Caroline proposed. "Like the Egyptians. When you have that sort of force beside you, and only your strength and cunning to keep it at bay, it drives you to make life beautiful and meaningful. Augustus told me the driving force behind art in the state was always the people of the Delta."

"Well, they had the money." Mack laughed. "You have to have money and leisure time to make art. Even the musicians who made the blues are indebted to wealth. That's how the musical instruments got here. You can make music on drums made of natural materials but it's not as good as trombones and saxophones and keyboards. You're not the first person to see the connection with Egypt. Think of the names of the river towns, Memphis, Cairo. Jean was interested in this. She wanted her ashes scattered on the levee near Mount Bayou, because it was the crevasse. She thought that was funny, but, of course, I didn't have a vote in that." He moved to the edge of the levee and looked out toward the river. "When Cortés first crossed this river he made his men build fires and melt down their stirrups to make nails to build rafts. They had Spanish pigs with them on the rafts. They got loose on the Arkansas side and became feral. Hence the wild razorbacks for which the University of Arkansas has named its athletic teams. I know a thousand river stories."

"Mack." She walked to him. "You didn't let her down. Dying is the enemy, not what you do with the body afterward. I see why she was fascinated by this. It's amazing to stand on this levee and to think of it going down the whole river on both sides. To imagine men thinking they could control and master such a thing as a river. It makes me proud to be a human being."

"Well, the Judeo-Christian tradition told us we were in charge of everything and could do with it as we wished. An idea I'm sure is always welcome in any group of humans."

She laughed and moved closer. They stood very close together looking at the Father of Waters. Then he put his hands around her waist and pulled her into his body, and they stood there long enough for many messages to be sent and received. Oh, shit, Caroline decided. This is the beginning of my major favorite fantasy. A man and a woman on a Sunday after church. He holds her against his growing penis from the back. Someone says, We'd better go home now and take care of business. *When we get behind closed doors. . . .*

Except, of course, that behind Mack's door is a dead woman he was sleeping with last week. I should know better than to mess with this. But I wouldn't count on it.

"I'm really worried about this thing with Jim," Mack said. "I told him a lot of things I wouldn't want repeated because they'd be misunderstood. Jean was thirty years older than I am. She was the mother I never had as well as my lover. She worried about it more than I did. I just live my life. But in the end the sex was about run out and Jim knew all that. I don't want him going around talking about my sex life. He talked to one patient about the other ones a lot. He told me all sorts of things about other people, Jean's friends, Celia, the governor, that I know shrinks aren't supposed to tell, but for a long time I thought it was just me he was telling these things to. I talked to William, the lawyer you met at the wake. He said Jim used to tell him all sorts of things about his other patients. Now what if he starts telling that stuff down at the police station or the coffee shop. Well, you don't want to hear all this."

The penis was going down. The moment had passed, not that Caroline Jones was going to forget it any time soon.

They walked back to the car and got in and were driven back down the gravel road and on to Oak Grove plantation.

"So what are we going to do all weekend?" CeCe was saying to her mother in the other car. "Just gossip about Jim?"

"This isn't gossip, CeCe. These are real problems. He's had a nervous breakdown. We have to decide what to do."

"I'm worried about him. He's a good man, Momma. He's been helping all of us, now we ought to help him. So he started taking his own drugs. Doctors do that all the time. It's nothing new, somebody getting addicted to a drug they thought they could control."

"You were in therapy with him, CeCe. A psychotherapist is not supposed to call up his patients and tell them his troubles. He's been calling people all over Jackson. I have to find someone else for you to see. I'm worried sick about what this will do to you."

"I never paid any attention to half the things he told me anyway. I knew half the stuff he said was a crock of shit. Especially this last spring and summer. He got into this crap about some translations of Vedic poetry. He kept showing me this meaningless stuff and trying to tell me it was poetry. I was only going to see him to keep you happy. I'll be glad to have my afternoons back. Why don't you give me the money you were spending and I'll buy myself a poetry magazine."

"CeCe, this is not about money."

"Oh, yeah. Well, sooner or later it will be. Everything always turns out to be about money. If I ever get a single friend sooner or later they turn out to want me to do something for them that involves money. Except for Daniel and George and that's just because they both have plenty of it themselves. So I could buy a poetry magazine and then people would want something else from me. They would want me to publish their poems."

"Don't be cynical, CeCe. It's unbecoming."

"Okay, I'll stop being cynical. I'll do anything you want, Mommy dearest."

"Oh, CeCe, don't be mean."

"I am mean, deal with it." They had come to the house now and CeCe let the dogs out and began to run with them across the lawn. Celia went inside to get ready for her guests.

~ 7 ~

MAYBE JIM JASPERS WENT CRAZY. Maybe he was driven crazy by his patients. If he had come to believe he was omnipotent, who had made him believe it? It was a heady thing to have the most powerful people in the state of Mississippi calling him day and night for advice, using him for their father and mother and spiritual adviser, asking him to forgive their sins, letting them turn him into God, since even godless people are always wanting something to believe in, especially something they create themselves. The creation of James Jaspers, M.D., was a group effort but it would be some time before any of the people involved began to arrive at that conclusion. For the moment they were busy with damage control, calling each other up, joking about things he might say, telling each other he was crazy.

Jim Jaspers drove around town for several hours on Friday afternoon. He was slipping in and out of sanity. Sometimes he had the intelligence to worry about what was going on. Then the mania would take over and he would call his patients on the car phone. He would tell them how well he was doing and not to worry, he'd be back in the office soon.

"I'm taking care of the equipment," he would say. "I'm not going to let anything happen to it."

The patients he had not been treating long were relieved to hear from him. They didn't mind stopping what they were doing to listen to him talk about himself. Actually, they were honored that this esteemed physician thought they were worthy of his confidence.

His old patients, the powerful ones, the cabal, were all away from their homes. All he got was a series of answering machines. They're at Celia's place in the Delta, he decided. They've gone to the blues festival. I'm going too.

He stopped the car underneath a tree and tried to call his old girlfriend. She had left him the month before and gone to Starkville to live. "It's me or those needles," she had said. "That's it, Jim. The last warning."

"I'm enlightened," he had answered. "I saw it, the why and how of all reality. I'm seeing God. I am God. If you leave me now you will never replace me. You'll never find another person who knows what I know. You are only a little, scared human being with a relatively low IQ. Whatever you did in your last life has come back to haunt you now. Don't you know that? Don't you know defective beings like you never get to know gods? And now you know one and you want to leave? Don't be crazy. This is the only chance you'll ever have to know divinity."

He had scared her to death. He had scared her so much she had spent the night and let him fuck her. As soon as she was sure he was asleep she sneaked out of the house and went home. She packed a bag and went home to Starkville where she had brothers to protect her. She had had all the genius she ever needed.

*   *   *

Jim kept on driving around town. Then he drove home and took a shower and drank a Coke. He took twenty milligrams of Ambien and went to sleep. Tomorrow I'll go to the Delta and surprise them, he decided. I'll get some sleep and then I'll go and tell them about God. I can't keep this to myself. I have to share this with my patients.

That night he dreamed that spiders and flies were getting into his house. In his dream he kept getting out of bed and stopping up the holes in the wall with chewing gum or else swatting the creatures or spraying poison. Finally out of a hole beside his bed two gorgeous figures about four inches tall emerged. They were half insect and half human. A beautiful man and woman with wings and antennae. They were dressed in gorgeous, colorful suits like butterfly wings. They smiled at him and danced in the air but he knew he must kill them too. For the rest of the night he pursued them around his house, hitting at them and scaring them and finally capturing one of them under a glass. He tore part of her wing as he set the glass on top of her. Still, she kept on smiling.

~ 8 ~

THE PLANTATION HOUSE sat at the end of a driveway lined with hundred-year-old oak trees. It was not what Caroline had expected. It was quiet and comforting and cool. There was nothing showy or tacky in the hugeness of its rooms, the height of its ceilings, the gorgeous perfection of its antiques and reproductions.

There were servants everywhere and the dinner was a dream. Meat from cows raised on the place without hormones or antibiotics. Milk and butter and cream from the same herd, vegetables raised in a garden without pesticides. "It's an experiment my husband started," Celia said. "He wants to see if he can re-create his childhood here. I wanted him to be with us, but he wanted to stay in town and rest. He hasn't been well for several years. It has been a sadness for all of us."

"I want to meet him," Caroline said.

"You will. He's just having a temporary setback. He'll be back in the swing of things before too long."

"After dinner we can go for a walk," CeCe suggested. "It's only a mile to the river. We can walk up on the levee but we have to spray ourselves. There are still mosquitoes this time of year. We have three

Indian mounds, you know. And we have a little cemetery if anyone wants to see it."

"I want to see everything," Caroline said. "And I've already been on a levee. Mack had them stop and let us walk on one before we got here." She looked at him and the look that passed between them was not lost on anyone at the table.

For dessert there was cherry pie made with cherries from trees on the place, topped with ice cream and whipped cream made from the plantation's own milk, all served in silver bowls. I love the rich, Caroline decided. This is okay. This is fine with me.

After dinner they went upstairs to change shoes for their planned walk. Caroline called Augustus to report.

"It's a paradise," she told him. "And I think Mack is trying to screw me."

"You lie."

"I am not lying. He took me up on this levee and got me in front of him. You think I ought to screw him if he asks me?"

"No. I think you'll catch ten diseases, you bitch. I think you should leave him for me. He's already had an older woman, what he needs next is a real lover."

"So tell me about Celia. Would she care if I screwed him in her house?"

"I would care. Don't you dare screw him until I get there."

"Hurry up then. What are you doing?"

"Writing a lecture on the Romantic poets. I can't come until Sunday. So what is everyone saying about Jim?"

"Not much. I guess they're waiting for you to get here. We had homemade ice cream on homemade pie. Is this the way to live, or what?"

"Mind your manners and they'll have you up in November for the quail hunts."

"I've got to go. We're going for a walk."

"Go on, then. Have fun. Don't fuck him, Caroline. It's too soon. Way too soon."

"So you say. You'd fuck him in a heartbeat if it was you."

She put on her running shoes and went out of the room and down the stairs in a wonderful mood, which was ruined when she found out Mack had gone to his room to go to sleep.

"He said he was worn out," CeCe said. "And everyone else chickened out so it's just you and me. Here's the bug spray. Really use it. These mosquitoes are not fooling around this time of night. When I was a child I was covered with bites all summer. I hate the little bastards."

Caroline sprayed herself thoroughly with bug spray and then she and CeCe started out of the house. A servant met them at the front door with two small flashlights. "We don't need those. There's a moon," CeCe said.

"Mrs. Montgomery wants you to have them. She said be sure you took them so you won't trip."

CeCe took the flashlights and held one in each hand. "Thanks, Danny," she said. "That was nice of you to get them for us."

The man stood watching them as they went down the stairs and then down through the grove of oak trees toward the front gate. When they reached the gate, CeCe turned and touched Caroline's arm with one of the flashlights. "We can leave them under a tree, but remind me to get them when we come back. I don't want to hurt Danny's feelings." She set the flashlights in the roots of a huge old liveoak tree, then took

Caroline's hand and began to lead her along a path that led to a fence. "We're going to the levee by the shortcut. You aren't afraid of cows, are you? There are cows back here, but they won't bother you."

"I don't know if I'm afraid of them or not." Caroline laughed. "What could they do to you?"

"Well, you could step in the patties. That would be the worst thing. Just follow me. Stay on the path. If anyone steps in it it will be me. There's a metaphor. Jim Jaspers stepped in it, for sure. It's hard for me to believe he'd take drugs. He hated drugs. It's all he talked about: don't drink coffee, don't smoke, if someone's doing drugs, call them on it. Never act like you don't notice. I mean, that's all he talked about."

"I only met him once. I really can't judge."

"Let's try to forget it. I didn't mean to bring it up. I love the book, by the way, but I won't make you talk about that either." They had come to a fence and CeCe climbed over it and held out her hand to help Caroline do the same. Then they walked across a field that seemed to be filled everywhere with the huge, dark shapes of cows. I was eating them, Caroline kept thinking. Now I'm walking by them.

The moon was full and high. There were beautiful and mysterious clouds moving very slowly across the face of the moon and making wonderful visions in the sky. They crossed the field and went up on the levee and walked along it for a long time without talking, then they went back to the house and collected the flashlights and said goodnight and went inside and went to bed. It had been a thoroughly delightful evening in every way. None of it had been anything Caroline could have expected.

9

AUGUSTUS CALLED CELIA at ten the next morning, just as the house party was getting ready to go to Greenwood to the opening of the blues festival.

"Celia," Augustus began.

"Yes."

"Is everyone there? Is Caroline with you? Is everyone all right?"

"Of course. We just finished breakfast. Callie made blintzes. I wish you'd been here. When are you coming?"

"Jim called me a minute ago. He wanted to know who all was there. He wanted to know if I was going. I lied to him and told him no. I could tell he was going to suggest he go along. You didn't invite him there, did you?"

"No. Heavens no."

"Well, don't be surprised if he shows up."

"Oh, God, don't tell me that. What will I do?"

"I don't know. Listen, I'll come on down this afternoon. Do you have room for me?"

"Yes. No one could come from New York or Memphis. It's just the four of us, CeCe and Caroline and Mack and myself."

"We can't be codependents for his addiction. He should be going somewhere to be treated. If he comes, we have to tell him that. William said he talked to Donna and she said Jim told her he didn't need any treatment. William's scared to death, with D. B. Duval breathing down his throat."

"Not to mention the governor. What did Donna suggest we do?"

"Stay away from him. That's what she told me."

"Donna's only a psychologist."

"Well, I'll be down this afternoon. Just hold on until I get there. Joe Biggs and Duval have both offered him planes to go anywhere he decides to go, but he hasn't called them back. The only person he's called today is me."

"He's lonely for us. That's understandable."

"We can protect ourselves, Celia. And we will."

"Hurry up then. I need you."

"I'm on my way."

Celia called everyone into a drawing room. It was decorated with yellow velvet sofas, white linen drapes, and beautiful Persian rugs so old they looked like they were made of silk. Coffee was served. "We have to decide what to do if he comes," she began. "This isn't just Jim Jaspers's problem. It affects all of us. He's refusing to be treated. He's running around the state of Mississippi like a loose shotgun."

"Loose cannon, Momma," CeCe put in.

"Whatever one calls it. He may be coming here. We have to decide what we're going to do if he appears. We have to be prepared. He could show up at the festival. He knows I have a party for it each year. He will know that's where we are. Well, there's nothing to fear, of course. I mean, the worst thing he could do is say things to us. But he was saying untrue things about people at the funeral. I wouldn't want him doing that. What if we are at the blues festival and he starts ranting in front of people?"

"Calm down, Mother," CeCe said. "Jim's not going to harm any of us. He's been useful to all of you. Actually at the beginning he was useful to me. He talked to me about *Catcher in the Rye*. He told me a lot of really useful things. He said the main thing wrong with all of us was we didn't have sex enough. He said people my age were supposed to have sex but our culture didn't allow it and besides there are too many diseases to catch unless we settle down with one good guy. I mean, he was useful to me. He made me understand a lot of things."

"He's refusing to be treated," Celia insisted. "Jim Jaspers injecting himself with a lethal drug is not the Jim Jaspers who gave you good advice a year ago."

"She's right," Mack said. "This isn't Jim, CeCe. This is a madman we don't know."

"Who are his friends?" Caroline asked. "Doesn't he have friends? Most doctors have other doctors for friends. Isn't there someone he trusts?"

"I don't know of any," Mack said.

"Well, none of you is capable of judging or helping him. I mean, I've never really been in therapy but I know about transference. Don't you transfer power to an analyst? I mean, doesn't he become a sort of father figure? So how can you solve this? You were his patients."

"We're all he has," Celia said. "He invested his life in us. If any of us were in this predicament, he would be helping us. I don't know, I guess we all got too involved with him, too dependent on him. We sent everyone to him. If anyone had a problem, we begged Jim to treat them. That's why he had to get Donna Divers. Because everyone wanted him to see their children."

"What can we do?" CeCe asked. "Surely we can think of something."

"We could have a doctor here in case he shows up." Celia stood up. She had finally hit on something that gave her hope. "I could call Royals Connell. He's in Memphis. I'll send the plane for him. I'm going to call him. He'll come if I need him. I know he will. Yes, that's the best idea I've had all week."

"He's a neurosurgeon, Mother," CeCe said. "What good will that do?"

"He fixes brains. It's brains that's causing all of this. I mean, Jim's brains, on drugs, like that advertisement on television with the fried eggs. You all go on to the festival and I'll follow you in the other car."

"We'll wait," Mack said. "We aren't going anywhere without you."

They were all glad to wait. Waiting to see if Celia had the power to make a neurosurgeon in Memphis give up his weekend to save them from their psychiatrist was definitely worth missing an extra hour of listening to ancient black men play songs about poverty and alcoholism and loss.

Celia went into the library and started leaving messages on answering machines in Memphis. Then she came back into the drawing room. "I can't get him but he'll call back. I'd better stay here and wait for him to call. You all go on. I'll join you later after I talk to him."

❧ 10 ❧

AUGUSTUS HAD A HARD TIME leaving Jackson because his phone kept ringing with calls from people who wanted to talk about Jim. The food editor at the *Clarion Ledger* had worked herself up into such a state he had to talk to her for fifteen minutes to calm her down. "He isn't going to tell your secrets to anyone," Augustus kept saying. "Face it, Peggy, everyone knows you're gay. There is nothing he can do to you."

"He armored me. He helped me. He gave me strength. I should be doing something to help him, but instead all I'm doing is worrying about myself."

"That's what armor is! You're supposed to defend yourself. You were paying him two hundred dollars an hour, Peggy. He wasn't doing this to be nice."

"Yes, he was. He loved me. He cared for me."

"That's an infantile reaction. He is a man in the business of making money just like everyone else. If you'd quit paying him he wouldn't have kept on seeing you."

"Where is he now?"

"God only knows. I hope he's not going to the Delta because I'm going there."

"I'm going to try to find him."

"How long has it been since you had a session with him?"

"Six weeks."

"You don't want to see him now. I'm warning you."

"What am I going to do? What if Helen leaves me? What if my mother dies? Who will I talk to? Who will save me?"

"You can talk to me. And there are other psychiatrists. Celia has a list of them. Call her Monday. Or call your internist and ask him who he recommends. Get an appointment and see somebody else right away. Look, Peggy, I really have to go. I'll give you a number in the Delta. If you get in a bind, call me there."

"Thank you, Augustus. You are an angel. I'll be all right. I just have to process this."

"Interview somebody. Get something done."

"If it gets out, it will cost me my job."

"It's out, Peggy. You're out. You're a fabulous editor. You work harder than anyone on that paper. You should demand a raise. That would be a good use for this anxiety. Tell them you need a raise so you can go to a psychiatrist to make up for the stress of the job."

"You sound like Jim. That's what he'd say."

"We have to stop now. I have to get ready to leave." He mocked Jim's voice and won a laugh from her.

"Call me if you need me," he added. "Or come on down. Celia would love to have you."

"I should be down there covering the festival but I gave it to Lyn

Moss. All right, I'm hanging up. Thanks so much, Augustus. At least I have you."

Augustus ended up leaving Jackson ten minutes before Jim Jaspers got into his car and started driving down the same road. Augustus was starving but he was trying to wait until he got to Yazoo City to eat because he adored the biscuits at the Yazoo City Kentucky Fried Chicken place. He had told dozens of people about those biscuits, how light, how buttery, how mouthwatering, melt-in-your-mouth, they were. Anytime he left Jackson on the highway to Yazoo City, the thought of those biscuits drove everything else from his mind.

So he drove fast and steadily. If he had not, Jim would have passed him on the highway. As it was he had barely parked in the parking lot of the Kentucky Fried Chicken place when he saw Jim go driving past, bent over the wheel, looking as mad as a hatter. He got back into his car and called Celia and told her what he had seen.

"Where are you?" Celia asked.

"At the Kentucky Fried Chicken place in Yazoo City getting ready to eat breakfast."

"You're eating fried chicken for breakfast?"

"No. Biscuits. I've told you about these biscuits. Haven't you ever tried them? I'll bring you one."

"So he'll be here in an hour."

"About that. He was going fifty through downtown Yazoo. Maybe he'll be stopped again."

"I got Royals on the phone. He's coming down this afternoon to help. I sent the plane for him. He's going to stay until tonight. What if Jim gets here first?"

"You could stay in your room. You could have the servants tell him you're not there."

"Hurry up. Start driving."

"As soon as I get my biscuits. I hate to eat them in the car. I disapprove of people eating in their cars."

"Augustus!"

"I'm on my way." He drove through the drive-in window, picked up six biscuits and packs of jelly, put the sack on the seat beside him, and drove on out of town. He could smell the biscuits, but he was damned if he was going to eat them until he got to Leroy Percy State Park past Belzoni. Augustus's grandparents had lived on a plantation near Greenville and he had been taken as a child to swim in the pool at Leroy Percy Park. It was a deep stone pool with water as cold as ice, and he remembered his afternoons there as moments in paradise, all his cousins by his side, chicken sandwiches with mayonnaise and Bibb lettuce. Thick cold pickles and potato salad and sliced tomatoes. Watermelons for dessert. A trip to Leroy Percy Park was planned days in advance. Now that Augustus was back in Mississippi, he never passed the entrance to Leroy Percy Park without stopping to at least walk around beneath the trees and be quiet long enough to remember being a small blond boy with beautiful cousins who adored him. "I think I started liking boys because of my cousins in the Delta," he had told Jim Jaspers, and Jim had not argued with him. "You were safe with them," he'd answered. "Safe to love them as much as you liked."

"We slept together on a sleeping porch. No one ever slept alone. I know it's supposed to be genetic, but there are behavioral reasons too."

"Why do you care? Just stay armored. Maintain your defenses. Don't be with people you don't trust to be glad you're who you are."

*   *   *

No matter what happens to Jim, he was useful to us, Augustus was thinking. I will not join a chorus to stop liking him. He had a midlife crisis. That's nothing new. I'll probably have one myself someday.

Jim Jaspers was driving on mania and aspirins. He had taken the aspirins with milk and now on top of his other troubles his stomach was bothering him. He refused to entertain thoughts about his stomach or digestion. It was the old wormlike part of the body. He was a god now and did not have a stomach.

His reason was cycling in and out on fifteen-minute stretches. On an in cycle he stopped and bought a bottle of Pepto-Bismol and swallowed some of it and then threw away the bottle. A Zen master can repair himself, he decided. Knowledge and power, that's all that matters.

He drove through the Delta in a manic dream. As he slowed down to go through the small town of Belzoni he began to think about CeCe. In the end it would be CeCe who understood what he was doing. The rest of them were too old. No matter how he tried to help them, their old minds slipped back into their old frightened ways. CeCe would escape. He had gotten her young enough. There was all that money. She would leave Mississippi and have a large fine life in the wide world. She would achieve and conquer and become enlightened too.

He slowed down and drove very carefully through the old worn-out town of Belzoni, being very careful of each speed sign and corner. He was thinking about Celia now. She would be glad to see him. She's my mother and my grandmother too, he decided. We love each other. We are deeply bonded. I need to tell her I'm okay. I want to tell her about the light I saw, about the dance of atoms and the spiral of DNA. I have to show it to her. I have to share this with Celia.

He pushed a button on his CD player. Kiri Te Kanawa singing "Se come voi" by Puccini.

He was outside of town now and could drive as fast as he liked. He was almost to the beautiful low plain where the levees begin when he reached into the box on the seat beside him and took out the hypodermic needle and the vial of enlightenment. He loved being able to drive ninety miles an hour with his left hand and prepare his salvation with his right hand. He was master of the universe. He was God.

It had not been simple to figure out the exact dosage it took to dissociate the mind from the body and still leave him able to function. He had started low and worked up. Too much put you to sleep. Too little didn't last long enough and you couldn't do it twice in one day. Which was still okay with Jim. Being God for several hours out of twenty-four was sufficient until he figured out how to do it full-time. Still, he was fairly satisfied. He could wait if he needed to wait but today he didn't have to wait. All he was doing was driving through the Delta to go and surprise his patients. To make sure they were all right. To let them know he loved them and wasn't going anywhere.

Augustus turned into the sweet fresh shade of Leroy Percy State Park and drove to a wooden table and got out and sat under a tree eating his biscuits. He cut each one open and put apple jelly inside and then ate them in huge, unchewed bites. He imagined the sounds of his cousins all around him, yelling and pushing and fighting, the smell of chlorine and the cold intense burn of the water going in. There was not another soul in sight. He had Leroy Percy Park to himself. He decided to waste as much time as he liked, remembering the past and shoring himself up for Celia's house party and the possibility that Jim would be there.

Augustus kept on sitting on the wooden bench ruining his clean khaki pants and eating his biscuits and practicing being recalcitrant. Because of that he was spared the sight of the highway patrol extricating Jim's body from the wrecked and burning car turned upside down in a cotton field just this side of the intersection of Highway 12 and Mississippi 1.

Jim had been going one hundred and five miles an hour when he went off the shoulder of the narrow, straight, flat, deserted road. The next vehicle to come down the road was a farm truck. It took the driver ten minutes to find a house and call the state patrol. If Augustus had not stopped to eat his biscuits he would have been the next car to the scene. He would have seen a sight that would have altered him forever. As it was he only saw a covered body being loaded into an ambulance. The surcease of biscuits, he always called it later. Never turn them down if they are near.

❧ 11 ❧

THE MORNING was lost for the blues festival. CeCe took Caroline off to see the horses and the barns while Celia waited for Royals Connell to call her back about when he could leave Memphis and come and help them.

"Why is everyone so afraid of this man?" Caroline asked. "You can just tell him to go away if he comes here. I'll tell him for you. You can all hide and I'll tell him to go away."

"You can't just do that to someone who was your psychiatrist. We have to get him into a hospital and get him well. But who can make him go, that's the problem. The governor called Mother yesterday. They're taking away his license to practice medicine because of the arrest. If that doesn't work, what can his patients do?"

"I can see how he could do a lot of damage if you let him near you, but you don't have to let him near. Say, 'I won't talk to you in this state,' or something like that."

"He could do a lot of damage in a sentence, Caroline. He knows everyone's fears. He can confront people with their demons. Think of the stuff he must know on Mother or on Mack. They've been going in there and telling him everything about themselves and saying things about other people. God knows what. He doesn't know much about me. I was very selective in what I told him. I knew he was conferring with Mother the whole time he was treating me. I could tell because they'd keep telling me the same things in the same words." CeCe climbed up on a wooden fence. Down an incline, in a small pond, was a life-size wooden statue of a fishing boat with a wooden fisherman. A motor pumped out rainwater and kept the boat from sinking. The fisherman's hook was always poised just above the water.

"I thought that was real," Caroline said.

"It's a Sheldon Mackie. I hate the goddamn thing. It sank last year because they forgot to change the battery in the motor. Mother went crazy. She thought someone had stolen it. When the police got here they found it at the bottom of the pond. I was so disappointed. I thought we'd gotten rid of it."

"I sort of like it. But I see how you could get tired of it after a while. Like hearing the same joke over and over. So what do they fear Jim Jaspers will say? What secrets could he know?"

"Well, the relationship Mother had with Jean Lyles. They were roommates at All Saints Episcopal School in Vicksburg when they were girls. I've always thought they were gay when they were there. I mean, they were locked up for four years. Then when they started the theater they used to go off to New York together for weeks at a time. Jean was such a power broker she'd use anything, and Mother can be used. I know, because I use her when I want to. That was one thing Jim always tried to cure me of. He thought it was a waste of energy to manipulate someone as easy to manipulate as Mother.

"Mother was jealous of Jean. She used to promise her money and then not give it to her for months. Stuff like that. She got really mad at

Jean for a year after Jean started living with Mack. I'd like to know the true story of all of that. Jean used to play people off against one another, make them jealous. It was her prime manipulative scheme. Anyway, there is a lot that could be uncovered, and Jim Jaspers probably knows more about all of them than they do themselves. They were so stupid, they would go in there and tell him everything they knew. As I said, I was careful with him. I was always on my guard."

"So what was it like, talking to him?"

"You'd get in his office and it was all cozy and he'd make you herbal tea and tell you that you were wonderful and exceptional and had great genes and could do anything you wanted to do and deserved to have whatever made you happy. He used to encourage me to spend money. I mean, like get new cars and things like that."

"Sounds nice."

"Well, you can see what we're afraid of then. What if he turns on us and says, 'You're really a bunch of selfish shits and you've been neglecting your children for this stupid theater and you didn't take care of your parents when they were sick' and things like that. He could say that stuff. Be careful of chiggers standing in the grass this near a barn. Stand on the gravel or get up here."

"Chiggers?"

"Red bugs. They get under your skin and itch for days. I hate them so much. I went out riding last summer and got about twenty ticks and a thousand chiggers in one afternoon. I hate nature, to tell the truth. Just because it's beautiful doesn't mean you have to go out in it. Everything trying to take a bite out of you. All this death. I'm about worn out with death."

"Madness and death. Drugs and drunkenness, the things we do to ourselves. I quit Yale to whore for the movies, I still can't get over that."

"You talk about that a lot, don't you?"

"I do?"

"You ought to stop thinking about it. It's the past. Don't let it bother you. I guess you learned your lesson." She smiled the dazzling smile again.

Caroline took a deep breath and dove on in. "Work for me this semester, CeCe. Don't goof off in my class and put me in a bad position. I want you for my friend. Make it possible for me. The Jews believe learning is prayer, an offering to God. I believe that too. It's a high privilege, to get to study great literature. Help me in the class."

"Okay." She smiled the smile again. "Okay, I will. I just goof off to get back at Celia for trying to live through me. She thinks about me twenty-four hours a day. I bet she's thinking about me right now. Did she tell you to make friends with me?"

"Yes. I thought it was a conspiracy. She told me, then the head of the English department told me. And before that, Augustus had suggested it. Listen, CeCe, I'm as hardheaded as you are. When people start trying to use me, I go into reverse. It's only because you're so nice, your smile is really wonderful, you know, that I want to be your friend. It's you and in spite of them."

"She wants me to be a writer because she wants to be one and can't."

"But what if you really wanted to be one? Where would that leave you? I mean, Bach's family expected him to be a musician and it didn't stop him from being a musical genius."

"Well, I'm not a genius. I don't want to do something at which I'll be second rate."

"What a terrible idea. There's only doing the best you can. There's no rating system. God, I hate this culture. Saying people are second and third rate. Those are ideas from the twenties. Like Hemingway thinking literature was a prizefight."

CeCe was quiet, sitting on the wooden fence in her shorts and a halter top, her hair tied back with a ribbon, no makeup, the dazzling smile turned into thought. "They're afraid Jim will come up here and tell them the things they think about themselves. That they are thieves and haters and scared to death. That they are cruel and selfish and secretly glad Jean is dead and they can dream of inheriting her power. No one will be able to because she was a monomaniac. She was the most narcissistic person I ever met. She used people shamelessly. She manipulated everyone. How else could you turn a small amateur theater into a thriving business with a board of directors made up of bankers? She was also a great artist, a great director and actor, and she never stopped learning and trying to improve. She drove people. I used to have to go to rehearsals with Mother. Jean let her star in Albee plays. I'd sit out front and do my homework while they argued and rehearsed. Mother used to cry driving home. But then the plays would open and here in this small southern town would be theater as good as anything on Broadway."

"As good as Broadway?"

"Well, we don't have the Redgrave sisters or Liam Neeson but she would pull performances out of people you wouldn't believe. Jean was something else. It was Jean who made Jim the psychiatrist to the stars, not Mother, although she thinks it was her. You see, people would go to him because they thought he could make them into Jean. Well, it's pretty complicated if you don't know the people."

"So what do you think he'll do if he shows up here? What's your worst scenario?"

"To tell the truth, I imagine it will be very understated and quiet, like a Bergman film. I guess he could tell Mother about my abortion, which Daddy arranged. I could have gone to her but I wasn't in the mood to deal with her second thoughts the rest of my life. What else wouldn't I want him saying in front of a crowd of people? That I'm afraid to compete for men."

"Are you?"

"I think so. Maybe I'm gay. I don't desire women but I like their company better than men, except for my two best friends. Of course, Mother was more interesting than Daddy, and Jean was more interesting than either of them. She used to try to seduce me — not physically, just to make sure I knew she was cuter than my mother."

"Tell me about this doctor who's coming from Memphis."

"Royals? I think Mother's in love with him. He calls her up all the time and asks her to serve on boards, which means give money, and she always does it. She's glad of an excuse to call in her markers. I'm surprised he agreed to come. Well, I guess the situation is interesting to someone who studies brains."

"What does he look like?"

"Like a movie star. He makes Augustus look like nothing. I mean, he's really a ten. You'll see. You'll be drooling. I always am."

"Let's go look at those horses. I really do want to see them." CeCe climbed down off the fence and they went into an air-conditioned barn where four dusty, cutting horses were waiting in their stalls.

"They don't keep them in stalls all the time, do they?" Caroline asked. "It seems so mean, to keep them penned up on a beautiful day."

"They brought them in in case anyone wanted to ride. I'd turn them all loose if it was up to me. I hate what we do to horses." She went up to a dun-colored mare and began to caress her neck. "Yes, yes, my darling, when I own all this I'll set you free. You can run around the pastures till you die. You won't have to carry me to the woods anymore. Not after those twenty ticks. I'm through with nature."

Caroline laughed. Nothing about this weekend was turning out to be what she expected. Really liking CeCe and wanting to be her friend was the nicest and most unexpected thing of all.

"We better get back," CeCe said. "We've got to go to Greenwood to this music thing."

∾ 12 ∾

AT ONE O'CLOCK the Lincoln pulled up to the front door and the party got in. They drove due east for forty miles to Greenwood, where an old friend of Celia's was waiting to take them to hear the blues. His name was Carl Reid and the blues festival was his creation. He had never dreamed it would be so successful or that musicians from all over the world would come every fall to Greenwood to celebrate the music black men had created on German instruments and Italian instruments and anything they could find to make a beat or pick a melody.

Carl Reid was indebted to Celia and Donald Montgomery. They had been his main support for the first five years of the festival. They had written him blank checks when he needed them.

"My angel," he said, getting Celia out of the car. "Wait till you find who's here. The Neville Brothers and this great band from Arkansas, the Cate Brothers. Wait till you hear their saxophone player. What else? Some young musicians from Kansas City who drove all night and ran out of gas. They had to buy farm gas from a farmer with a shotgun. Introduce me to everyone."

Caroline and Mack were introduced and the Lincoln drove off to wait for them at a car dealer's lot. Carl had arranged all that. Now he led them to the white tents where the musicians were playing.

Mack took Caroline's arm and walked beside her. "I'm so glad you're here," he said. "I need people now. I'm so glad you came. You can't know what it means to me."

She didn't look at him but she went over her sexually transmitted diseases mantra just in case. You don't sleep with anyone until everyone's been tested. You don't kiss on the mouth or exchange any fluids. Don't break the rule. It wouldn't be worth it. These are theater people. Wild as gypsies. You can masturbate.

Plus his girlfriend's barely cold in the grave. Plus she was older than my mother. What does that say about his psyche?

They arrived at the first tent where an ancient black man was playing a guitar and singing ancient songs of poverty and woe. "Is this poetry too or just keening?" CeCe whispered to Caroline.

"It's the stuff of poetry. Women being stolen by other men, then someone gets killed. That's Homer and Aeschylus, isn't it?"

"Yes. And Jim Jaspers was Sophocles, when he was well. 'It is the courage to make a clean breast of it in the face of every question that makes the philosopher. He must be like Sophocles' Oedipus, who, seeking enlightenment concerning his terrible fate, pursues his indefatigable inquiry, even when he divines that appalling horror awaits him in the answer. But most of us carry in our hearts the Jocasta who begs Oedipus for God's sake not to inquire further . . .'"

"That's beautiful. What is it?"

"A letter from Schopenhauer to Goethe. Anne Sexton used it as an epigraph in a book. Mother showed it to me a long time ago when she wanted me to start seeing Jim."

"Say it again."

"I'll write it down for you. Anyway, that's how they got me into therapy."

They had found seats in the back of the tent, which was packed with black and white people, all dressed in their best clothes, all making a point of being extremely polite and pretending that racism doesn't exist.

"What are you thinking about?" CeCe asked.

"Nothing. About how hard it is to be human, to be mindful and kind. Black and white thoughts, that endless mess. It seems so hopeful here."

"It's poverty and disease and lack of education," Mack said. "Jean said if you don't remember that you can't believe it can be changed. We loved that movie *The Year of Living Dangerously*. With the dwarf quoting Saint Paul. 'What now shall we do? What now shall we do?'"

"I've seen it a dozen times," Caroline said. "I watch it to see the Y Yang, the puppet show. All the tapes of it are so old now, the color has faded. I'd give anything to see it on the big screen, a really good print of it."

The musicians were beginning a new song. It was very hot. This was music made for late at night, not the middle of the day with dressed-up people in tents as though for a revival.

CeCe got up. "I'm going outside," she said. "It's too hot in here."

Outside the tent people were drinking beer in plastic cups. A woman from Natchez had cornered Celia and was trying to interest her in a new magazine they were publishing to promote tourism in Mississippi. "Send it to me," Celia kept saying. "I'm so glad you've found something you like to do."

The woman would not be stopped. She had had two glasses of wine at eleven that morning and now she was drinking beer. She was going to get a commitment from Celia if it took all day.

"Momma," CeCe said, stepping in. "I need you to come with me a minute. Hi, Mrs. Allensby. How you doing? What do you think of the music?"

"I'd like to put CeCe on the cover of an issue," Mrs. Allensby said. "CeCe, would you like to model for the cover of our magazine?"

"No," CeCe said. "I don't like to be photographed. It steals your karma. Sorry." She pulled her mother away.

"What is it?" Celia asked.

"Nothing. I just thought you would want to be rescued. When is Royals coming down? I might go home and wait for him."

"Wasn't the music good in the tent?"

"It's too hot for this. I've got work to do for Tuesday. I want to go home. Where is the car?"

"By the Pontiac place on Main. You want to go home by yourself?"

"Yes."

"Then go on. Augustus is on his way. I don't know when Royals will be here."

CeCe gave her mother a kiss on the cheek and walked back through the town to the car. Halfway there she got her cellular phone out of her pocketbook and called the driver and told him to come get her. She walked another block in the heat before the Lincoln pulled up and she got in the front with the driver. "Jesus Christ," she said. "What a waste of time."

When she got back to the house she decided to go upstairs and masturbate. It would at least put her to sleep. She giggled at the thought and went into the kitchen and got some whole wheat bread and turkey and made a sloppy sandwich and put it on a plate. She went upstairs and into her room and closed and locked the door. She got her new vibrator out of her suitcase and put it on the pillow. Then she picked up a book and started reading it. She read while she turned down the bed and while she was pulling off her clothes and while she was getting propped up on the pillows. It was a book about astrophysics by her new heart-throb, Timothy Ferris.

"You can meet Timothy Ferris," Jim had said when she told him about it. "You can do anything you set your mind to. Read his books and write to him. Ask him where he's going to speak and go and shake his hand. Everyone you admire doesn't have to end up being a lover, CeCe. You could just be friends with the man and admire his work."

She delved down into the book, forgetting her plans to masturbate. She had read the book twice already and this time she was really understanding it.

She had fallen asleep when the phone rang. It was already taking a message by the time she picked it up. It was Augustus.

"Celia, it's Augustus. Something terrible has happened. I'm on my way there. . . ."

"Augustus, it's me. It's CeCe. I'm here at the house."

"CeCe. I'm about twenty minutes away. Oh, God, there's been an accident."

"Tell me what it is, Augustus. Don't do this. Say it."

"Jim's dead. In an automobile accident. I was there. I saw the car. It was on fire. Flames were shooting out of it. This huge column of fire from the red car. Oh, God, it was unbelievable. Who's there with you?"

"That's three," CeCe said. "Now I guess it's over."

*   *   *

She hung up the phone and started to get up. A dream Jim had told her came to her. About a beautiful fairy that came to him and danced around his room and made him believe in beauty and the sanctity of life.

She picked up the vibrator and held it to her left temple and turned it on. She moved it to the other temple and vibrated that one for a while. Then she began to cry. She turned off the vibrator and began to cry deep, old, terrible tears. Death was all around them. Death of the bayous from the green scum and insecticides, death of music from festivals, death of people from cars and craziness. Everyone was crazy and now the only one who had protected her was dead. Not just crazy anymore and to be pitied, but dead and gone.

There was nothing left to do but cry.

13

ROYALS CONNELL was coming to the Delta with information. While he was finishing his rounds for the morning he had called an old friend who was a criminal attorney. "I need everything on a psychiatrist named James Jaspers, who's been practicing in Jackson, Mississippi. Everything you can find. It's for Celia Montgomery. Well, that doesn't matter. Just get it for me."

By the time Royals was back at his house and changing clothes, a four-page report was in his e-mail. It wasn't the first time Jim Jaspers had gone crazy. The first time was after his father died. He had ended up in a hospital for medical students who were in trouble. He had been saved by a team of psychiatrists, which explained the specialty. He went back to school, finished his degree, and went to work to save other people. Residency at Barnes Hospital in St. Louis, then practice in Philadelphia until he came to Jackson in the nineteen eighties. His career since then had been brilliant, his credentials were sterling. There were a handful of citations for speeding. Then nothing, until last spring when he was treated for two weeks in a hospital in Dallas.

So they didn't really save him, Royals decided. They just put it off for fifteen years. Death does him in, drives him crazy, then the shrinks calm him down and get him back on track, but nothing has been explained because there are no explanations. He finishes his education. He goes to work. He spends ten hours a day letting people dump their terror and confusion in his lap. He thinks he's armored. He thinks it won't bore in. Then one day he sticks a needle in his arm and suddenly it's quiet. No more questions. Nor more terror, no more death.

Royals put on some khaki pants and a soft, blue shirt, stuck his feet into old worn Birkenstock sandals, picked up his bag, and left the house to go to the Delta. He went back in the house and took the printed copy of the e-mail and stuck it in his pocket. I feel sorry for this guy, he decided. I love a man who keeps on trying. It should be a lesson to me. Treating illness, playing God, is an addiction. All I do is take care of people. I don't even try to stop thinking about them. I don't even have a family. I'm thirty-eight years old and I don't have any kids. When I get home I'm going to seriously start looking for a wife. I want a real woman with a real education and a career of her own and I want some babies. Surely there's someone who wants to give those things to me.

Mack and Caroline were sitting outside a tent listening to "BoBo" Haddad play the steel guitar. They were having a strange conversation underneath a magnolia tree.

"I won't be over Jean for a while," Mack was saying. "She was my life. I loved her so much, you know. I was thinking this morning how much I wanted to ask you to go to bed with me and I thought, for what? So I could use this wonderful young woman for a poultice."

"Well, I don't know what to say to that." Caroline moved back a step. "I mean, well."

"No. I owe you that. We're attracted to each other. Who wouldn't be attracted to you, you're so fresh and funny and you have that wonderful book and more to come I'm sure. I want us to be friends. I want us to start on the right foot."

"Telling me you thought about sleeping with me but then decided not to is not the right foot for me. I mean, you have no reason to think I'd do it anyway. I'm careful about who I go to bed with. My God, this is the weirdest conversation I've had in a while."

"Don't be like that. Let me be honest and be my friend."

"Why did you start this then? I mean, why in the world would you bother to tell someone you didn't want to sleep with them. I have plenty of boyfriends, by the way. I have too many. I was thinking the other day that I needed to get rid of some of them."

They were interrupted by Celia. She was walking toward them with a terrible expression on her face. "Jim's dead," she said. "A car wreck, near Belzoni. We have to go. CeCe's alone at the house. Carl's gone for the car."

They followed her to the Lincoln, which was waiting ridiculously in the middle of a crowd of people moving between the tents.

They got into the car. Caroline made sure not to sit by Mack. She was mad at him. He had pushed her worst button, the one where her father tells her she is not good enough for something, hasn't won the blue ribbon, hasn't taken the field. Mack sat looking at his hands. Celia was crying. The car went slowly through the field of blues fans and out onto the road and through the town.

"Call CeCe and tell her we're coming," Mack suggested.

"Yes." Celia reached in her purse for her phone but the batteries were dead. Caroline found her own and handed it to her. Celia rang

Oak Grove. A servant answered the phone. After a long time the servant came back to the phone. "She doesn't want to talk on the phone. She said she's okay."

"What else? What is she doing? What else did she say?"

"She's in her bed crying. She said she didn't want to talk on cell phones and broadcast to the whole Delta. Can everyone hear on these phones, Mrs. Montgomery? Who can hear on them?"

"Satellites, I think. Okay, go back up there and tell her we'll be there in twenty minutes. Has Mr. Augustus come?"

"No, but Doctor Connell called and said he was on his way."

"If either of them gets there find them rooms in the guest house. Go make sure the rooms are ready and call CeCe if anyone comes. I don't want her to be alone."

"She's got those dogs in there. Those Australian dogs. One's on the bed and the other one is on the floor."

"Thanks, Amy. Keep an eye on her. Don't worry about the rooms. They'll be okay."

"What did she say?" Mack said.

"She said CeCe was in bed and she had her dogs in the room, those Australian shepherds she takes everywhere. I told her not to bring the dogs to the Delta but she brought them to the airport and I had to let them on the plane. Now I'm glad I did."

"She's very well defended," Mack said. "She takes care of herself. Jim did a good job with her."

"He's dead," Celia said. "I don't know what to do with all of this."

Royals Connell was there when they got home. He had come to pay Celia back for the one hundred thousand dollars she had given his boys' camp fund and the ten grand she'd contributed to the scholarship fund and also because he liked the woman. He approved of rich people who stayed involved in the culture. He approved of her theater and her support of liberal politicians and her pretty little feet and legs, which reminded him of his mother. He had been to Oak Grove for quail hunts and parties but this was the first time she had asked him for a favor. He was glad to be able to pay her back for her generosity.

He was standing on the front porch when the party got out of the Lincoln. Caroline got out first. She was wearing a short cotton sundress the color of butter. Her legs were long and tan and her toenails were painted like some delicious offering or promise. She was the height of his mother. She had the same color hair and eyes. When she was introduced she gripped his hand as though it were a tennis racket. Then she smiled. The string of pearls around her neck lay against her skin like a caress. Royals kept on looking at her and she returned his look.

Before they got into the house Augustus arrived. He walked up the steps and began hugging people. "I'm done in," he said. "I'm shaken. I want a drink and I don't want to be alone for a second."

CeCe and Caroline embraced him. "It's the third death," CeCe kept saying. "That means it's over. That means it won't happen again."

"If I'd brought him with me this would not have happened."

"I wouldn't have let you bring him," Celia said. "Don't say or think that. Never think that again."

Later, when everyone had had a bath and changed clothes and rested, they all convened in the drawing room to talk it over. Celia put Satie on the stereo, Pascal Roge playing Erik Satie.

Royals told them what he had learned, Augustus told them of coming upon the wreck. CeCe said, "From the moment he got sick, we were tracking him. Everyone was telling each other everything he said and did and where he was. He was like one of those bears that come into Greenville in the spring and the wildlife bureau catches them and puts a tracking signal in their ear. He was tagged. There wasn't a place he could go that someone wasn't calling Mother and telling her what he'd said and done. We were worried about him talking about us but all we were talking about was him."

"We were doing what we could," Augustus said. "Donna Divers and William and everyone he knew were offering all the help they could. If anyone's going to feel blame, it's me. I may have been the last person he called before he started driving."

"He was injecting himself with something when he died," Celia said. "The state police said there was a needle in his hand. The man I talked to a while ago told me that twice. I think he was as shocked as we are."

"They were putting him in the ambulance," Augustus said. "A dead body. All that kindness, all that good humor and the good advice he gave us. He used to tell me things about Celia that made me love her even more than I already did. He told me about the health problems you overcame. I know he wasn't supposed to tell us those things, but he did, and they mattered."

"He told me about your uncle who worked with Jonas Salk," Celia said. "It was when I really began to know who you were. You're right, it was his own brand of psychotherapy. It wasn't the party line. He made it up for us, because he wanted so much to help us." She stood up. She didn't want to cry anymore in front of the others. She wanted to be Jim Jaspers for them. She wanted to remind them of the world outside their sorrow.

"Please, everyone have a drink," Celia said. "It's going to be a long night. I have to talk to the police again and then we have to decide what to do. The bar is open in the library. Please help yourselves."

Caroline got up and went to the bar and fixed herself a Diet Coke. Royals was standing there as she filled the glass. "I want one of those too," he said. "That looks like a good idea." He smiled at her. She was wearing a soft white sweater set she had bought to amuse Augustus. It clung to her breasts. Above the neck of the inside sweater her soft ivory skin was young and alluring.

"Celia says you are a poet," he added. "That makes me afraid to talk to you. Is it safe to talk to you?"

"I don't know." She handed him the Diet Coke she had fixed and poured another one for herself. "This has put me in a strange mood, that's for sure. I teach Shakespeare, for God's sake. I thought he piled up the bodies, but it's nothing to what I've seen in Mississippi . . . I'm safe enough, I guess. As long as you don't start anything you don't want to finish."

"I finish what I start," he said. "You can count on me for that."

~ 14 ~

THE POLICE had called Jim's partner, Donna, and she and her husband had driven to Greenville and identified the body. Jim's only close relative was a brother who lived in New York City. He was in Italy with his wife and a child who was recovering from a lengthy illness. It was impossible for them to return to the United States for several weeks.

There were no other close relatives. Both of his parents were dead. There was an elderly uncle in New England.

After many phone calls to and from the police and the intervention of several lawyers and a United States senator, Celia reassembled her guests in the living room to tell them what had been decided.

"It's going to be up to us," she said. "There should have been an autopsy but the senator had that waived. So now we have to decide how to bury our friend. Donna says he was insistent on being cremated. Since that sounds like Jim and is all right with his brother, I think we should do that, and the sooner the better."

"Cremation!" CeCe got up and went to stand in the doorway. She had been sitting by Caroline on one of the velvet sofas. "This is too morbid. It's totally morbid."

"Death is morbid," someone said. "There's no good way to dispose of a body. If that's what he wanted, that's what we should do."

"Where is the body now?" Caroline asked.

"In Greenville at a funeral home. It wasn't easy to make that happen but I did it." Celia sighed and looked at her hands. She always tried very hard not to seem privileged or let the power show. Who am I playing now? she asked herself. What role is this?

"The police took the body to the funeral home. They've been very respectful, very helpful," Augustus added. "We all should wish we had Celia around when things need getting done. She was magnificent on the phone." He went to Celia and took her hand. "We decided there was no reason to transport Jim's body to Jackson if it was going to be cremated anyway. I mean, most of us are here, the ones who might want to be there for something like that. Not want, I mean, feel the need to be, whatever."

"We were thinking we might be able to go on and have the cremation on Monday," Celia said. "It's Labor Day but we hope that won't be a problem."

"Call the funeral home and ask," Royals suggested. "Get some information on that." Augustus went to a phone and confirmed that for an extra hundred and fifty dollars they could have someone cremated on a holiday. "They can do it tomorrow if we'd rather," he added.

"His brother is faxing permission to the police in Greenville," Celia said. "Power of attorney to me and what not. So why wait until Monday? We could do it tomorrow and get it over with. What do all of you think?"

Everyone was nodding yes. "What can I do to help you?" Royals asked. "Tell me what I can do."

"Stand by me," Celia said. "Catch me if I fall." She looked at him and laughed at that. "I will go in the other room and call a few people in Jackson and let them know. Some of them might like to be here. I'll call Governor Jamison and Judge Williams and Donna. Who else should I call?"

"I'll call William Harbison and Monte Ne Presley over at Tougaloo," Mack said. "Let Augustus call the folks at Millsaps. That ought to do it. That's who he'd invite if he was here."

"He wouldn't invite the governor," Augustus said. "He thinks he's a fool."

"All right. I won't invite him to the cremation but I have to let him know what's going on. He is the governor, whether you like him or not."

"Go on and call them then. If there are two lines, I'll be using the phone in my room." Augustus stood up. He put his hands in his pockets and bowed his head. "Everyone think of something to read. We don't want this to end up like Jean's funeral. I want Jim to have some voices raised, some wailing."

"I could wail," Celia said. "I could keen and wail all night for him. I loved him. He was my child and my brother."

CeCe got up and went to her mother and put her arm around her waist. She held her mother's small, slight body against her own and thought of bodies going up in flames, in India and all over the world as people burned their dead, tossed the people they had loved into the earth and into furnaces and onto pyres. This was it. This was the day they had to look that in the face and be part of it.

"Buddhist monks say you should think of death each day," she said. "So you will be prepared for it. Jim told me that when Daddy was sick. He came to the hospital when Daddy was being operated on. I won't forget that. How I felt when he came walking in the door."

" 'Every day without knowing it I have passed the anniversary of my death,' " Caroline added. " 'Never send to know for whom the bell tolls. It tolls for thee.' I always fall back on poetry. Poetry is always about death. Even when it seems to be about love, it is really about death." She raised her eyes and looked at Royals Connell. Death had made her bold. She was going after what she needed in the world, starting this afternoon, starting today. "When it cools off, I'm going for a walk," she added. "CeCe has supplied me with my own personal can of insect repellent. I'm going to test it against the Delta mosquitoes. Does anyone want to go along?"

"I will," Royals said. "I run every day. I'll go with you." He disengaged himself from Celia and walked over to where she was. He had made up his mind about Caroline. He had decided what to do. He was tired of waiting for life to happen. He was going out and confront it the way he used to do before he spent his afternoons worrying about his mornings.

"Count me in," CeCe said. "What time?"

"Six o'clock," Caroline said. "Then we can be back in time for dinner."

"I'm going to call these people," Celia said.

"I will too. Then I'm going to watch the U.S. Open," Augustus said. "Then I'm going to take a nap. I may go hike with you but I'm not promising."

They moved out slowly to different parts of the house. Royals followed Caroline to the stairs, then watched while she walked up them to the landing. Her legs were long and finely wrought. Her hair was thick and wild. Her hips were thin and tight. Her mind was quick and interesting. She was a winner and plenty ruthless enough to be a mother and a doctor's wife. The more he thought about it the more he wanted to fuck her. If they knew what we thought about them they would slap us every time they saw us, he thought. He had heard a comedian say that on a late night television show. He had thought it was the most profound thing he had heard in years.

She turned on the landing and looked down at him. Whatever he knew, she also knew. He drew in a deep breath. His body seemed to fill with breath. This is how it used to be, he remembered. I want it back. God, I've missed this feeling.

She kept on looking at him. "So how far do you run?" she asked.

"Two or three miles. I'm out of shape."

"I used to run," she said. "I ran a couple of marathons. I'll run with you if you like. I can keep up for two or three miles."

"All right. I'll see you at six then." He kept on watching her. Now he was intimidated. He didn't want to compete with Caroline. He wanted to fuck her and take her home and keep her.

Caroline started to walk on down the hall to her room. Then she changed her mind. She walked back down the stairs instead and put her hand on Royals's arm, which was on the post at the bottom of the stairs. "I'll use you for a grounding wire," she said. "Are you a stable man, Royals Connell? Could you keep a mass of carbon atoms from turning back into carbon? Could you save me from myself and from the world?"

"I can't save people from death," he answered. "But sometimes I buy them time. Sometimes I make them worse. Sometimes I make them better."

"If you could be anyone you wanted to be, anyone at any age, who would you be?"

"I'd be the pitcher for a baseball team of twelve-year-olds the year they win the state championship and then go to the Little League

World Series in Williamsport and either win it or come in second. I guess we'd win it. Yes, we would win it."

"Could you have done that?"

"Nope. The same strange eyesight that makes me a good surgeon was not very good for sports. I have very keen, fine, near vision but it doesn't work as well at a distance."

"How do I look under those circumstances?"

"Perfect with my contact lenses. I'll have to see what happens without them. What would you be if you could be anyone at any moment?"

"I like this fine," she answered, and moved her hand until it was on top of his. "Right here is all right with me."

"I'll meet you at six then." He didn't move his hand. It lay beneath her small, moist palm and fingers. Finally she took her hand away and went on up the stairs to her room.

Caroline had brought her running shoes and a pair of very short yellow shorts and a sleeveless top but she had forgotten to pack a sports bra. She tried on a small pink silk brassiere underneath the running top. Her nipples showed through the material. Well, Augustus would get a kick out of that. And as for Royals Connell. Well, she was going to bed with him before she left the Mississippi Delta if she had to show up in his bed in the middle of the night. Except that he was staying in that stupid guest house and Augustus was there.

She went down to the library where Augustus had finished making calls and was watching Steffi Graf play a young player from Switzerland.

She sat down beside him on the sofa and cuddled up. "I've had all the death I can take," she said. "You know what is supposed to happen at funerals to make up for that, don't you?"

"There's no one here who's gay," he said. "Besides, I'm shy. I have to be invited."

"I'm not talking about you. I'm talking about Royals Connell. I'm going after it. I mean it, Augustus, and the problem is, you're both staying in that guest house. Can I get in his room without it seeming like you know about it?"

"But what about Mack Stanford? Yesterday you were going to fuck Mack."

"I was only teasing about that. Not to mention he took me off at the blues festival and told me he had decided not to fuck me although he wanted to. What a prick teaser. It made me so mad I started lying." She cuddled closer, smelling Augustus's Brooks Brothers polo shirt. "What did you put on this shirt? It smells like heaven."

"It's just me, honey. Just my natural goodness. So Mack's out and Royals is in? And I have to vacate the guest house?" He pulled her close to him and held her. His girlfriend, his precious Caroline. "What did you lie to Mack about?"

"I told him I had so many boyfriends I was thinking of getting rid of a few. Isn't that pitiful? Doesn't that make you sick? And I don't want you to vacate the guest house. You could change rooms with me. I could say I'm allergic or something."

"I'll be sound asleep with the lights off after having announced I'm taking a sleeping pill. Will that do?"

"You are my angel." She kissed him and got up to leave. "The gods reward generosity. You will be rewarded for this day."

"They'd better hurry up. I'm not getting any younger."

At six CeCe and Caroline and Royals and Augustus met in the front hall. They proceeded out the door and down the front lawn to the deserted Delta road. Caroline and Royals began to run. CeCe and Augustus walked along behind them.

"Who'd you get on the phone?" CeCe asked.

"I got William Harbison. He's driving down in the morning. He's going to bring Peggy Dillan and her girlfriend and maybe Lauren Gail Lyles. They read the will, by the way. Jean left three-quarters of the estate to Lauren Gail and made the boys divide up the rest. William said they're all mad as hornets. The boys are mostly mad at Charlie but it's Lauren Gail who got the money. Anyway, he might bring her down."

"What are we going to do?"

"We're going to stand there while they burn up the body. Then we're going to keep the ashes for his brother. We'll read things. We'll be there. I don't know what to do. I've never had to do this."

"Mother got a lot of people on the phone but I don't think any of them are coming."

"Did she get Donna?"

"She said Donna doesn't want to be here. She already had to iden- tify the body. I wonder who'd come if I got killed. I bet nobody would come except for Mother's friends."

"Then you'd better live until you have more friends, hadn't you?"

She shoved him and picked up the pace. They had already lost sight of Caroline and Royals, who had disappeared down the road.

Caroline had not been running for a month. She was having a hard time keeping up but she was not going to admit it. "Let's slow down," he sug- gested, when he heard her laboring to breathe beside him. "I'd rather talk to you. It's too hot to run, even at this time of day. I'm used to doing it at dawn."

She slowed down and they began to walk. The closeness on the stairs had turned into shyness now. She was shy and she knew that he was also. This dance of sex, she decided. This attraction, this chemistry, it never changes, does it? There is not a bit of difference between this and the tall, skinny boy I loved the summer I was seventeen. I want to kiss this man. I want to put my hand back on top of his. If life has taught me nothing else, it has taught me that he is as scared as I am, if he's worth a damn. Good men are scared to death of sex, as they should be. It's the arrow Cupid shoots. It's the honey to end all honeys. It's the thing we have to have. He's been denying himself this as much as I have been. And now we're here and I'm going to have to think of something to say.

"Tell me what you do on an ordinary day," she said. "Tell me how you live your life."

"I am lonely," he answered. "I've become a lonely man. I chose this profession because I wanted to make money. I'm good at it. I like doing it. I see more miracles than I expected. The human body is so resilient, so powerful, it's a greater miracle than I dreamed. What I said a while ago about not being able to defeat death. Well, I don't really believe that. I think I can sometimes defeat it, if the patient helps me. I see things every day that astound me. I operated on a famous baseball player. He willed himself to heal. I've never seen such courage, such will. Other times, people want to die and I can't stop them." He stopped for a minute, then went on. "Tell me about yourself. Are you in love with anyone? Are you free?"

"I guess you can call it free." She waited, then she said, "I'm sick of death. I want to get laid, to tell the truth. There's an eighteenth-century bed in my room. You ought to see it. It's like something in a museum.

What am I doing sleeping alone in that bed? That's what I'm asking myself. What's it like in the guest house? Is it fabulous?"

"Very nice. But it's not antiques. I think it's modern furniture. I don't know about such things."

"I need to get grounded," Caroline said. "Don't be surprised if I show up in your room." She was laughing at him. He couldn't tell if she was serious or not.

"Yes," he said. "Absolutely. Anytime you like. I mean, it's fine with me." He was laughing and smiling too. He had become a child in the presence of her candor. "I'll be there," he added. "Starting now."

"Well, it won't be until after dinner." She began to run again. As fast as she could run. Past the rows of scraggly drought-blighted cotton, with the wide levee in the background and the frustrated mosquitoes being brilliantly repelled by the chemicals she had sprayed on her body. Why do I always think doctors don't have AIDS, she asked herself. Well, everyone has to believe in something.

Royals Connell followed her. He wasn't asking any questions. He was taking what was offered. He was there for the taking.

After dinner that night Augustus stood up and said, "I have five Halcion that I'm willing to share. I'll leave the bottle in the kitchen. It's a discredited drug nowadays, but remember, it was Halcion that made the Bush foreign policy work. How else do you think they flew back and forth across the Atlantic Ocean and ended the Cold War? Well, that's for history buffs and trivia collectors. For now, for me, ten hours of sleep to prepare myself for tomorrow." He came to Celia first and kissed her and thanked her for dinner, then he embraced CeCe, then Caroline. "It's a terrible occasion," he added, "but the best of company." He went to

Royals and shook his hand. "If you need me it will take a bucket of cold water but I'll rally," he said. That was overdoing it, and Caroline gave him a look that almost brought them both to laughter.

The moment passed. Augustus went into the kitchen and left a bottle of four Halcion on the kitchen table. "They're sleeping pills," he told the cooks. "In case anyone needs them. We have to see to the cremation of a friend tomorrow. Everyone needs to get their sleep."

"I could use one of them myself," the older cook replied. "I've always had a hard time sleeping."

"Take one," Augustus said. "The secretary of state of the United States used to take them all the time. Then they decided they might harm your heart or something. Don't take it if you've had any health problems." Augustus had had three glasses of wine and was not in the mood to appear ungenerous. On the other hand giving prescription drugs to your friends and letting the help take them were two different things.

"Maybe you should ask a doctor before you take it," he added. "I wouldn't want anything to happen to you."

"I'm not going to touch your pills," the cook said. "I got some Tylenol P.M. that works like a charm if I take it."

Augustus's ploy and terrible acting job turned out not to have been necessary. Royals came to her instead. As soon as everyone had gone to their rooms he walked up the stairs and into the huge, old, quiet room that had seen sixty years of interesting activities. A child had been born there in a storm. A girl who had grown up and gone off to be an architect in New York City and design the ballet wing of Lincoln Center. She was Celia's long-lost sister. A painting of her wearing a red dress hung above the fireplace.

It had always been a guest room but Celia's parents had used it for their afternoon naps. They had loved one another passionately and loved to sneak into the room and make love while their children played around the house.

The huge old lock they had installed on the door was still in place. When Caroline threw the bolt into the casing she had déjà vu. Then she turned to the man who was sitting on the edge of the bed looking shy and worried and began to ply him with her poet's voice.

The only thing that happened that night was that they learned to make love to each other. Nature was saving her tricks for later. All she wanted on this Saturday night was to open them up and meld them and let them flirt with pleasure.

The next day was Sunday. At nine thirty a car came up the driveway carrying the head of the theater department at Millsaps and Jim's partner, Donna Divers, who had changed her mind and decided she could take it if she had Darley Hitt for support.

They had barely gotten out of their car when a Jeep Cherokee carrying Lauren Gail Lyles and Peggy Dillan and William Harbison came and parked by the steps.

They all assembled in the living room and drank sherry and talked while they waited for eleven o'clock. Eleven thirty was the time set for the pre-cremation service.

"He was the mainstay of Jean's life," Lauren Gail said. "She told me so many things he told her that I used to think I was in therapy with him myself. I used to think she just went to him to find out things to tell me."

"That's like Mother," CeCe said. "He and Mother used to plot to keep me from being crazy. There's no telling where I'd be if they hadn't kept on trying. He told Mother I was using drugs long before he met me. She would tell him things I did and he kept saying, 'She's doing drugs.' He was the one who wasn't fooled. Then he fooled himself."

"We don't know why he did it," Mack said. "We will never know what caused it. That day at Jean's funeral was the first time I ever saw a side of him that wasn't in control. It started when William and I went over to tell Charlie and Robert they couldn't have that song at her funeral. I'm sorry, Lauren Gail, I don't mean any disrespect for your husband."

"It's okay. It was a stupid song. I begged them not to have it. I think Robert's having an affair with that soprano and she wanted to sing it. I'm glad you stopped it."

"Anyway," Mack continued, "I looked up and there was Jim tearing down the aisle of the church with this really crazy look on his face. The reason they backed down on the soprano was Jim's behavior. He looked like he'd do anything, kill someone. I wasn't surprised when he took off his clothes later and started dancing. I'd already seen it in his eyes."

"We'll never know what sadness drove him to drugs," Peggy Dillan said. "When I think of all the times I called and woke him up at night. I'd get drunk or something and get depressed and call him up. I didn't have to call and wake him up. I could have left him alone at night. But he let me do it, so I did. I quit doing it after I hooked up with Helen and got a life for myself. But I used to do it. I bet plenty of other people took up the slack. I blame myself for not doing more. After that night at Mack's I should have gone and found him and refused to give up until he went into treatment."

"Don't do that, Peggy," Celia said. "Don't beat yourself up. We were his clay. He made his life from our problems. It isn't our fault we had problems. He didn't hate us for having them. He just wanted to throw more light on them. Give us information, guide us out of our mazes."

"I was going to get Caroline to go to him so he could get her unblocked," Augustus said. "I had already called to see if I could set up an appointment."

"I got unblocked by myself," Caroline put in. "In case anyone cares." She walked across the room and found Royals and stood very near him. She could still feel and smell the night. And she didn't have the slightest desire to keep it a secret.

"I wrote a poem for Jim," William Harbison said. "It's sort of a sonnet. I'd like to read it when we get there, to the funeral home, I mean."

"He was very sick." Darley Hitt stood up. He was crying and he didn't try to hide his tears. He had cried playing Horatio in *Hamlet* when he was twenty years old and had been such a hit he had never again tried to hide honest tears. "So very sick and all I did was sit on that couch and bitch because the dean wouldn't let me buy new gels for *The Boyfriend*. That's how I spent the last two sessions I had with him. Bitching about the lighting for *The Boyfriend*."

"You can always borrow our gels," Celia said. "Anytime you want them. All you have to do is send for them."

"What time is it?" Peggy Dillan asked. She was crying too.

"Time to go," Augustus said. "Let's go and get it done."

"We should be on time," Lauren Gail put in. "Let's go tell our friend goodbye."

They drove into Greenville and to the funeral home. They filed into a reception room and stood around while the body of Jim Jaspers was rolled into a crematorium and turned into ashes.

*   *   *

"Let's stand in a circle and say our goodbyes," Celia said.

"We should say a prayer," CeCe suggested. "I brought the *Tibetan Book of the Dead*. You want to read something from it, Mother?"

Celia took the book and held it. "I marked some passages with those yellow Post-it tags," CeCe said. Everyone was quiet. These were theater people. They knew how to create an atmosphere. Celia bowed her head, lifted it, and began.

"We are gathered to bemoan the passing of a good soul who was kind to us and helped us. May he rest in peace. May the goodness that was in him always stay in the universe and in all of us. Amen." The group continued to stay still with their heads slightly bowed. Celia opened the book to the first of the passages, read it over, shook her head, then quoted Shakespeare instead.

> *"Our revels now are ended. These our actors,*
> *As I foretold you, were all spirits and*
> *Are melted into air, into thin air;*
> *And like the baseless fabric of this vision,*
> *The cloud-capp'd towers, the gorgeous palaces,*
> *The solemn temples, the great globe itself,*
> *Yea, all which it inherit, shall dissolve;*
> *And like this insubstantial pageant faded*
> *Leave not a rack behind. We are such stuff*
> *As dreams are made on and our little life*
> *Is rounded with a sleep."*

"You aren't going to read from the Tibetan book?" CeCe asked.

"He gave me that book. He liked it."

"You read it, then." Celia handed the book to CeCe, and CeCe opened it and read a chant. "Om, mani, padme, hung. Om, mani, padme, hung. Om, mani, padme, hung."

Then William Harbison read his poem.

> *"I never told you what you meant to me*
> *Such things are never said*
> *We take it all for granted*
> *Until a friend lies dead*
> *Then we begin to really talk at last*
> *We say, you knew how hard I tried to be civilized*
> *And you did not laugh*
> *You energized me with kindness*
> *Week after week you sent me forth*
> *Like a kind mother, armed with a lunch box*
> *Full of the food of love*
> *We will miss you, Jim*
> *We will remember you and all you taught us*
> *And helped us do."*

No one knew what to say to that but everyone was proud of themselves for managing not to giggle.

Peggy stepped forward and shyly said, "A few lines from 'East Coker' by T. S. Eliot. If you all remember he had these framed on his desk with all those little knickknacks people had given him and those rocks from the Ganges. Okay, here're the lines.

> *"Whisper of running streams, and winter lightning.*
> *The wild thyme unseen and the wild strawberry,*
> *The laughter in the garden. . . ."*

Lauren Gail stepped forward. " 'To be alive becomes the fundamental luck each ordinary, compromising day manages to bury.' Author unknown. Amen."

"I loved you, Jim," Donna Divers said. "I owe you so many things. I did what I could but I wasn't strong enough to save you." Donna began to weep.

"Okay," Celia said. "I think we have run out the time. Augustus, take us out of here."

Augustus stepped forward. " 'We carry nothing into this world and it is certain we can carry nothing out. The Lord gave and the Lord hath taken away; blessed be the name of the Lord.' "

"His brother is going to bury the ashes with their people in Pennsylvania," Celia said. "The funeral home will send them to him."

After a while the undertaker appeared and told them it was accomplished.

They filed out of the building to the cars. Darley and Peggy and Lauren Gail got into Darley's car and drove slowly off to return to Jackson. Donna Divers and William Harbison and Mack were going up to Oxford to visit Dean Faulkner Wells on their way home and see the new statue of "Pappy." Caroline and Royals and CeCe and Celia and Augustus stood on the steps of the funeral home waving until they were out of sight.

"I wish Jim could have seen this," CeCe said. "Everyone typecast as themselves and playing their roles to the hilt. He liked ceremony. He said it was the best idea man ever hit upon. Acting like we aren't animals until maybe it becomes true. Well, he said that to me."

"We will have the most beautiful memorial service ever held in Jackson," Augustus said. "Darley said he'd help me with it. We might have it in the theater instead of the cathedral. Of course, if we did that we couldn't get John Paul to play the organ. Well, we'll see. We'll work on it next week."

"Does anyone need anything before we go home?" Celia asked. "Is there anything anyone needs in town?"

"Let's find a newsstand and buy all the papers we can find and take them home and read them," Caroline suggested. "Surely there's somewhere around here where you can buy a *New York Times*."

"Big grocery stores," Augustus suggested. "That's where I find them on the coast."

"I have to write obituaries," Celia said. "If I don't do it today Peggy Dillan will write one. We can't have that. I need a London *Times* for inspiration. Sometimes you can find one around here. Sometimes not."

"We'll bring what we can," Augustus promised. "We'll meet you at Oak Grove."

CeCe went with her mother. Augustus and Caroline and Royals were in the second Lincoln. The driver took them to a large grocery store in a mall and they found the *New York Times* and the *Commercial Appeal* and the *Times-Picayune* and the *St. Louis Post Dispatch,* but no London *Times*. They bought the papers and got in the car and started reading. They read obituaries all the way back to Oak Grove Plantation.

It was a long strange day. Sometime in the night that followed Caroline Denegue Jones and Royals Hardy Connell made love again in the eighteenth-century bed with its beautiful pink satin bedspread and pillowcases and its linen sheets from the Lylian Shop in New Orleans. The sheets had been made in the Netherlands and were embroidered with tiny blue and pink and yellow and lavender flowers, so dainty and perfect they gentled the heart of anyone who looked at them.

"Are you on the pill?" Royals asked. He had asked the night before but now he asked again.

"Yes," Caroline lied for the second time. She lied because she hated rubbers and she was pretty sure she couldn't get pregnant anyway because she never had and she'd taken plenty of chances in her younger, crazier days. Besides, it was the wrong time of the month and besides, the trip to the mortuary had made her ruthless.

Royals wasn't exactly drunk but he was closer to being drunk than he had been in years. He was thinking of the ashes too and of going up in flames. He was thinking of the brain and what it looked like underneath the knife. He was thinking of Shakespeare's brain. How could such a wonder be contained in flesh? Nothing remained but words. Shakespeare's progeny had died without passing on the DNA. But Royals wasn't thinking about his DNA or how he might have a chance at immortality by passing it on. He was thinking he wanted to fuck Caroline again. He wanted to get laid some more in Celia's eighteenth-century bed and pretend he was a king.

So Julie McEvoy Stillman Connell was conceived and, half an hour later, William Royals Connell, which may explain why Julie got all the black Irish genes and naturally curly, thick, black hair and Will got mostly English genes and thin, blond hair that would begin falling out in his thirties.

They were the only children Caroline and Royals would ever have. Carrying them was a huge burden. Caroline had to leave her post at Millsaps in January and move to Memphis and get married to Royals and find a house and furnish it and then spend the last seven weeks of the pregnancy in bed.

"That's it for me," she told Royals when they were delivered. "If you want more children than this you'll have to get another wife."

"Maybe we don't have a vote," he answered, looking down at the wonders they had created. "Maybe we're just vessels, Caroline. Maybe there is a god." He kept on looking at his babies, looking back and forth from the quiet little boy to the larger, dark-haired girl. He was thinking he didn't know what was underneath that hair. He could not bear to know how fabulous it was, how fragile.

POSTSCRIPT

THAT WAS NOT absolutely all that happened that should be noted. CeCe Montgomery spent the following summer at her parents' beach house writing a roman à clef about Jim Jaspers and his patients. She made her mother into a thirty-six-year-old tennis champion who had aborted four fetuses in an attempt to hold on to her career. She made Augustus into a short, balding history professor who made out with his students in his office. Mack Stanford became a lonely painter in the Ozark mountains with a wife and six mistresses. She, CeCe, was the narrator, a young girl dying of AIDS, which she had contracted while caring for patients in an African hospital.

Jim Jaspers was an eighty-year-old Freudian who analyzed his patients over the phone and by e-mail until he was killed by an anti-abortion activist who had gotten the wrong address and the wrong doctor. Ironically, he was just typing up an e-mail to the tennis champion begging her not to abort a fifth pregnancy when the shot came through the window and blew his brains all over the computer.

When she had a three-hundred-and-sixty-page manuscript in hand, she drove up to Memphis to show it to Caroline. The twins were four months old at the time of her visit.

"I don't know, CeCe," Caroline said when she'd read it. "I think maybe you'll have to tone this down a little bit. I don't know how to tell you what's wrong with this, but it isn't finished yet. I mean, it's plenty long enough, but somehow it just isn't as believable as I'd like it to be."

"I'll just write the real story then," CeCe said. "Do you think that would be better?" Caroline was holding Julie. CeCe was holding Will. They were sitting on swings on a porch. CeCe didn't want to say anything, but she was sick of holding babies. She'd been holding them for two days while Caroline read her book.

"Let me read it one more time," Caroline said. "Go get the stroller and take them for a walk, would you, so I can concentrate."

"No. I don't want you to do that. If it was any good you'd have already said so. Give it here. I'll trade you for this baby." CeCe gave Will to Caroline and took the stack of papers and went in her room and threw it in her suitcase. "It's the part about the abortions that got her," she told herself. "I'll have to make it three abortions maybe. Or maybe two. I knew four abortions was too many. No, the best thing to do is throw this away and write the real story, if I could find it out. But I can't. The real story's gone. It died with Jim. God bless him for what he taught me."

The babies were crying in the other room. When she had been holding Will she had been sick of holding him. Now she wanted to see what he was doing. They are funny little things, she decided. You keep wanting to see what they are doing. You keep wanting to talk to them. I was thinking I never wanted to have one but I might change my mind about that. I might take out some eggs and leave them in an egg bank just in case I ever change my mind. You're supposed to have a supply that lasts until you're forty, but you can't tell, it might run out.

Caroline had brought the babies inside to the nursery, which was next door to the room where CeCe was staying. CeCe went to the nursery and picked up Julie and took her to a chair and looked at her.

It was definitely a possibility. If she had one and got tired of it she could always take it to the Delta and make Celia take care of it. She put her nose down into Julie's neck. It smelled so good — that was the strangest thing about babies, how fabulously sweet they smelled.

"I saw this nature movie on television," she said to Caroline. "And this mother tiger kept licking these babies and cleaning off their navels. The announcer said she was doing it to keep them from having infections. Now how does a tiger know to do that, would you tell me? So I was smelling Julie and I thought it might be smell. Maybe the smell tells us what to do? What do you think of that?"

"I think you better quit holding these babies," Caroline laughed, "before they get you in a whole lot of trouble."

Which may have something to do with the fact that as of January 2000, the official roman à clef about Jim Jaspers and the Jackson cabal has not been finished or published. This manuscript is just a holding action.

STORIES

THE SANGUINE BLOOD
OF MEN

LeLe Arnold woke from a deep, long sleep. It was eight o'clock. She had broken her record of sleeping without a sleeping pill. Perfected, she decided, and rolled over on her stomach to stretch her legs. Fifteen days at the health club and she was back into her tightest jeans and ready for something to happen. She rolled onto her back and opened her eyes just enough to see that the sun had risen above the Berkeley Hills and was shining gorgeously in a blue sky with broken clouds. Lovely, lovely, lovely, LeLe decided. This day would do the trick. Caroline couldn't leave on a day like this.

She got out of bed and stuck her feet into the fluffy white house shoes they had bought on sale at Sears for five dollars. They had bought matching pairs, then celebrated their bargain by going to the most expensive Japanese restaurant in Berkeley to eat sushi.

LeLe padded into Caroline's bedroom. She wasn't worried about whether Caroline would be awake. Caroline woke at dawn no matter what time she went to sleep. Caroline was as terrible an insomniac as LeLe had been before she started listening to her self-hypnosis tape and cured herself of worrying while she slept. "Nothing is wrong and nothing needs fixing," the voice on the tape chanted. "You are safe to go to sleep."

"Caroline," LeLe began as she came in the door of the room. "You cannot leave me. You do not need to leave San Francisco just because you ran out of money. I make lots of money. You can use my money until you find a job. You don't have to go home. I won't have it."

Caroline had been stacking piles of sweaters and underwear when LeLe came in the door. She kept on folding and stacking them. "We should have bought ten pairs of those house shoes," she said. "They are the absolute buy of the year."

"I need you," LeLe said. "I don't want to live alone. I'll go back to eating in restaurants. I won't have anyone to work out with or borrow sweaters from or take care of me if I get sick."

"You never get sick. I've never known you to get sick."

"What about the flu? What if I get the flu and you aren't here to say I told you so?"

Caroline giggled. She had spent two years trying to get LeLe to take a flu shot but LeLe was deathly afraid of needles because her father was an anesthesiologist.

"You're the only cousin I have who can write poetry," LeLe said. "You can't give up now. You can't quit San Francisco just because those whoremongers don't like your script."

"They won't pay me for it, LeLe. I don't give a fuck whether they like it or not. I don't like it. I wrote what they told me to write and now they won't pay me."

"You haven't heard from Fine Line yet. About the time you're driving through Colorado in a snowstorm and dying of hypothermia in your car they'll call and say they loved it."

"Don't tell anyone I sent it to Fine Line. Don't spread that around. For all I know I'm still under contract to EnterTrain."

"You're under contract to not leave me alone in California without a single person I can trust." LeLe threw herself down upon the pile of sweaters and underwear. She put her face down into the pillows. She was not joking with Caroline. She was going to be *devastated* if her cousin drove out of the driveway never to return.

LeLe Arnold was thirty-seven years old. She was a reporter for the *San Francisco Chronicle*. She had worked in the campaign to elect Jerry Brown mayor of Oakland. She sometimes thought she was in love with Jerry Brown but she had never told him so. To impress him she had become a member of the board of the John Muir Society. She was a Big Sister to three young black girls in the ghettos of Oakland. She had a rugby player who fucked her whenever she could find him and sober him up. She had a good body and an interesting face. She had never been sick a day in her life with anything a round of antibiotics couldn't cure. Her parents were alive and still married.

Still, she couldn't stand to be alone. She got lonely just thinking about living alone in a house. It was a disease, she had often decided. When she was alone a strange, black melancholy came over her. Maybe I have to have an audience, she had once told a psychiatrist. Maybe I can't maintain the illusion of happiness without applause. Maybe I am afraid to die.

"If you leave, I'm going down to the sperm bank and get inseminated and start having babies," she said. "I will not stay here alone. 'I cannot maintain this great fortress without you.'"

"Who wrote that?"

"I've forgotten. Maybe Sexton. She's so underrated. They put such terrible poems in the anthologies. I think the men poets are trying to keep anyone from knowing about her."

"When I teach I'll revive her, and Millay too. If I ever teach again."

"You will. You'd get a teaching job out here if you'd go on and take the education courses. I'll support you while you do it, Caroline. You don't have to have a job to stay."

"I could not do it. It is not in my genes to let anyone support me. I'm going to go home, LeLe, and regroup."

"You'll let your parents support you, but not me?"

"It's not the same thing and you know it."

"I don't."

"Yes you do." Caroline threw herself down on the other side of the bed and put her arm around her cousin. "I'm leaving you the red cable-knit sweater. I know you covet it. It's yours. You can send it back if you get fat."

"Let's go eat breakfast. My editor wants me to write a piece about the King George Hotel. We can charge it to the paper if we go there. Come on. Stop this packing. I don't have to go in until eleven. Let's go have some fun."

"All right. Get dressed. I wanted to start this afternoon but I can wait until tomorrow. Turn on the television. See what the weather's doing in Tennessee."

"You're going to have to go the southern route. You'll never make it through Colorado this week."

"Damn, I wanted to stop in Boulder and see Stacie. I told her I'd stop and spend the night with her."

"You ought to go over to EnterTrain and talk to those people before you run off. Movie people change their minds about everything on a daily basis. When I was in Los Angeles I used to interview those people all the time. They don't know what they're doing from one day to the next. They'll cancel a project and then something happens to make them think they were wrong. Someone shoots a film like it that makes money or they hear something and the next thing you know they're hot on it again."

"Sidney Mills is not going to be hot for *The Sanguine Blood of Men* anytime soon. He doesn't keep his promises and they didn't pay me the rest of the money and I'm through."

"Let's get breakfast. Then we'll finish talking about this. I asked around about him. Why does he have his offices in San Francisco, for example? This isn't where the action is, it's in L.A. Well, it turns out his wife won't live down there and he's such a pussy he lives here because she wants to. That is not the stuff studio heads need to be made of. If she can manipulate him, so can we."

"That's dreaming, LeLe. It's over. The project's done. I need to go home and get a job teaching in college."

Caroline was still taking clothes out of drawers and folding them on the bed, but she was smiling now, her shoulders were straighter, she didn't look as distraught as she had when LeLe first came into the room. LeLe had the drop on Caroline because she had been the oldest cousin when all of them were children and went to Denegue family gatherings in Nashville. LeLe would arrive from Jackson with her curly blond hair and her seven years of tap and ballet and her will like a hurricane and life would change for all the younger Denegue cousins. LeLe's ambitions were to be the star of Broadway musicals and also a newspaper editor like her uncle George. In the summers she would make up plays for them to put on and their grandmother, May Garth Denegue, would allow her to tear up the house and enlist the services of the servants into their projects. May Garth did back exercises every morning on the rug in the solarium, and LeLe would lie beside her and do them too. LeLe was the oldest granddaughter and May Garth couldn't help preferring her over most of the other people in the world. So Caroline had always thought LeLe Arnold was the most interesting, fascinating, and divine creature in the world. She was too shy to lie down beside them while the exercises were happening, but she would lie on the rug in an adjoining room and watch them through the door. One year LeLe brought her toe shoes with her and let Caroline try them on. This was when Caroline was six years old. The fix was in. She had believed LeLe was a magical person who could transform the world and she still did.

LeLe padded back into her room to get dressed. She wore wonderful inventive costumes that were never what anyone else in California was wearing that season. If everyone else was wearing loose outfits made of soft materials she would begin to dress in tight, hard clothes. This winter she was into cord jeans, fitted jackets, and flat, black riding boots. She had spent a weekend at a seminar given by Ralph Nader and was on a mission to only buy clothes made in the U.S.A. This meant she had begun shopping at Sears and Penney's and big department stores at the malls, reading labels and giving lectures to salesladies about the plight of garment workers in the United States.

She hadn't written about it yet. She was still gathering information, but while she was in the malls, she had hit on this tight, American horseriding look and it suited her. It gave her an edge when she was interviewing actresses wearing Prada or boring old Donna Karan or tragically boring Armani.

"There must be a way to make me forget that I love you," she was singing as she stepped into the shower. "There must be a way to make me forget that I care. . . ."

She shampooed her short, curly hair and was in and out of the shower and dressed in five minutes. She threw on some foundation and blush, added mascara, and went back into Caroline's room. Caroline had stopped folding clothes now and was putting them in a suitcase.

"No, no, no," LeLe said. "If you leave, then Cameron will move back in. His goddamn rugby stuff will be all over the living room. His drunken rugby mates will be sleeping on my sofas."

"I thought you were going to be artificially inseminated as soon as I left." Caroline had put on black slacks with a blue cotton sweater set. She was wearing her high-heeled black loafers from Banana Republic. She was softening. Maybe she wouldn't leave for a few more days. "I'll stay a few days," she said. "If you promise to be impregnated with Irish genes. We need some more really crazy people in the family. We're running out of wildness on the Denegue side."

"So you say. Come on. Let's blow off the King George idea. Let's go to Andromeda and get a waffle."

They got into LeLe's Bronco and drove down into Berkeley to the Andromeda Grill which was run by a black man from Arkansas and his Chinese wife. The Andromeda served breakfast twenty-four hours a day. It was a favorite hangout for journalists and the faculty at U.C. Berkeley. A table full of astrophysicists were there when they arrived, all wearing T-shirts and sloppy jackets and bad hair. "They vie with each other to look like they slept in their clothes," Caroline whispered. "To think I was in love with one of them. He drove me nuts staring off into space all the time. Even when he screwed me he acted like he was thinking about something else."

"When was that?" LeLe asked. "I don't remember an astrophysicist."

"At Yale. Before I quit to come here."

"Don't start that. Coming here was a good idea. Being here until something breaks is a better one. Come on, let's grab that table by the window." LeLe moved past the astrophysicists and captured the table. Caroline joined her.

"Now," LeLe began. "Let's get down to business. I'm older than you are. I've been covering the movies for years. I know how it happens, Caroline. The people who stay are the ones who get the prizes. I've seen it over and over again. They don't have to be the best writers or the smartest. All they have to do is wait. If your name's out there sooner or later someone needs a scriptwriter in a hurry and it will be you. You need a better agent though. Gill is a whore. You should never have trusted her. That contract you signed with EnterTrain is out of another century. She worked for them on this and she screwed you. It doesn't have to happen again. You're not under contract to her."

"Well, it wasn't her fault they didn't like the screenplay."

"You were supposed to be paid for writing it, not for them liking it. I don't know how many times I have to tell you that."

The waiter brought the waffles. They covered them with syrup and ate them and Caroline's spirits began to lift. "I might go over to EnterTrain and try to talk to Sidney," she said. "He acted like he was sorry when I told him I was quitting. Well, it was just on the phone but he sounded sorry. Maybe I'll give it one more shot. You're right, I might catch him in the right mood and he'd agree to pay for a rewrite."

"Leave Gill out of it entirely. Let her sue you if she finds out. Fuck her. She sure fucked you."

"Sidney might not do it that way."

"If he wants a rewrite, he'll do it any way you like. If they want something, they don't care what they pay or how it happens. They're like spoiled little children who are used to having their way. Not *like* — they *are* spoiled little children." LeLe paused, thinking of the producer she fucked when she first came to California. She had been fascinated by what a babyish, chickenshit, physically cowardly, second-rate man he was. Her perception of who ran Hollywood had been formed by that encounter.

Nothing that had happened in the ensuing years had changed her perception. "Be sure and ask him if the rights have reverted yet. They think about rights all the time, it's their metaphor. If you ask him he'll start thinking you're going to sell it someplace else."

They finished the waffles. The astrophysicists kept looking at them. The astrophysicists were definitely getting a hard-on for them. That gave the morning a lift and gave Caroline an edge as she got on BART to go downtown to the San Francisco offices of EnterTrain Films, the failing enterprise of a small, neurotic man who lived on coffee and massages and was terrified of women.

Here's what happens, Caroline was telling herself, getting ready to pitch the new version of the script she wanted to write. A young girl in the Ozark Mountains is getting ready to go teach school. She looks like LeLe and has that kind of kinky, reddish-blond hair, but hers is long and falling all over her shoulders. She is a beautiful, unspoiled person with a good mind and a great outlook on life. Her mother is a stupid bitch who still tries to work out things through having boyfriends. Her father was a Danish sailor who met her mother and impregnated her in the Virgin Islands while her mother was on a vacation there. He married her and she lived in the islands until the girl, I'll call her DeDe, after LeLe, was one year old, then she left him and went home and was never even nice to him again. She wanted to keep DeDe all to herself because DeDe was so cute and smart. So one day there is an accident and they call DeDe and tell her that her father is dead or missing. She flies to the islands to see about his memorial service and when she gets there she falls in love with the guy who called to tell her her father was gone. They have this beautiful love affair and in the end the father wasn't dead, he had been able to make it to a deserted island but there had been a hurricane and no one found him for a while. He had lived on fish and finally was able to dry out some wood in a cave and make a fire by rubbing flint on stone. I always wanted to use firemaking in a movie. Well, I wrote that poem about it. He could know the poem by heart. It has the procedure and he would remember how to do it by the poem. That's how our progenitors passed down knowledge from generation to generation.

I was a poet. Well, now I am a whore but not for long. As soon as I get paid for this script I'm going back to literature. Maybe I'll marry a rich man and let him support me while I write but that's just one more way to be a whore. No, I'd better teach.

Caroline was so deep into her thoughts she almost missed her stop, but at the last minute jumped up and got off at the Civic Center station.

The president of EnterTrain was named Sidney Mills. He had a little bitty dick the size of a finger and sometimes, but not often, it got hard and became the size of a thumb. It got hard at the sight of big breasts if the woman wasn't tall or fat. It got hard at the touch of a woman's tongue. If she would lick him and lick him and lick him, it would stay hard and he could come.

Sidney didn't care that his dick was small. But he cared that he couldn't keep it hard when he tried to fuck someone. He tried not to worry about that, however, and made sure to get a blow job nearly every day so his dick wouldn't lose the ability it had until medical science invented a way to keep it hard that didn't entail putting himself in danger of a heart attack. Then I'll fuck them, he told himself. I'll tie those bitches to a bed and fuck them until they beg for mercy.

He adjusted his four-hundred-dollar tie on his handmade three-hundred-dollar shirt and squirmed around in his leather desk chair. He had been on the phone all morning and now he was getting ready to go to lunch with the famous actress Tia Volare. I wonder if she would do it to me, he was thinking. I'll ask her what she wants to do to me this afternoon.

He looked at the clock. It was twelve fifteen. He needed to be at the restaurant at one. In twenty more minutes he would need his car. He was just pushing a button to call his chauffeur when his secretary's voice came over the intercom to tell him Miss Volare had called to cancel the lunch.

He got up and began to pace around the room. The fucking bitch, he decided. That fat whore. Cancel on me? If I had a hit all that would change. If one of those goddamn useless writers living off of me would give me one goddamn script worth filming I could go and get my share. Now who will I have for lunch and where will I get a blow job this late in the day?

I'll show her, he added. She'll be sorry. She'll pay for this. Nobody cancels a lunch with Sidney Mills.

Sidney had had two huge successes in the eighties. A film called *The Baby in His Head* and a sequel called *Will the Baby Never Shut Up?* In both films the baby a man used to be follows him around and asks for things. "Hungry," the baby cries out, or "Scared," or "Mommie," or "Sleepy." Only the audience can see or hear the baby but the man's behavior is affected by the cries. For some reason audiences had howled with laughter at these films and it had become chic to always be saying "Hungry" or "Tired" or "Mommie" at the appropriate moments.

Sidney had stolen the idea from a short story a southern woman had written in the 1930s. He still lived in horror she would appear some day and sue, but ten years had gone by and nothing had happened yet.

Anyway, he had made a lot of money on the films and he was still running on the credit. It's about run out, he decided, and stopped in the middle of his silk carpet to look down at his five-hundred-dollar leather loafers with lifts in the heels.

She cancels on me? She leaves me horny? He felt for his tiny little penis. It was a little bit stiff. Just a little bit. He pulled his silk trousers back so he could see it in his crotch. Definitely stiff. Very definitely aroused. "Arous-Ed," he said, remembering the high school production of *Romeo and Juliet* in which he had played Benvolio to much praise. I could have been an actor, he decided. I could have acted rings around Tia Volare's fat ass. I could have left her in the dust.

He walked over to a wide curving window and looked out upon the new San Francisco Public Library. It was a beautiful sight and it cheered him up to think his name was on the brass plaque beside the wall of writers' photographs. How much money has she given to public works? he asked himself. Where is her name known, here or in L.A.? How dare she cancel without talking to me herself.

He walked back over to the desk and pushed a button and asked his secretary who had called to cancel the lunch.

"Her agent," the secretary said. "He said she wasn't feeling well. Mr. Mills, there's a Caroline Jones in the office. She wrote a script for you called *The Sanguine Blood of Men*, do you remember? She wants to talk to you."

"Send her in," Sidney said. "Tell her to come on in."

Caroline was reading a fashion magazine she had found on an ivory table. She was as shocked as the secretary when she was told to go in Sidney Mills's office.

She threw her cardigan over her arm and went on in the office. She was wearing the sleeveless blue sweater LeLe said made her breasts look too large and she was in a really hot mood. These guys were a bunch of whores and she was a poet. She had something to sell. If they had any sense they would buy it. If not they could kiss her ass. She was going home to Tennessee.

"Come on in," Sidney said. He had gone to open the door for her. "I'm starving. I was just going to order lunch. Will you eat with me? I've been so busy all morning I haven't had time to eat. Come over here. I'll show you the menus. There are three or four places near here that deliver." He took her hand. He pulled her over to a leather sofa near his desk. He sat down beside her. He watched her breasts move around in the soft blue sweater. He was so glad she was here. He turned his big brown eyes on her. He hoped she noticed the eyelashes. It had cost him a lot of pain to have them thickened. The dye had gotten in his eye and almost blinded him. Half the makeup department on the prequel to his *Baby* films had been fired because of that. The prequel had never been finished. The star, Carlos Summers, had quit because of a fight with the director. He had the right to quit if he could prove the director was forcing him to do something that might harm his image or career. He had proved it and walked away without losing a thing but half the million point two he had been given. He had never wanted to do the prequel to begin with, had hated the script, and had only signed on because he thought he needed the money. Then he married a wealthy woman and went off with her to suck up to the Clintons at fund-raisers.

The last Sidney had heard was that Carlos and his bride were spending every weekend in the Lincoln bedroom. It made Sidney sick to think about the failed project. It had been especially dear to him. It had been called *Babies Know Best* and had scenes from the baby life of Carlos's character Dave's own life interwoven with the baby life of a woman Dave falls in love with. At one point their babies are both at the same cocktail party and quit bossing their adults around long enough to eat half a cake and throw the rest into the swimming pool. Sidney had written the cocktail party scenes himself and was very proud of them. The babies would eat a piece of cake, then take icing and smear it on each other. The male baby began to pinch the female baby. Then she began to pinch him back. Cut to Dave in the living room with the woman. Dave is talking about politics but the audience hears the baby's voice-over saying "Hungry, hungry, hungry."

Sidney had gotten that idea himself. He got it from a film he saw about Buddhism. He thought his babies were modern versions of the Buddhist "hungry ghosts," which signify the endless cravings of man. He thought at last he had hit upon an idea that would get him some respect from the critics.

Instead, Carlos Summers quit and the movie project fell apart.

"Are you wearing mascara?" Caroline asked. His face was so close to hers, he seemed so distraught, that she blurted it out.

"No, they grow this way." He moved back. "Won't you look at the menus? I want to talk to you about your script, but I'm starving. First things first."

"Get something from the Chinese place. I just had a big breakfast, waffles, with my cousin. I'm not very hungry but I can always eat Chinese. Whatever you're having will be fine."

Sidney gave her his sweetest smile. He had a beautiful face and the soft, endearing little smile had gotten him everything he wanted for the first ten years of his life. Then his mother had lost interest in him and he had been forced to learn to rely on his wits. It hadn't been his mother's fault. She had breast cancer and became terrified and self-involved, then dead. He had never liked school when she was alive. After she died he became a better student, sailing through the public schools in the little town of Petaluma where they lived, then on to Berkeley for four years, then to Los Angeles to work as an assistant director in a distant cousin's films.

Now he was thirty-six and he owned a production company and he could pick up a phone and demand any sort of service or have hand-made sofas made for his living room or trade in his Rado or do anything he thought of to make himself happy except Tia Volare had broken a luncheon appointment with him and that made him think his career was on the downslide and that scared him. You could lose anything in the world, your mother, your power, your little bitty dick, your ability to get a hard-on.

"I'll have the secretary order shrimp and snow peas and what else?" he asked. "Come on, what do you like? Tell me, Caroline."

"I love shrimp and snow peas. Get that and wonton soup."

*   *   *

Sidney got up and went to the desk and pushed a button and told his secretary the order. Then he came back to the sofa grouping and sat across from Caroline. "We didn't have an appointment, did we?" he asked. "And your agent didn't call. So what's up?"

"I've changed my mind about the script. Not because I think you were right but because I need some money. I'll write it again with some of the changes you suggested if you'll pay me. I want the rest of the money I was promised in the original contract. That money was owed me for writing it, Mr. Mills, not for rewriting it twice. I think I've been screwed."

"Well, of course we'll pay you for the rewrite. Where did you get the idea that we wouldn't?"

He was getting more and more interested in Caroline. He liked the barely noticeable southern accent. He liked the casual getup and the sweater. He got up from the sofa and went to the side of the room and framed her with his hands.

"I bet you're very photogenic," he said.

"The opposite. I'm too pale. So, listen, tell me again what you want changed about the first scenes. I thought it was so crucial to start it off in the small town where she lived, to really set up the character so the audience knows her well enough to understand her behavior when the call comes about her father. Did you ever see *Badlands*? The camera spends about five minutes on the male lead going from house to house on the back of the garbage truck. But it's a pretty little midwestern town and it's spring and he's so young and good-looking. Of course, he's going to become a criminal. I want the audience to know DeDe's going to be hard to scare or fool. She's strong, made strong by her family and her roots, her useful life as a teacher."

"Something has to happen. The audience won't sit there for a travelogue."

"Something is happening. We run the credits over the hurricane on the island if you want. I don't want it that way but I could do that. We could show her father's boat being pushed this way and that. I meant to write this as a murder but then I changed my mind and decided the world has plenty of murders. It's a romantic comedy." Caroline was on her feet now and walking around the office as she talked. "We had Winona Ryder interested until she saw that doctored script you let that man write. If you had shown her my script she would have liked it. This has been a real mess, Sidney. I'm glad to get to talk to you in person about it without all them around talking too."

"I know. It's a difficult profession, Caroline. You may not be temperamentally suited to it." Sidney liked the way he sounded saying that and went over and took a seat behind his beautiful dark walnut desk. He usually waited to sit behind his desk until he wanted to make a point about money. "Why don't you just give the script another try and do it your way and let us see what you get. I'll call Gill Reed and talk to her about the money."

"Do you have my original script here?" Caroline asked.

"I may. Let me look." Sidney pretended to be looking for the script in the drawers of his desk and then on a wall of scripts in binders. He didn't want Caroline to think he hadn't *respected* her enough to keep a copy in his office.

While this was going on two secretaries came scurrying in the open door carrying trays and set up lunch at a table by the window. Sidney came around the desk and took Caroline's arm and led her to a table. "Do you worry about the cholesterol in shrimp?" he asked. "I never do. I never gain weight. I have great metabolism."

He began to eat with gusto. All he had eaten that morning was coffee and a bagel. He liked to save himself for lunch, then off to bed for the afternoon, then back to the office at five to do the hard part of his work, which was make phone calls to people who weren't in his pocket.

He waited until they had finished lunch and were having coffee before he made the pass. "I'm going home for an hour to take a nap," he said, smiling the endearing, little-boy smile. "Come spend the afternoon with me. Life is short, Caroline. No one in this town remembers to be alive, but I do because my dead mother was a happy woman who taught me to love life. I like pleasure, is what I mean. I like to give it and receive it."

"Not today, Sidney." She got up and walked around the table and gave him a kiss on the cheek. "I have to work all afternoon. Besides . . ." She decided to give him a bone. "I might not want to leave." She stepped back. "So you'll call Gill this afternoon and talk to her?"

"Or tomorrow." He put his napkin carefully beside his plate and stood up. Now that she had turned him down he was aware that he was shorter than she was. Not much. With his best posture and a better pair of shoes he would be her height. He looked down at her shoes. She was wearing one- or two-inch heels. You couldn't tell about those squared-off shoes.

"I have two films in production," he added. "Burt Reynolds is finishing a project with us for PBS. I've got Tia Volare coming in to audition. I'll call Gill as soon as I have time. I don't know when it will be."

"Thanks for lunch," Caroline said. My grandmother was a founding member of Tri Delt at Vanderbilt, she was thinking. My great-great-grandfather was the governor of Tennessee. My cousin is an All-American. My father is a physician. I do not have to take this shit from a midget but on the other hand I do not have to be rude to him.

All I have to do is negotiate about forty feet of carpet and get out of here.

She's looking at my dick, he decided. No, she didn't look at my pants. She's looking at her hands. I wouldn't pay that bitch another cent if she was William Goldman.

"Wonderful visit with you," Caroline said, and reached out and touched his arm. "This office is absolutely gorgeous, Sidney. I love knowing I'm in business with someone with such perfect taste. It makes me think we'll work this out and have a film someday."

She made an exit then, turning at the door to wave.

Sidney went over to the desk and sat in his chair and called his psychiatrist. Amazingly, the man answered the phone. "I've been rejected twice in an hour," he told the doctor. "I'm dealing with it. They are not my mother. I know that. I am five feet six inches tall, which is a normal height. My dick is big enough to bring a woman to orgasm or if not I can use my mouth. I am an exceptionally talented and successful man in the hardest business in the world." He was crying now. His personal secretary had heard this before. He didn't bother to get up and close the door. Some woman needed to hear him suffer. Someone had to share his burden.

"Calm down, Sidney," the doctor was saying. "I have a five o'clock open. Do you want to come in?"

"I want some happiness," he cried into the phone. "I want a little respect and some happiness."

"You have your wife and children right there in your house."

"They aren't there. They're in Houston with her family. They've been gone for three days. They aren't coming home until Wednesday."

Caroline walked out of the building into beautiful, blinding sunlight. She was smiling like a child. She was amazed and smiling and absolutely free. The dwarf had made a pass at her and she had fielded it like a pro. She would no more write another word for that fool than fly to the blue moon.

There was not enough money in the world to get her to touch the script again. Well, not that she was going to be offered any by Sidney Mills.

She stopped by her automobile. I didn't ask him about the reversion of the rights, she remembered. But that's Gill's department anyway. Not that I trust her either. I'm getting out of here. LeLe can stay here and be the reigning southern expatriate to her heart's content. I'm going home where people know who I am. Did he actually think I'd go to bed with him? Do you think he actually believed there was a chance I'd do that? She kept shaking her head while she got into her car and drove off to finish packing. LeLe would just have to deal with it. She, Caroline Denegue Jones, was going home.

Sidney closed the door to his office and pulled his Buddhist prayer bench out into the exact center of his Indian rug and began his chant. I am a good man who has done good and useful work in the world. I create jobs. I let the craziest people in the world come into my space and I do not let them drive me crazy. I deal with egos so inflated and wounded and crazy any psychiatrist would not let them in his office. I let them in mine. Writers and painters and actresses and actors, the scum of the earth, are the clay I use to mold a world where paychecks are delivered, house payments are made, and food is put on the table. I do this with my balls. My dick may be small but my balls are huge. My dick may be small but my balls are tremendous.

In a few minutes he got up off the prayer bench and went to the phone and called his CPA and told him to send a check for twenty thousand dollars to UNICEF. Then he told him to send a check for ten thousand dollars to the Bosnian Refugee Relief that had been bugging him for a month.

Then he felt better and decided to go home and take a nap. His beautiful house was waiting for him with his big soft bed, and at five he would go see Doctor Glick and really do some work on his mother. It was his mother who had passed on his small stature. His father's family were tall, Russian Jews. It was his mother who had cursed him with her small, French genes. Yes, she had had enormous, soft breasts. Yes, she had nursed him until he could talk. Yes, she had died before he stopped needing her. It is an imperfect world. Everyone has burdens. At least I don't have to fool with that stupid southern woman anymore, he decided. That project's finished. She doesn't understand this industry. She'll never make it out here.

Caroline stopped at the grocery store and bought some angel hair pasta and Romano cheese. She had decided to cook dinner for LeLe to soften the blow when she told her she was going home.

As she was leaving the grocery store it came to her. How to take the script and turn it back into a murder mystery with a mysterious half brother in Miami who was five feet five inches tall and who kills his father. No, he has him killed by the Mafia to inherit his fortune, only the father has left most of it to the heroine, the good schoolteacher in the small town in Arkansas. His mother is from some small, dark race. I won't be specific. He looks nothing like his handsome father. He can't get laid except by whores or people he buys. He has to have the money but he's so stupid he leaves a trail a Girl Scout could follow.

She drove home filled with happiness. If she wanted to stay in California, which she did not, she could finish the script and so forth but she was leaving anyway.

Oh, God, what a wonderful world, she was thinking. So full of opportunities and possibilities and surprises and invitations and danger. What a lucky thing to get to be here at all.

That's all I'm going to think about all day. I could write a poem about it, but who wants to read a poem about joy. Joy doesn't need any minstrels. Joy just hangs out like the air, waiting for anyone who wants to take or breathe it.

Caroline rolled down the windows of the car and drove on home to cook dinner for her cousin.

LeLe Arnold's day had been equally eventful if not as dramatic. The moment she arrived at the paper she became involved in a dispute about who was going to cover the just broken Monica Lewinsky scandal in Washington. The Washington bureau chief wanted it all coming out of his office, but the editor in chief in San Francisco wanted to send a reporter to set up a special desk. "It isn't going to last that long," the managing editor kept saying. "This is it. He'll resign. It's happened. By the time we get a desk set up it will be over."

"Are you kidding?" LeLe kept arguing. "This has weeks to run, maybe months. This is a centipede. It's got legs to last into the new millennium."

*   *   *

Nothing was decided during the day, but the newsroom was a beehive until LeLe left at six to drive on home. In the meantime, she had managed to finish a story about Habitat for Humanity's getting into a fight with a group of Realtors over building on donated land in a gated neighborhood.

Then she finished up an interview with a young movie star named Boots Macnamee, whose real name was Doris Coleman. She returned a lot of phone calls from people who had thought up things for her to do that she had no interest in doing.

Finally she called the rugby player and left him a message. Then she drove on home. If Caroline leaves I won't have anyone to come home to, she was thinking. I have to find her some work, so she won't leave, but I don't have any leverage with the movie world. She shouldn't have gotten mixed up with that whore Gill. That was her first mistake. Well, I want that job in Washington if it pans out. Who knows, I might have to be there a month. I could tell Caroline to stay and house-sit. She knows I don't like to leave the place alone.

LeLe was driving along, completely oblivious to the beautiful blue skies, the people in other cars, the delight and possibility and order and beauty of the world. All she was thinking about was the mess in Washington and its potential for advancement and the fact that her cousin Caroline was probably going to leave no matter what she did.

Just as she started out onto the Bay Bridge, the rugby player called her back. His name was Cameron Harlow and he was more than just a rugby player, although LeLe thought it was unhealthy to admit to herself that he was also the handsomest man she had ever seen in her life, plus one of the sweetest. When he wasn't playing rugby he ran a small

renovation company and made a good living fixing up houses and selling them at reasonable profits. He was a man who liked being reasonable. The only unreasonable thing he did was fall in love with neurotic
women. LeLe was the third neurotic woman he had loved. "She's not as
crazy as Sally was or Chile David," his best friend liked to remind him.
"She might not be crazy if you'd marry her and get her pregnant. She's
lonely, Cameron. That's why she acts so crazy. Women that age need to
have babies. They leave you alone after they get some children. The only
way to get them to stop thinking about you and messing in your shit is
to get them pregnant."

Cameron's best friend was from South Africa. He was half Masai
and half Dutch. Cameron thought he was the wisest person he had ever
known. When he was sober, he was the wisest. When he was drunk, he
was so wild LeLe wouldn't let him in her house. Once he had climbed
the telephone pole near her house and threatened to electrocute himself
for world peace when the police came. Africa, he called himself. He had
ditched his last name and wouldn't have one. If he had to put one down
when he applied to have his green card renewed, he called himself
Africa Man.

"Where've you been?" Cameron asked, when LeLe answered the phone,
one-eighth of a mile onto the bridge.

"Working for a living," she answered. "What are you doing later?"

"I'll be waiting for you. You want to have dinner?"

"No, Caroline's cooking for me. Then I have to go back to the
office for a while, then I'll come over. A lot's happening. I might be
going to Washington, D.C. Caroline might be leaving."

"Whenever you get there. I'll be waiting. LeLe, may I ask you something?"

"Of course. What?"

"Are you still on the pill? I read this thing the other day about it isn't good to stay on it more than five years."

"Ten years, and no, I'm not on it right now so have some rubbers."

"I have everything you need, LeLe. If you'd only let me give it to you. I don't know why you get so mad at me."

"You're a drunk, Cameron. You ruin everything you do with whiskey."

"Well, I'm not drinking this week. I'm working like a dog on this place on Powell Street."

"I'll be there by ten. Maybe sooner."

"I love you, baby. Do you know that?"

"Oh, well. Listen, I have to hang up and get off this bridge." She giggled then and he laughed with her. He could always make her laugh. It was the fatal flaw in her attempts to stop seeing him.

She turned off the bridge singing to herself. "There must be a way to make you believe that I love you," she was singing. It was one of the songs from musicals she used to put on in Nashville with her cousins. They had had a very limited supply of albums to use for production numbers. "There must be a way to make you believe that I care. . . ."

Caroline was sitting on the stone wall by the driveway. She was holding the mobile phone and she was crying. As soon as LeLe's car pulled into the driveway she jumped down from the wall and stood waiting.

"What?" LeLe asked. "What's happened?"

"It's Grandmother. She's had a stroke. They think she's dying. We have to go to Nashville. I made us reservations. There's a plane at nine through Chicago."

"Oh, God." LeLe got out of the car and embraced her cousin and they hurried into the house.

"I packed for you. Your bag's on the bed. See if it's okay." They went on into LeLe's bedroom and LeLe looked at the suitcase without seeing it.

"That's good. When did they call? Why didn't you call me?"

"I didn't want to tell you while you were driving. I tried once and the line was busy, then I decided to wait. I was going to call again if you weren't here by six thirty."

The phone rang. It was the travel agent saying she'd found them a flight at eight with better connections if they could make that.

"Let's go, then," Caroline said. "I fixed you a sandwich. It's in the kitchen. Take it with you."

"I have to call the office. Well, I can do it on the plane. I have everything done for the Sunday paper. I need to stay here. Well, I can't. Did you call Miss Freddie?" Miss Freddie was the caretaker of the condominiums where LeLe had her place. She was always good about watching over the house if they had to be gone.

"She said just leave. She said she'd do what needed to be done."

"Let's go." They closed the suitcase and carried it out to the car. Caroline's luggage was already in the carport. They climbed into LeLe's Bronco and began to drive.

"What did we forget?"

"Everything. What does it matter?"

"I put the message on the answering machine. I just said, 'Call Caroline or LeLe's mother or leave a message.' That's all I could figure out to do."

"Oh, shit. Cameron. Call him, will you, and tell him what's happening. I don't like talking on the phone on the expressway. I think it's nuts and dangerous. Did you see that truck? Did you see that son of a bitch?" LeLe began honking her horn furiously at a Wonder Bread delivery truck that had done nothing but stay in its own lane when she veered illegally into it.

Caroline got Cameron on the phone and talked to him. "He said to tell you he was sorry," Caroline said, when he had hung up. "He said to let him know if there was anything he could do."

"He can quit drinking is what he can do, but he doesn't even *entertain* the idea."

"He's a good man, LeLe. You've been going out with him for ten years. Why don't you go on and marry him and get it over with?"

"Because I won't marry someone who drinks and that's the end of it. What else did they say? Do they know anything at all?"

"They're going to do an MRI as soon as they can. She's asleep, LeLe. She may not wake up, you know. She could be dead right now."

"Well, don't say that. I can't stand it if I never talk to her again. I want to talk to her. I want to hear her voice." She swerved around a Celestial Seasonings truck and back into the center lane and then gunned it to make a light. "Don't breathe like that. I've never had a wreck in my life. I can't have one. I have perfect reflexes. Cameron says the reason I don't have wrecks is that my reflexes are so good."

"I don't care how you drive as long as we don't miss this plane."

They got to the airport at seven fifteen. Caroline got out and took the bags and LeLe parked the car in the short-term parking lot and ran for it.

They got onto the plane with ten minutes to spare. The sandwich Caroline had made was in the bottom of LeLe's purse. She took it out and gave half of it to Caroline. It was seven-grain bread with four slices of tofu and lettuce and sprouts and tomatoes. It was food for the soul and they took their time and ate it. They were a marvelous-looking pair of mourners, travelers, young women of the contemporary world. Caroline had changed into a short silk skirt that was black with white and yellow flowers. Underneath the skirt she had on black silk hose and a pair of black drawers with lace around the edges. On top she had a white silk camisole and a navy silk jacket. She was wearing her mother's pearls and little pearl earrings LeLe had lent her so long ago she had forgotten they didn't belong to her.

LeLe still had on her American riding costume, which was a good thing because as soon as the plane reached cruising altitude it became very cold and there weren't enough blankets to go around.

Over the Great Salt Lake in Utah they fell asleep with their heads touching. LeLe's strawberry-colored curls and Caroline's darker curls. Asleep they looked like the sixteen-year-old colleen who had been their great-great-great-grandmother. The curls were hers and perhaps the will. Things LeLe felt in the night when she slept beside the rugby player were also the Irish girl's because some genes are so useful nature never loses track of them. Caroline had it too but she had never found the match to start the fire. It would happen, but not for another year.

Their grandmother, May Garth, was awake and able to recognize them when they arrived at the hospital at seven the next morning. They had slept on the plane and been met at the airport by their cousin William. They dumped their bags at Caroline's parents' house and went on up to the hospital. "It could be a week," William warned them. "Or it might be this afternoon. She isn't letting them do anything else. We're going to take her home tomorrow if we can."

They didn't talk anymore until they reached her hospital room. Three members of their family were standing outside the door. Caroline's mother was by her mother's bed.

"Come here, my darlings, my little chickens." May Garth held out her hand to them. "You didn't wear that on the plane, did you, Caroline?"

"No, ma'am," she said. "I just threw it on. It's too short, isn't it? I think they shrank it at the cleaners."

"Don't worry about that, Grandmomma." LeLe approached the bed and began to cry. "We flew all night. We are so worried about you. I love you so much." She leaned down and let her grandmother embrace her with the hand that was still hooked up to an IV.

"My little girl, my LeLe," her grandmother said. "I was waiting for you to get here. And you too, Caroline. It was hard on you to fly all night, I know."

She reached her other, freer hand to Caroline. Then she gasped. Her body jerked and her head fell to the side.

They watched as she died.

LeLe could never remember what happened next but Caroline wrote it down that night and many months later sent her a copy of the notes. "We watched our grandmother die. She was the bravest woman in the world and lived through the depression and raised her oldest daughter, Annie Moss, who died in a car wreck, and my mother, Jo Anne, and a daughter, Ella, and a son William, and a son Philip. She thought LeLe was the reincarnation of her daughter, Annie Moss, and used to tell us so. She let us do anything we wanted to when we were at her house in the summer. She had a playhouse for us built in the backyard and a tree house with steps. She taught us to play bridge and she let us take drags off her cigarettes. She let us drink Cokes. Here she was about to die and she noticed the length of my skirt.

"We ran out in the hall and got Uncle William and Aunt Edith and they came in but she was already dead. Then the funeral home people came and they had to take the body away. I wanted to go with the body but no one would let me. I always got left out of her life for being so young but I loved her and I know she loved me. She got about twenty copies of my book of poems and gave them to all her friends. She was the only one who didn't bitch about my language in the poems. She was glad I was getting published.

"So after they took her away we had to go to our house and call people all day. Then we had everyone there and then we had to have that funeral and bury her by Granddaddy and that's that. The death of a loved one. The goddamn terrible fate we all share. 'No possum, no sop, no taters,' as the poet said. This is what poets do, they try to talk about death but who can talk about such a thing.

"I don't want to write poetry. I want to live in the golden present and do something normal for a living. I want to have a child so when I die someone will be standing by the bed. It's so late now I guess I won't have many. You have to start early if you want people standing by the bed. I guess LeLe will be there. LeLe will probably live forever. But that's what we thought about Grandmother and it didn't happen, did it?"

Caroline and LeLe flew back to California the day after the funeral. "I'll be fired," LeLe told her parents when they begged her to stay.

"I'll lose my chance to rewrite the script," Caroline told hers. So they escaped and found themselves on a six A.M. flight wearing old, comfortable clothes and part of the jewelry May Garth had left them.

Caroline had on a white gold bracelet and LeLe had on an emerald and diamond ring.

They were sad. And they were changed. Neither of them had ever seen a death before. LeLe had spent most of her career covering the arts. "There was slaughter," she said out loud. "But not death. I was thinking about my career," she added. "I knew there was a reason I never wanted any of the harder beats. I could have had them. I could have gone to Bosnia several years ago but I turned it down. I was afraid I'd see starving children. I see plenty here. But not someone I loved leaving forever. Forever, Caroline. She will not return. There isn't any reincarnation, like the way she used to say I was Annie Moss. No one is anyone else. There's no heaven. There's no afterlife. It's bullshit about the DNA. We're just here and then we're gone. Right back into the dark matter."

"You don't know it's dark. It could be light. She could be sailing around in the air like light or electricity and it isn't bullshit about the DNA. DNA is a physical fact that can be measured and manipulated. She is in every cell in my body. Through my mother into me. And there might be an afterlife. There's no surety in saying there's nothing after death. There might be. All you can say is you don't know."

"I know there's nothing. How could there be? . . ." They were interrupted by the stewardess offering coffee. Caroline said yes but LeLe decided to sleep.

What do I believe? Caroline asked herself. The coffee came. It was Starbucks with real cream. There was a note on the tray saying American Airlines had a new partner in Starbucks from Washington State. Caroline drank the coffee, strangely, childishly glad for this small pleasure, favor, treat. She closed her eyes and remembered tea parties with May Garth and her cousins. Playing ladies, making the world a courteous and gracious place in the middle of an afternoon. I'll live like that again, Caroline vowed. I'll write thank-you notes and not on stupid postcards. I'll flaunt my intelligence instead of my legs. Well, I won't do that. I like short skirts. I look great in them. But I'm going to remember stuff she taught us. I'm going to hold my neck up and tuck it in when I want to look regal, and what else? I don't know. Maybe I'll stop being rude. Maybe I'll be polite to every single person in the world whether they deserve it or not. I'll write a thank-you note to Sidney Mills and thank him for the lunch. God, what a move that would be. He'll go crazy trying to figure that out.

They got home at two in the afternoon Pacific time. While they were gone Cameron had brought over a crew and built the flower gardens LeLe had been wanting for five years. Islands of daisies and hostas and red salvia and blue salvia with circles of Dutch iris and tulips, bare now, but marked with flags saying what they would become.

"I love you," read a note on the door. "Call me when you get home."

"My God," Caroline said.

"I'm touched," LeLe admitted. "I'm really touched. Now you can't leave, Caroline. He's trying to marry me again."

But five days later Caroline did leave. She packed her little Cabriolet with her clothes and CDs and a box of manuscripts and left everything else she had accumulated for LeLe to keep or sell or put in storage. "I'm going home and start applying for real jobs," she told LeLe. "I have a life if I'll go find it and it has to happen in the South. A degree from Vanderbilt doesn't mean enough out here. They don't know it and besides, they judge everyone on their political correctness scale and they want you to teach those stupid women writers who whine and moan all the time. The school of resentment, that's all there is out here in the English departments. I'm tired of pretending to think that's valid. I'm going home to where someone knows John Crowe Ransom and William Faulkner and James Baldwin. Home to my own world."

"All right." LeLe had given up. Caroline was leaving. It was done. "But your stuff stays in your room in case you change your mind."

Caroline climbed into the Cabriolet and pushed the trip odometer to zero. She had thousands of miles to drive and she wanted to count them. She had a route planned that took her in two days to Albuquerque, where she planned to pick up an old high school friend who was going to share the driving from there to Nashville. They were going to stop in Oklahoma to see friends from college, then on to Nashville. Come on, Caroline, she told herself as she buckled her seat belt. People crossed this country in wagons and on foot. All you have to do is drive this car and try to have some fun along the way.

She shoved a CD into her portable CD player and Michael Bolton started singing. "You made me leave my happy home. Took my love and now you're gone. . . ."

She had meant to listen to Mozart all the way to New Mexico but she had forgotten to put those CDs on top. "Since I fell for you," she was singing. "Since I fell for you."

LeLe went back into her empty house and sat down on the sofa and cried. I'm crying for Grandmomma, she decided, and for every damn one of us in this fucking vale of tears.

The phone was ringing. It was Cameron, wanting to come over and see how the flower beds were doing. "Have you got any rubbers?" she asked him.

"I've got some Häagen-Dazs coffee ice cream," he answered. "How about that in the meantime?"

She started fucking him as soon as he got in the door and had his shirt off by the time they reached the living room. They had fucked each other on that carpet a hundred times on winter nights with a fire in the fireplace, but this was the first time they fucked each other there on a winter afternoon with the sunlight streaming in the windows and all the curtains open while a four-dollar pint of ice cream melted on the floorboards of his truck.

I don't know what this means, Sidney was thinking. He was pacing around his office with the letter in his hand, stopping every now and then to look out the window at the roof of the Civic Center and the towering majesty of the library, *which his generosity had helped build.* He was in a marvelous mood. Tom Hanks was about to sign for the role in *Babies Know Best*, the film Carlos Summers had quit. With the proviso that Robin Williams be the voice of the baby, but that could be solved with money. How much could it cost to get Robin to say fifteen or twenty lines into a microphone? Of course, no one had talked to Tom, but his agent was on board.

Plus, his wife had come home five pounds thinner and in the mood for love. Plus, the PBS show on orphans was edited and off to earn him thanks and praise. Plus, the little southern bitch had written him this letter on this funny, old-fashioned, creme-colored stationery lined with some sort of satiny paper that made it look like a wedding invitation. Dear Sidney, it said. Thank you so much for the lovely *lunch* and for taking the time to talk to me about the script. It's so nice when we can get past all the agents and go-betweens and just talk as fellow artists. Good luck with all your projects. Yours most sincerely, Caroline Jones.

What did that mean? The lunch was probably about what she *didn't eat.* She had *not eaten a bite.* Listen, she was supposed to be some sort of poet who had won awards. There was no way she would have written that unless she wanted him to read between the lines. Poets were always doing that. Trying to squeeze meaning out of some little everyday piece of language.

Well, let her wait. Give it a week or two and then he'd call her late some morning and get her to meet him at the apartment. There is nothing in the world, not in the whole wide world, Sidney believed, as good as fucking someone who had turned you down. It had everything. Poetry, justice, juice, juice, juice.

Caroline had just passed the little town of Madera. She had decided to memorize the Michael Bolton tape before she changed to Mozart. It's good for poets to stay in touch with the culture, she decided. Besides, it gave her a chance to stretch her voice. "If you ever change your mind. About leaving, leaving me behind. Baby, bring it to me. Bring your sweet loving. Bring it on home to me. Yea, yea, yea, yea, yea . . ."

LeLe and Cameron were asleep when Sidney Mills called looking for Caroline. Anyone can play the waiting game, he had decided. It takes balls to just ask for what you want and take a chance on being rejected.

"She's gone home to Nashville," LeLe told him. "She's driving. Who is this?"

"I'm sorry. You sound like you're asleep. Were you asleep?"

"That's okay. I had to wake up anyway."

"It's Sidney Mills, at EnterTrain. So does she have a phone in the car?"

"I think so. She has one. I wouldn't bet it was on. She's driving to Nashville, Tennessee, Sidney. She'll be there Friday or Saturday."

"Friday? How could it take that long?"

"She's stopping several places. If she calls me, I'll tell her you called. She'll probably call when she stops somewhere tonight. She's taking the old southern route. Have you ever driven that?" LeLe was waking up, sitting up in bed but still talking very quietly so as not to wake Cameron. "Wait a minute, will you." She got out of the bed and walked into the dressing room and sat on a chair before the dressing table. She closed the door to the bedroom. "I'm sorry. There's someone here. I was trying not to wake them. If it's something important I could get you her mobile phone number, but I doubt if you'll get her to answer. She never turns it on."

"Well, give it to me. I'll try. When she calls, tell her I got her letter and I called to thank her for it. Just tell her to call my unlisted number. Do you have a pencil to write it down?" He was getting turned on by LeLe's husky, sleepy, southern voice. "Who am I talking to, by the way?"

"LeLe Arnold. I'm Caroline's cousin. We've met. I work for the *Chronicle*. I covered the premiere of *Pigs That Fly*, the film you did last March."

"Here's a number then." He gave her two unlisted numbers he knew better than to give a reporter. "Don't put those in a computer or a Rolodex, Miss Arnold. If you don't mind."

"Of course. So what's happening with Caroline's script, if you don't mind my asking? I hated to have her leave. I wish something would break to bring her back. We lived together."

"It's still in the works," Sidney said. "Those things take time. Well, I better go. Come in and visit the office sometime, Miss Arnold. Any late morning. We have some really interesting projects now."

"Okay. Here's her mobile phone. Good luck. I'll tell her to call when I talk to her." LeLe hung up the phone, brushed her teeth, combed her hair, and went back to the bed. "Who was that?" Cameron sleepily asked.

"Movie people," she answered and cuddled up in his arms. His endlessly welcoming and sheltering arms. Oh, fuck, she was thinking. I'm sucked back in. How many times has this happened? "They always sense when they're losing something," she added. "They can't stand to think something moved out of their range of possibility. They can't believe they can't buy any artist on the earth."

"They buy a lot of them." Cameron pulled her closer to him. "Go back to sleep. I love this afternoon. Don't let it end."

Caroline was driving in beautiful country. To the east the mountains rose up from the plain. Caroline had cut off the CD player so she could drive and feast on beauty. Now's the time for Mozart, she decided. No, I'll just be quiet and think about this incredible piece of real estate we call the United States. We stole California from Mexico, of course, just like we bought the Lousiana Purchase for peanuts. Maybe I'll teach history but literature is a truer picture of a time. Christopher Marlowe and Ben Jonson and William Shakespeare tell a truer story of the sixteen hundreds than all the history books. Who will tell the story of our age? There are so many of us. So many realities. Maybe Sidney Mills and his stupid movies are as valid as Timothy Ferris and Larry McMurtry and Gabriel García Márquez. Maybe it's going to take all the writers we can muster to tell this story, Gore Vidal and Kurt Vonnegut and Amos Oz and John McPhee and Seamus Heaney and Joan Didion and William

Buckley and William Faulkner and John Fowles and Annie Dillard and hundreds more, all telling their stories, documenting, and journalists too, for all their hurried insults and bad decisions. LeLe's part of it and maybe I will be too.

The mountains were too beautiful. She was driving south. She began to sing songs from home. "Amazing grace," she began singing. "How sweet the sound, that saved a wretch like me. Oh, I was lost but now I'm found. Was bound but now I'm free."

Sidney gave up trying to get Caroline's mobile phone to answer and decided to go home and get his wife and drive to Las Vegas to spend the night. I want to be on a long car trip, he decided. I want to be behind the wheel, burning dinosaur juice, listening to the stereo, having some fun for a change. I haven't taken the little Porsche out for a spin in a long time. It just sits there. What good does it do me? I never have any fun. All I do is work, work, work.

Having made up his mind to change that, he became filled with happiness and made a note to remind himself to give five grand to the United Way when he came back to the office on Monday. Or ten, if I win at the tables, he decided. That will bring me luck and keep me from feeling guilty about gambling.

He went singing out of the building and down into the parking lot to pick up the Lexus his wife had made him buy from his brother-in-law and drive it home. I'm giving this piece of junk away, he decided. I don't have to drive a Lexus to town just because Sam Walton drove a truck.

HEARTS OF DIXIE

THIRTY-SIX GOLD KRUGERRANDS. At four hundred dollars apiece, that equals fourteen thousand, four hundred dollars. I want to keep these Krugerrands. I can't help it. Just because I'm a Presbyterian doesn't mean I'm perfect. This is not like when some poor child finds a sack of money that fell off a Brinks truck and gives it back because his mother taught him to be honest. This is not like finding someone's bill-fold. No one even knows these Krugerrands exist, unless it is some coin dealer who sold them to her. I don't even know when she put them there. She told me she wanted the safe deposit box because there were a lot of letters she had written over the years and managed not to mail and she wanted to keep them to remind herself of the tangled skein of human love, not to mention she thought they might make a play some-day, like that piece of junk called *The Love Journal* the Little Theater puts on every couple of years to give their aging prima donnas a vehicle in which to wear negligees.

Jean Lyles refused to become an aging prima donna. When she started getting old she founded her own theater and became a director. She brought Albee to Jackson, Mississippi, and Harold Pinter and Tom

Stoppard and did Shakespeare and Shaw and Ibsen and played the music of Philip Glass in the lobby.

I was only the typist. I guess that's what I'll say when the police come to the door to get the Krugerrands.

The safe deposit box had nothing to do with Jean's dying. It wasn't there in case she died. Besides, the chances of her dying seemed zero. She ran two miles every day on her treadmill. She was as thin as a girl. She didn't smoke or drink. She drank bottled water from France. She had a twenty-nine-year-old lover who adored her. Then, two weeks after her sixtieth birthday, she woke up and had a fatal heart attack.

Leaving five sons to fight over the estate, the young lover moping around town like a ghost, and this goddamn safe deposit box in my name full of those letters and all this money. Maybe she wanted me to have it. Maybe she was hiding it from the IRS. Maybe it belonged to someone else.

I can't tell her people about the Krugerrands unless I tell them about the letters, can I? Here is one of them. See if you think I'd be doing her family a service by turning this over to them.

Dear Anderson [her third son],

I named you for my father and grandfather. I thought by doing that I would endow you with the intelligence, kindness, and goodwill for which they were known. Thank God they are dead and can't see the way you have wasted your life. Your father was not brilliant but neither was he a stupid man. What on earth would lead you to believe that *gambling* is a way for a man to make a living? What dark insanity drives you to lay your honor down in the service of a pack of cards? I give up on you, Anderson. I don't want to see you anymore. I will not give you another cent in any form.

In answer to your tirade I have not given any family money to the theater. I *raised* the money to buy that building and now the theater is self-supporting. If you could rouse yourself from your self-absorption for an hour, you might find many reasons to be proud of me and to tell me so.

Your out-of-patience
Mother

Here's another one. I just grabbed these off the top of the pile. After I saw the Krugerrands I was so paranoid I didn't want anyone to see me leaving the bank with my pockets bulging. The letters are hand-written on thick paper. Each one is in an envelope with initials on the outside. I can't believe she'd keep this next one. This is too mean.

Dear Ann Claire [her son Jimmy's wife],

For God's sake, stop drinking. For the sake of your children, stop sitting in the kitchen at night with a water glass full of wine and your teeth turning pink while you talk on the phone to your friends. Don't make my granddaughters watch you get drunk and sink into sadness. You are sinking into sadness, my precious one. I used to love you so much, Ann Claire, not just for the gift of my grandchildren, but for yourself, for the promise, the possibility, the brilliance, the charm.

I know the causes. I know your own mother drank and died before you were old enough to cure the harm she had done to you. I was there at your wedding, remember. I remember the fool she made of herself and how your father was too inhibited by his own crazy mother to make her stop.

Your daddy couldn't make her stop drinking any more than you can stop Jimmy from running around with every waitress in town. I know those causes also. I know he has to have those women because he didn't have me enough when he was young. He had maids and baby-sitters and now he has to have all those women to make up for that. I have been in psychoanalysis for twenty years to find out why we do the stupid things that ruin our lives.

Ann Claire, for God's sake, for the sake of your children, get well from this addiction. It is not Jimmy's fault or your mother's fault now. It is your fault.

I will do anything to help you quit. I will send you anywhere. I will stop everything I'm doing and move in and run your house while you are gone. I will go with you to AA meetings. I will do anything, pay anything, to get you to stop or help you stop.

I will help you divorce Jimmy. If you stop drinking for one year I will see to it that you get the house and car and plenty of money to live on the rest of your life. I will testify against him. You will have custody of the girls. You will have a life if you quit now and leave him. If you keep on drinking you will die of liver failure or heart disease and leave the girls as your mother left you, unfinished, with the terrible burden of guilt the children of alcoholics bear. They believe they are responsible for your drinking. I heard your daughters talking to each other a few days ago. Ann Chatevin was saying to Alice, "Clean up your room, you pig. Mother told you to clean it up. You never do anything she tells you to. No wonder she gets drunk."

ALCOHOL IS A CENTRAL NERVOUS SYS-TEM DEPRESSANT. It is self-treatment for depression, powerlessness, anxiety, feelings of worthlessness, guilt. It works for a few hours, then there is the terrible price to pay. I wish I could mail this letter, pry up one board of the coffin of your denial.

The language of AA is not a joke. CENTRAL NERVOUS SYSTEM DEPRESSANT, DENIAL, SADNESS, HELPLESSNESS, DESTRUCTIVE BEHAVIOR.

Love, Jean

I better start at the beginning. The writer of the letters was named Jean Andry Lyles. My name is Sally Shelton. I am a tennis professional and a professional typist. I also do clerical work for selected clients. My relationship with Jean Lyles goes back fifteen years, to before she started her theater. I typed things for her and straightened out her bank accounts and house-sat for her when she was out of town.

Now she is dead and I am in the unfortunate position of having twenty-two terrible letters in my possession and thirty-six gold Kruger-rands worth four hundred dollars apiece that I didn't know were in the safe deposit box. If I tell her family about the coins I have to tell them about the letters.

I should burn these letters. She can't make a play out of them now because she woke up one morning and had a heart attack. She didn't give them the letters when she was alive. Why should I give them to them now?

Thirty-six times four hundred is almost fifteen thousand dollars, although I read in the financial pages that the price of gold was falling.

Later: I just found out. They are only worth about three hundred and fifty dollars apiece at today's price and that's if they're in good condition.

I didn't even go to her funeral because I was so upset about finding those coins in there. As soon as I heard she was dead I went straight down to the bank and took everything out of the box to look at it and there they were, thirty-six gold Krugerrands from South Africa, doubly, triply cursed.

I was scared to go to the funeral after that. I was right not to go because the sons had a fight with her lover right in front of the cathe-dral and didn't let him go to the burial. Then, the next week they opened the will and she had left nearly all her money to one of her daughters-in-law and there are lawsuits being filed by every one of her sons. If they find out about the safe deposit box I'll be called to testify in all the lawsuits and made to reveal the contents of the letters.

I feel like somebody who's been caught up in the Whitewater mess or the Monica Lewinsky scandal.

I should get a lawyer and let him handle this but what if they find out about all the money Jean paid me and never reported to the IRS? Mostly she paid me in cash but sometimes she gave me checks. I'm used to being paid in cash from teaching tennis and I'll admit I'm not good at keeping records. I barely make enough to live on and I sure can't spend my time keeping track of every grimy twenty-dollar bill some ten-year-old kid has wadded up in his pocket to pay for his lesson.

I CAN'T KEEP THIRTY-SIX GOLD KRUGER-RANDS THAT DON'T BELONG TO ME. On the other hand, the Lyles family sure doesn't need them. Even the sons she didn't like got half a million apiece. It was just the big money and the property that she left to the daughter-in-law.

Five into thirty-six goes seven and a fifth. Do you think seven and a fifth gold Krugerrands would be worth having to read these letters to her children, who are already in a rage and maybe even grieving? Of course not. Common sense tells you it would be better if I just burned the letters and kept the money.

I could give part of the money to French Camp Academy, the children's home in Madison County. Jean was on the board of that. In her obituary it said to send money there instead of flowers.

Here's another letter. See if you'd want this delivered four months after your mother's death.

Dear Jodie [her second son],
   I was ecstatic when you were born. You were such a funny-looking little baby. The doctor or someone said you were ugly and I cried and

cried. My first and only experience of post-partum depression. You were not ugly. You were the prettiest and sweetest baby I ever had. You were my favorite. And now you are a drunk. You get drunk and make a fool out of yourself. You embarrass your nieces and nephews. You come into town from the drunken escapades you pretend are adventures and go to their houses and say stupid, embarrassing things in front of their friends. They don't want you to come to their houses, telling your stories of crazy trips to South America or Antarctica or wherever you have been going to escape yourself. You come into town and go find whichever of your brothers or sisters-in-law are currently lonely or drinking themselves and you settle in for a few days and make the teenagers' lives miserable. No one wants a drunken uncle coming to stay in their house. Once you were a beautiful, happy child, a child everyone wanted to have around. Now you are the drunken uncle. How did that happen, Jodie? How it happened doesn't matter. It's your fault now. Do something about it. I'm through with drunken fools.

Love, Mother

Am I supposed to deliver that? Here's where I am in my thinking, as of today.

1. I want the thirty-six gold Krugerrands.

2. The price of gold keeps falling. I have to sell them soon or they won't be worth a thing. But I don't know where to go to sell them. I can't go to the bank. They turn all their records over to the government.

3. I should burn this journal. I should not keep this in my room. Also, I need to get a different hiding place for the coins and letters.

4. I have been an honest person all my life. Why would I even think of keeping the coins? I could give the coins to Jean's

lawyer and throw the letters away. But the letters are the only proof I have that I came by the coins honestly. Someone might think I stole them or got them selling dope.

Here is a letter I wouldn't mind delivering. It is to Charlie, Jean's oldest son. He's the biggest asshole in Jackson, Mississippi. It was his wife who got all the money in the will.

Dear Charlie,

You have let me down and, more important, you have let down your children. What is your daughter going to think when she finds out about the child your mistress is bearing down in Hattiesburg? Did you think I wouldn't find out about that? The girl called me in the middle of the night looking for you. It was two A.M. She sounded crazy. I can only hope for the sake of the unborn child she was drunk. If it was drugs I guess you know the child will be born addicted.

I have not had much sleep. I slept from about three to four and here is what I dreamed. I dreamed a little girl who belonged to you fell down a hole in the ground. It was an abandoned well or something like that. Deep down in the hole your daughter was curled up like an oyster in a place she found to hide. She was not moving. She would not talk. She had become still.

Workers were trying to reach her, but the hole was too small for any of their equipment to be of use. She sank deeper and deeper into the hole. She became quieter and quieter. I begged you to reach down into the hole and touch her, just touch her to let her know it was all right, but you would not come near. You were leaving her rescue to other people. When I had given up on you, I reached my arm down into the hole. I thought I would lose my arm in the terrible, cold, dark hole but I kept reaching until I could get my fingers into the shell she had built around herself. I began to stroke her tiny arm. She was without movement but I kept on trying and finally she began to respond. She began to grow. She rose up out of the hole. She became two beautiful girls. Then they split and became two beautiful boys also. She was four beautiful children, like the ones you have, and all of them were dancing in the sunlight and the air. All around us the workmen were cheering and I said to you, "See, all you had to do was touch and love them."

Instead, you are down in Hattiesburg screwing whores and getting them with probably addicted children. I hate you, Charlie, for what you are doing to my grandchildren. I know Lauren Gail is not the sort of woman you wanted for a wife and that you married her because she was pregnant, but you did marry her and had other children and they are your responsibility. You are going to be punished for this, Charlie. I am going to punish you. I am going to change my will and leave your share to Lauren Gail. Maybe I'll leave Jodie's share too. I am so mad at you I cannot contain my rage.

Your mother

JANUARY 1, 1999

I don't know where those coins came from. I don't even know if it's legal for me to have them. I want to take them out of the box and trade them in for a new car. I'm only human. Anyone wants to keep thirty-six gold Krugerrands worth three hundred and twenty dollars apiece if they can. I need to find out where to sell them but I don't know who to ask. Who can I trust with such a story?

JANUARY 2, 1999

I went down this morning to the BMW place and looked at the convertibles. There's a secondhand one for sale that used to belong to Davenport Keith, the National Public Radio announcer who went to Nashville to be on television. It's a work of art. The salesman said

Davenport almost cried when he turned it in for the five series car he bought to drive to Nashville. He turned it in because he was sick of getting tickets on the highway. A BMW convertible is a red flag in a patrolman's face.

I wouldn't care if I got tickets if I could find a way to sell those cursed coins and trade them in for that baby blue dreammobile.

After I left the car dealership I went down to the OxBow Coffeeshop near the Millsaps campus to see if anyone knows anything about gold coins, but I was afraid to bring it up. These coins are hanging over my head like the Sword of Damocles. That convertible won't sit there long. I'm thinking of going to the man who runs the place and just putting ten of them on his desk and saying, "My daddy was giving these to me for birthdays over the years. He died last year. I think it's time to trade them in for a car."

Who could say it isn't true except Mother, and I don't guess she'd turn state's evidence against her own daughter, but I'd have to tell her not to or she might. If someone from the IRS called her and said, "Did your husband give gold coins to your daughter, Sally Shelton of 555 Belhaven Street, or not?" she would say, "Of course not, why would he do anything like that?"

Of course, it would be my word against hers, but then the IRS would try to find records of Daddy buying them and then what?

The more I think about it the more I think Daddy did give me these coins.

Here is a letter Jean wrote on an airplane. She was flying back to Jackson from her summer house in Destin, Florida. Look at the writing. She was so mad her hand was shaking.

The letter is to her niece, Charlene, the only daughter of her sister, Callily. Charlene was a tennis star when she was at Jackson Academy. I gave her her first two hundred tennis lessons.

Dear Charlene,

I can't believe this past weekend. I had spent two days getting the beach house ready for you and your friend, buying groceries, sweeping the porches, making up beds, arranging to have the boat cleaned up and delivered to the dock, putting out toys and books for your friend's little children. I wanted it to be a beautiful Easter weekend for all of us. Instead, I was up all night Friday night trying to get your friend's three-year-old to stop crying while the two of you were out doing God knows what with those men who came to pick you up. WHO WERE THOSE TWO? You have hit rock bottom, Charlene. I don't know why I thought my being nice to you was going to make a difference in the course you have set for yourself.

Then, after we talked on Saturday and I told you not to drink anymore at my house, you went off and got even drunker Saturday night, although at least you took the children with you that time. Where did those little children sleep? Did either of them even have a bath while they were here?

I left Mack alone in Jackson rehearsing a play and came down here for you and look at what it got me. It got me what one always gets if one thinks they can make a difference in the life of an alcoholic.

Is this how you pay me back for ten years of tennis lessons, not to mention the times I paid your tuition when your dad was too messed up to do it?

I give up. You were my favorite niece. The daughter I never had. I make you one last offer. If you will go into treatment for your addictions I will pay for the treatment. It can be anything from going to a treatment center to going to AA meetings. I'll go with you to the meetings. I'll fly with you to check in to a clinic. What I won't do is have anything further to do with alcoholics. I'm through.

Your aunt, Jean Andry

JANUARY 8, 1999

I had to let somebody else in on this so I drove down to New Orleans to spend the weekend with my cousin, Clark Mallison. He is a computer programmer and has a wonderful little house right off of Prytania Street near Commander's Palace. I didn't tell him right away. I got there Friday night and we went to a party with some of his friends and slept late on Saturday morning. I was sleeping on the futon bed in the living room with his Labrador retriever sleeping by my side.

When we woke up we made coffee and went out to sit on the front porch and watch New Orleans waking up.

"I have thirty-six gold Krugerrands in a lockbox in Jackson that don't belong to anybody but I'm not sure I can keep them," I began.

"You have what?"

"Thirty-six gold Krugerrands worth about ten thousand dollars and I want to cash them in without anybody knowing it. Do you know how I can do that? I'll pay you a commission if you'll do it for me."

"Where are they?"

"Well, they were in a safe deposit box but now they're in the trunk of my car. Do they always keep records of things like that? I mean, how do you turn them into money?"

"I don't know. I'll find out." So he went back into the house and got the phone book and found a listing for a coin dealer in the French Quarter and called and the man said to come on down, he'd be there all day.

"Where did you get them, Sally?" Clark asked. "You haven't been selling your body, have you?"

"You won't believe it, but here goes." So I told the story, not leaving out a thing, including the fight at the funeral and the lawsuits that were starting. "So I think they're mine," I finished up. "I think I can justify keeping them and if you'll help me sell them I'll give you a commission."

"Jesus, Sally, I don't know."

"What did the man say?"

"He said come on down, he'd be there all day."

He kept looking at me. Our family used to have money. Our grandfather was one of the founders of Treadway Insurance Company in Jackson. There hasn't been any money in a long time, but there used to be. We have a taste for it. Still, we are good people. No one in our family has ever been dishonest.

"All right," he said. "If she put them there she must have wanted you to have them."

We went down to the Quarter and parked the car at the Royal Orleans and walked over to the coin dealer's little store on Conti Street. It was squeezed in right next to the side door of Prince of Conti Hotel, near the old Evangeline Academy. The brass on the door was brightly polished and the coin dealer, Mr. Maxim, was a nice man, tall and elegantly dressed in a gray suit.

He looked at the coins one at a time, then wrote down some figures on a piece of paper.

"My dad gave them to me on birthdays or when I made good grades in college," I said. "I know he'd be happy to think they finally were some use to me. I need a new car to get to my job."

"You ought to keep these three," the man said, holding out three coins in red cardboard folders. "These are in very good condition. They will increase in value if you keep them. The price of gold is depressed right now, as you said you knew."

"No," I said. "Too many memories. They make me sad. I'd rather just get rid of them all." I was surprised at how easy it was for me to lie to Mr. Maxim. Still, he kept looking at me like he knew I was lying. It was getting very close and uncomfortable in the little closet-size office.

"There's the total then," he said. He held out the pad of paper. The total was nine thousand, nine hundred and forty dollars. I took it. He wrote me a check for that amount and I put it in my pocketbook and Clark and I walked out into the sunlight.

The Quarter was very beautiful that morning. Cold and clear. The old stones that were ballast in the great sailing ships that came into the port so long ago reflected the brilliant sunlight. They made the old part of the Quarter look like Paris. We walked over to the Café du Monde and had beignets and café au lait. Then we walked over to Royal Street and went to A Gallery for Fine Photography and looked at the photographs. I had almost enough money to buy a Karsh print of Muhammad Ali but, of course, I didn't buy it. You don't have to own everything that's beautiful. You can remember what things look like.

We walked around for an hour and inspected the paintings being made on Jackson Square and talked and giggled and had a good time.

When we got back to his house I wrote Clark a check for five hundred dollars and told him not to cash it until he heard from me. I made him take it. I wanted him involved.

Then we ate lunch and watched the highlights of the Australian Open and then I got in my car and drove on home. Clark had a date that night and I felt I'd be in the way if I stayed any longer. The great thing about first cousins is you can come and go in each other's lives without worrying about how polite you have to be.

*   *   *

It was hard waiting until Monday morning to put the check in the bank. I've stopped worrying about how to account for it to the IRS. I'm going to tell Mother to say she gave me nine thousand, four hundred and forty dollars as a gift. You can give ten thousand dollars to your children every year if you want to. Maybe it would give her an idea.

While I was at the bank depositing the money I took the letters out of the safe deposit box and put them in a bag and closed the box. "I don't need it anymore," I told old Mrs. Pendergraf, who handles safe deposit boxes at the branch. She was my grandmother's banker and is my mother's and my brother's and mine. She is about as old as God, but she keeps on going to the bank. No wonder there aren't any good jobs for young people in this town.

"Be sure to have copies of any deeds or birth certificates if you keep them at home," she couldn't help advising.

"I don't have any deeds," I answered. "All I have is a typewriter and six tennis rackets."

Shakespeare in Love was playing at the Metroplex. Naturally we are the last city in the United States to get it. I called my friend Kathleen from a phone by the music store and asked her to come meet me and go to the movie.

Half an hour later we were munching three-dollar popcorn and watching the show. Jean didn't like it when people made fake biographical plays out of the lives of geniuses. It was the first time I'd really missed her since she'd died. I knew if she were alive I could have called her up and she would have told me why I shouldn't have had such a good time at the movie and liked it so much. She was highly critical of any art except plays she directed herself, and she was critical even of those. I have been to plays she directed that I thought were perfect and had her tell me a week later why what I saw wasn't as good as I thought it had been. Maybe that's why she died so young. Maybe it's like a red hot fire to be that passionate and talented and ambitious and thin. Well, I miss her. Now that the problem of the Krugerrands is solved I can take some time to grieve. I really am going to send a check to French Camp in her name. I would send them a hundred dollars but I guess the Lyles would think it was pretty odd for a typist to send a memorial that big.

JANUARY 20, 1999

I waited a week before I spent any of the money. The first thing I bought was a leather jacket on sale at Maison Weiss. It is the most beautiful, soft leather you've ever seen in your life. I took it home on approval but I've already worn it twice, so I guess I'm keeping it.

That night Clark called from New Orleans to ask if he could put my check in the bank.

"Go ahead," I told him. "I'm already spending mine. I bought this gorgeous leather jacket. It's dark brown with a deep collar and it's so soft you wouldn't believe it. I want to hang it on a wall and look at it."

"I thought you were getting a car."

"I don't know if that will look so good. All of a sudden I turn up with a new car when everyone knows I don't even have a job."

"You ought to get a job, Sally. You're getting too old to be living hand-to-mouth."

"Well, I was thinking of going over to Millsaps and applying for something in the administration office. They have this big development project going on. Madison Hale is making fifty thousand dollars a year raising money for them. She was my big sister in Chi O. I've been thinking of putting in an application to her."

"You ought to do it. It would take two hours of your time."

"I might. I'm out of people I can stand to type for now that Jean's dead. I didn't realize how much of my income she accounted for. Oh, God."

"What? Oh, God, what?"

"What if this was her plan. To force me into the real world by leaving me thirty-six gold Krugerrands I can't account for unless I have a job."

"Go apply at Millsaps. Look, Sally, I better get off the phone. The girl I told you about is coming to dinner tonight and I need to clean up this place."

"Oh, so that's still on?"

"She's got this coal black pubic hair. It's driving me crazy. I want to marry her, Sally. I had this fantasy about getting her pregnant. I have it every time I'm with her."

"Jesus. That reminds me of this poem I read the other day by Robert Frost. It's about a milkweed pod. It starts, 'Calling all butterflies of every race . . .'"

"What does that have to do with it?"

"Never mind. Just remember, nature is not on your side, Clark. Don't go taking off your rubber just because there's something fluffy in your bed."

"You are so wise, Sally. Every time I talk to you I learn something new."

"Shut up. I'll talk to you tomorrow."

So there goes my cousin Clark. Pretty soon I'll be the only single person left in my family or anywhere I know except the theater. Even that's changing. The world is completely unpredictable. One minute everybody's single and having a good time and the next minute I'm applying for a steady job.

FEBRUARY 1, 1999

So I got the job at Millsaps. I start in nine days. I'll be making twenty-one thousand dollars a year and have health insurance and be able to use the gym and swimming pool and tennis courts just like I did when I was a student there.

Plus, I get to work in the new building in a beautiful office and get dressed up every day and help Madison convince our alumni to give us money, money, money. I'm already guilty of keeping money that doesn't belong to me. Why should laying guilt trips on wealthy alumni bother me?

I'm sorry. I was going to get carpal syndrome if I kept on typing term papers. Plus, I'm sick of teaching tennis. One in twenty of the kids really wants to learn anything. The rest just come because their mothers want them to do something they didn't get to do. To hell with it. I don't have to apologize for getting a job.

FEBRUARY 3, 1999

I need a better car if I'm going to be driving to Millsaps every day and maybe having to take important people out to lunch and meet airplanes. So I went over to Mother's and told her some lies.

"I don't know if you know about this," I began. "But Daddy gave me some gold coins before he died and last month when I went to visit Clark we took them down to the Quarter and cashed them in. If I had a few thousand more I'd have enough to buy a car. I can't depend on that old Volvo to get me to Millsaps every day."

"What gold coins? He didn't say anything to me about it."

"Just some coins he had. I wanted you to know about it in case anyone asked about them."

"Who would ask?"

"The Internal Revenue Service for one."

"I'm delighted you have a job, Sally. I'm thrilled you'll be working with Madison. She's a lovely young woman. I want you to be careful what you wear over there. Get some really nice shoes and please don't wear pants all the time."

"I can't afford to get new clothes. I'm worried enough about getting a dependable car."

So of course she walked over to her desk and took out her big checkbook, the one that goes to her savings account, and wrote me a check for two thousand, three hundred dollars. It was the first money she'd given me in two years. She had told me she wouldn't give me money and she meant it. "Go get your car and buy some clothes that make you look like a serious person," she said. "How many gold coins did your father give you? I never knew him to have any coins of any kind."

"Thanks so much," I answered and kissed her on the hair so I could smell her perfume. She used to wear Joy but now she wears Chanel Nineteen. I really love my mother. I admire her. I just live on a different wavelength than she does and never the currents do meet.

"And stop running around with all those theater people," she added, turning around to face me from her little rosewood desk. She was wearing the helpless, I'm-about-to-tremble look she wears when she's going to deliver a lecture. "Now that Jean Lyles is dead I don't think that theater's going to last much longer. That play they put on about those people in San Francisco with AIDS was about the last straw. Nice people aren't going to pay to see things like that. If you want to be successful at Millsaps you are going to have to start acting like someone from a nice class of people. You can't just throw your reputation around in this town. Let this new job be a beginning. . . ."

"I have to go meet Madison and talk to her about my computer," I lied. "What time is it? I don't want to be late." I ran out of there and went to the bank and added the two thousand three hundred to my nine thousand two hundred. I was getting so rich I felt like Midas.

FEBRUARY 13, 1999

I have decided what to do about the Krugerrands. I will declare their sale a capital loss. I was talking to a CPA at this party Madison had me go to. It was a cocktail party for the class of 1949 to plan their fiftieth reunion. This old skinny CPA cornered me and I let him look down my new blue velvet dress while I picked his brain about the IRS.

"I just sold some gold coins my daddy gave me," I told him. "They sure weren't worth much. I don't know how to declare them on my tax return."

"That should be a capital loss," he answered. "You can set it off against any capital gains you make this year."

I am starting to like being in the normal working world. It looks a lot more manageable than I thought it would be.

I still haven't gotten a car. I'm looking at secondhand Audis and Toyota Corollas. Just because I have money doesn't mean I have to spend all of it.

Clark is calling about three times a week to get advice about the Cajun girl he's screwing. He wants her to marry him but she keeps saying no. He cannot believe she's saying no.

Mother's obsessed with the Krugerrands. She can't believe Daddy did something behind her back. She keeps bugging me about them. She wants details. How many were there? Where did he get them? When did he give them to me? She should work for the Central Intelligence Agency. Am I going to have to listen to her questions for the rest of my life or should I tell her the truth and let her know she raised a dishonest person for a daughter?

Life is one damn thing after another. Nothing ever is resolved. Not as long as it has to do with people.

"Don't ever mention those Krugerrands again," I think I'll tell her. "It could get us in a lot of trouble. He may have been hiding money from the IRS, for all you know."

It wouldn't hurt a fifty-six-year-old widow to have some mystery in her life. It doesn't hurt to question your reality. Jean Lyles has sure forced me to question mine. God, I loved to talk to that woman. Not a day goes by that something doesn't happen I want to hear her opinion of.

Not all the letters I took home were terrible. Some were kind and full of good advice. Here's one I opened the other day. It's to her daughter-in-law Laura. Laura's a good woman. I always like to run into her at the grocery store. She always looks like she never combs her hair. You have to love that in a woman.

Dear Laura,

Just a note to tell you how proud I am that you have joined the staff of the *North Jackson Star*. I think you are wrong to call it "a little, hippie newsletter." It has been doing good service in the community for ten years now and I think anything that gets you out of the house and out into a larger world is good for you and good for the children. I think you should stop worrying about Laura Jean not getting along with the other girls at dance school. She is so creative that a group arts activity may not be the right outlet for her talents. Why don't we try her in a different dance school for a while? Just because all your friends from the Junior League send their children to Prime Arts Academy doesn't mean it's the right place for Laura Jean. I thought their recital last year was dreadful, really uninspired, which means the teachers don't inspire. The only good thing about it was the costumes, which must have cost a mint. If that is all Miss Caitlin can do with girls she has had for twelve years no wonder Laura Jean is bored and doesn't want to go.

There is a dance studio over in West Jackson run by a woman who danced with Alvin Ailey. She teaches all the classes herself. The dancers she has sent to our rehearsals at the theater are amazing. One was a ten-year-old boy. So maybe we could try Laura Jean there for a while. Of course, it's an integrated academy so you might have a hard time selling that to Anderson. I'll talk to him if you want me to.

Keep up your own good work on the newspaper and try not to worry about Laura Jean so much. I'm worrying with you and maybe we are both wrong to worry. She may know what she's doing.

Love, Jean

That letter piqued my interest. I wanted to know if Laura Jean got to quit Prime Arts, where I had also been tortured for years, and go to the studio in West Jackson. I got the rest of the letters and threw them down on my bed. I found one with Laura Jean's initials on it and read the sad news.

Dear Laura Jean,

I'm sorry that they won't let you go to West Dancers to dance with Mackie Young. You and I know it isn't because it's too far away because I volunteered to drive you every time you had a class. This is a racial thing, Laura Jean. We live in Jackson, Mississippi, and this is a fundamental part of our lives and a continuing problem neither of us created.

Your father is worried about your safety. Your mother is worried about what people will say. So it goes. I can only do so much. Meanwhile, you will have to plod on at Prime Arts or I can get Sally to teach you to play tennis.

I love you, Grandmother

Then I saw the letter with my initials on it. When I spotted it a cold chill went over me but in a minute curiosity won out over fear and I opened it and read it.

Dear Sally,

I am getting on a plane to go to New York in a few minutes and decided to write you a letter about what to do with this safe deposit box in case anything should ever happen to me. I'll be putting some gold coins in here with the letters as it occurred to me that the reason you never seem to move on with your life might be fear. A few thousand dollars won't remove your fear but it might buy you time to step back and think. It's a dangerous thing to write this letter and put it in the box. If I died in a plane crash you'd be left to read things no human should ever say to another. I can remember when you were a star, Sally. You were the most graceful and polite champion who ever stepped out onto a tennis court. You won gracefully and you played like a dream.

I want that Sally back. Maybe it's partly my fault that you have lost your discipline and focus. I pay you too much for too little work and I waste your time.

I thought being near me would teach you by example. That you would see how hard I work and remember what it takes to succeed. I know it broke your heart when your injuries ended your career. I had a career in New York City that ended when I got pregnant.

Maybe the difference was the money. Hence this pitiful little mound of coins. Go coach some great stars, Sally. Or go on to medical school. It's not too late. It's never too late to fulfill a dream.

If anything should happen to me, burn the letters as fast as you can and be nice to my children if you run into them, even Charlie. Charlie was the one who ended my career. What if he had been the last child I had? Well, there I go again. Bitch, bitch, bitch.

It wasn't signed.

So then I felt like a piece of shit and I put all the letters into a basket and carried them out to the charcoal grill and doused them with charcoal lighter fluid and set them on fire and watched them burn. It took a really long time. That was good stationery she was using.

As if I could start medical school when I'm thirty-seven years old. Well, thirty-seven isn't dead. Thirty-seven is a pretty good place to start. I can start. I'm not Charlie or Laura or Anderson or pitiful Ann Claire or Jodie. None of them ever did a thing in their lives but live off their inheritance. I WAS AN ALL-AMERICAN THREE YEARS IN A ROW. I can do anything if I can remember how to try.

That letter she wrote me hurt me so much it took me a month to get over it. It's hurting me still but I'm starting to forget it. I'm starting to see it going up in flames instead of seeing what it said.

I'm starting to change too, but I don't want to say too much about that until it's finished. After all, I'm going to be working at Millsaps. I can take classes for free. I could take biochemistry and see if I could pass. I could start running every day and see if I could get my body back in shape. I could start teaching young kids.

I am starting to change, but I don't want to say too much about it. It might be bad luck. Tennis players are suckers for believing in luck.

THE SURVIVAL
OF THE FITTEST

JO NELL JENNINGS had discovered Darwin and she could not get it out of her mind. Not that it hadn't been taught to her at Paris High School, because it had been, but she must not have been listening then, what with Donald Semmes having his hand up her panties every night after football practice and her daddy getting her out of bed every morning before dawn to cook breakfast for everybody so her mother could get to work. It had been a happy life. Later, when she married a boy from Fort Smith instead of Donald, it didn't mean she hadn't kept on being happy.

"Donald Semmes is a big man down in Little Rock now," her mother never failed to tell her, whenever she was stupid enough to go and spend Christmas or Thanksgiving down in Paris. It wasn't often, thank goodness, since she had three kids of her own and worked eight hours a day delivering babies at the Washington Regional Medical Center in Fayetteville where she lived.

Her husband, Harlon, worked for Dillard's out at the mall. They had a good life and loved to screw each other still.

* * *

Perhaps they had taught her about Darwin at nursing school, but she doubted it. Nursing school had been a blur of classes and working and being pregnant. She couldn't remember if they talked about him or not. Still, she had heard Charles Darwin's name plenty of times. She was certain of that, but it was only when she was thirty-six years old that his books came into her hands and she read them and the ideas sank in.

The Origin of Species and *The Descent of Man*. The *descent* of man, coming down from a long chain of one-celled, then two-celled, then multi-celled, then more and more complicated *animals*. Animals. She was kin to animals and so were her kids and Harlon and her mother. Her own kids, Angela and Robert and Terry, who could talk a blue streak. What animal do you know that can talk? she asked herself. Except that nasty little dog on television that sells tacos.

Still, once you started thinking about it you could not stop. Dogs give birth just like people do, except they have more puppies because human babies' heads are so big you can only fit so many in a human womb. Except that disgusting story about that woman in Chicago having eight babies. Everyone at Washington Regional thought they ought to put the doctors in jail who implanted that many embryos in a woman's womb or kept on giving her hormones when she already had two or three in there. "If any of them live, they will wish they were dead," her favorite obstetrician told her. He was a really darling man who was always flirting with her because he wasn't afraid of getting accused of anything like most of the staff.

But back to Darwin. *"The inhabitants of the world at each successive period in its history have beaten their predecessors in the race for life. . . . Old forms have been supplanted by new and improved forms of life, the products of variation and the survival of the fittest."*

*   *   *

Of course, it would be just as she was really getting into the books that Donald Semmes shows up in Fayetteville to be on some panel at the business school and calls her at the hospital.

"How'd you know how to find me?" Jo Nell asked.

"Your mother told me. I called her last night. She said you had three kids. I can't believe it. I'm sorry we lost touch with each other. So much has happened to me, Jo Nell. I'd like to tell you about it, if you could get away for lunch today. Or tomorrow."

"I probably can. It depends on if someone starts delivering. I can take off at twelve thirty if nothing happens before then. You want to take a chance on that?"

"Sure. Just tell me where to go. I went to school here, you know. I know the town."

"Come to the entrance of the hospital on Highway 71. I'll come down to the lobby. If I don't come right down at twelve thirty I'll page you there."

Jo Nell was looking forward to Donald seeing how good she looked. She hadn't gained a pound since high school and she hadn't gotten any wrinkles and her coal black hair was as dark as it had ever been. With a little help from the drugstore.

Harlon kept her satisfied and Jo Nell believed that was all a woman needs. Besides, he had given her a diamond ring for Christmas, so big she was embarrassed to wear it to work. "Why didn't you give this to me sooner?" was all she could think of to say.

"I wanted to be sure you were going to stay," he answered. "Besides, I heard on the radio that if you go bankrupt the only thing they can't take are your wedding and engagement rings."

"We are not going bankrupt," Jo Nell answered. "We have twenty-six thousand dollars in a savings account. I know how to handle money. That's one thing you can say for me."

Donald Semmes looked good but he had gotten fat. He started apologizing for it as soon as he hugged her. "I know I'm fat," he said. "I'm definitely going to do something about it soon." They walked out of the hospital and across the parking lot and got into his huge gray Mercedes and he reached across the seat and put his hand on hers. Fat or no fat it all started coming back, all those nights with his hands up her panties, all those hot, frustrated nights.

"I think about you every day of my life," he said. "I'll never understand how we drifted apart."

"Momma says you made a lot of money," Jo Nell answered. "How'd you make it?"

"Working my ass off and being nice to people. The business is home supplies. I got in on the ground floor with a company down in Little Rock and now I own half the stock. I'm thinking of retiring when I'm forty."

"So did you get married?"

"For a year once. I don't have much to report except owning stock, Jo Nell. Sometimes I think I've wasted my life."

"No, you haven't. Don't say that." He still had his hand on her hand. I'll have to tell Harlon about this, she was thinking. He'll be glad I was wearing my ring to work for a change.

"I'm reading *The Origin of Species* and *The Descent of Man*, by Charles Darwin," she said, to change the subject. "Did you ever remember reading them in school? I think they talked about Darwin but I don't remember reading any of his books. They're so good. They were such important books. It's like there it was, right there for anyone to see and only this one man thought of how it all fit together."

"I heard the Restaurant on the Corner had moved out by the old drive-in. Have you been out there yet? You want to go there?"

"If we have time. I have to be back at one thirty."

"Should we try?"

"If you want to."

So who is at the Restaurant on the Corner but Harlon's little sister, Jamie, having lunch with some of her friends. Jo Nell almost fainted when she saw her. She took Donald over and introduced him and tried to make a joke out of it. "Don't tell Harlon I was out to lunch with another man until I get a chance to tell him," she said, but Jamie didn't look like she was buying that.

"She's filling me in on the survival of the fittest," Donald said, trying to help. "She's telling me about evolution."

They found a table and told the waiter to hurry and ordered sandwiches and coffee.

"I could look at you all day," Donald said, sitting across from her with his hands on the table, those hands that had been inside her panties nearly every night from when she was fourteen until they graduated from high school.

"Don't say it," Jo Nell answered. "We shouldn't even talk about it, Donald. I'm a happily married woman. I have three children and a husband that I love. That's not going to change."

"You can let me say it."

"No, I can't."

*　　　*　　　*

The waitress delivered the sandwiches and they ate them without talking much more. Then Donald put a twenty-dollar bill down on the table and took her arm and they went out the door and got back into the car and drove back to the hospital. It was so hot and intense inside that car. Jo Nell's panties were so wet. It was so sad and hot and full of meaning she could hardly breathe by the time she got back to the fourth floor and scrubbed her hands with antibacterial soap and went to the desk to read the charts.

At four she called Harlon at work and told him about it. "My old boyfriend from Paris came by and took me out to lunch," she said. "You better be glad I have on this ring. You better get on home this afternoon and get ready for some action. I mean it, Harlon. I need to fuck you."

"I'm leaving now," he said. "I'll be there waiting."

"We'll send the kids out to eat," she said. "I'll tell your momma to come get them and take them out to dinner."

"What old boyfriend?" Harlon asked, starting to get a little mad. "What's his name?"

"Donald Semmes. You've heard of him."

"I'm going to kill him," Harlon said. "I'm going to fuck you and then I'm going to kill him." He was laughing but somewhere down in his heart he meant it. "Don't have lunch with him again, Jo Nell, unless I'm there with you."

The kids came home from school full of news. The oldest one, Angela, had been picked to go on a field trip to Washington, D.C., in April. Only fifty people at Ramey Junior High had been picked. It would cost a thousand dollars but she had to go.

Robert had a note saying Jo Nell had to come in and talk to his English teacher about him not doing his homework.

Terry had three papers with one hundreds on them. He had to be rewarded for that.

"I'm sending you all out to dinner to celebrate," Jo Nell said. "Momma Lee's coming to get you at five thirty. Go get your faces washed and don't turn on the television until you've done all your homework."

Angela went up to her room and turned on the television with the sound practically off and watched it while she did her math homework. She was thinking about how she was going to have to get some new clothes to wear to Washington, D.C., and she had better not make her mother mad until she got them.

Terry and Robert went into their bedroom and turned the television on and watched *Beavis and Butthead* without worrying about their mother. They knew her too well to think she was going to follow up on anything after she had been at work all day.

They could hear her shower running in her bathroom. She was getting dressed. You could do anything while she was doing that.

"The extinction of old forms is the almost inevitable consequence of the production of new forms. We can understand why, when a species has once disappeared, it never reappears. Groups of species increase in numbers slowly, and endure for unequal amounts of time; for the process of modification is necessarily slow and depends on many complex contingencies. . . ."

The kids were hardly out the door with Harlon's mother when Donald called her on his car phone from right outside Russellville. "I can't get over seeing you," he said. "I just had to talk to you again."

"I don't want to talk to you, Donald," she said. "Don't call me any-more. It's going to make my husband mad."

"I know you were glad to see me."

She took a deep breath, she looked out the window at the barren winter trees, she did the first mean thing she'd done in weeks. "You're too fat," she told him. "Even if I wasn't happily married I wouldn't want to go out with a fat man. I'm a nurse, Donald. I look at you and I see a heart attack waiting to happen. If you call me up again all you're going to hear is more of this."

"Then what should I do?" he asked. "I want to lose some weight. What do you suggest?"

"I'm hanging up," she answered and she did. She went back into her bedroom and took off her bathrobe and her red silk crotchless under-pants and stood naked looking at herself in the mirror. When she heard Harlon come in she just walked stark buck naked into the living room and cuddled up against his winter coat. "You better fuck my eyeballs out," she said. "You better fuck me like there's no tomorrow. I've had a crazy day, Harlon. You better get me settled down."

He rubbed his hands up and down her back and butt. He pushed her into the bedroom and took off his coat and went to work on her. He had a great body and he had great taste in clothes and he was her husband. He was the one she had picked out to be with her forever and to help her get the species another step along on survival.

Just about the time she was getting ready to go down on him to see if he could get it up for the third time, she noticed the book on the bed-side table. This one's for you, Charles Darwin, she told the book. I'll show you survival of the fittest. I'll show you how old homecoming queens get their business done.

She laughed and almost lost her concentration, and Harlon turned around in the bed and took her into his arms and held her so tight she was afraid he'd break her ribs. "What are you laughing about?" he asked. "What was this Donald guy like? How'd he look?"

"He was really fat," she said. "It was all I could do to stand to have lunch with him." She slipped her hand down into his and he squeezed it so hard the ring cut into her finger.

"Let me take off my ring, please," she said. "And lie back on that pillow until I'm done with you."

Down at the Burger King the kids were taking advantage of what they sensed was an opportunity. "Could we get one of those watches?" Robert began. "They only cost a dollar ninety-eight if you buy a meal plan."

"I don't know," their grandmother said, but she was beaten before she could finish the sentence and bought three of the watches, adding six dollars and forty cents to an eleven-dollar meal.

"You all spend too much money," she said, to make it better in her mind. "I don't know how your daddy stays afloat the way you ask for things."

"These watches will be worth a lot of money someday," Robert insisted. "Things like this double in value once they quit selling them."

"I could just get the watch and not get food if you want me to," Angela added, as if she wasn't already eating her chicken nuggets.

"Can we get a movie on our way home?" Terry begged. "It's on the way. We have to go right by the store."

The next night the Arkansas Razorback basketball team was playing at Auburn and Harlon was having his friends over to watch the game. Every time there was a road game his friends came over to their house to watch it. They never went anywhere else, and Harlon and Jo Nell didn't want them to. The den was plenty big enough for everybody and there was a big new television set and people have to have some fun or what's the point.

Harlon's two best friends were identical twins who were six feet seven inches tall and had been the stars of the Fort Smith High School basketball team when Harlon was the point guard. The three of them sat in their appointed seats, Harlon on a recliner to the side, the twins positioned to the right and left of him on sofas. They watched the game as if their lives depended on it. Other friends came and went but those three were the core. They screamed at the television set, they went outside and wished they could smoke a cigarette and sometimes smoked one, they dived into and became the game, they won or lost, it was so much like life, Jo Nell often thought, it was just like life, it was almost worse than life.

The Auburn game was worse than life. The Razorbacks, rated 19 that week, had come to play, but the Auburn Tigers, rated 14, were red hot and nothing could defeat them. They had a little six-foot-tall white kid who could not be stopped and a seven-foot-tall black kid who could shoot. The Razorbacks kept the score in a five-point range until almost the end, then they folded and Auburn won 89 to 79.

When the game was over, Harlon's friends got up and put on their coats and left without saying goodbye. Harlon came into the kitchen and made himself a drink and stood leaning on the counter while he watched Jo Nell finishing up a dress she was making for Angela to wear in the Sweetheart Pageant at the junior high.

"You can't win them all," she said. "That's what sports are supposed to teach you."

"It was a five-point game until the last two minutes. We could have won it as easily as they did."

Harlon was really suffering. She decided to comfort him. After all, he was her husband, her lover, her boyfriend. "I'm not tired of making love if you aren't," she said. "I can finish this tomorrow." She put down the dress and went over to him and started moving her hands up and down his butt. She loved the rough feel of his pants and the man of him. She made him laugh and then she made him want her and then she made him forget the basketball game, at least until the morning.

So of course she gets pregnant because Jo Nell can't take the pill because her aunt had breast cancer and it's too dangerous and using rubbers is okay but not perfect and it's hard to know when to take a diaphragm out and so forth and so on.

"Eight years we kept it from happening," she said to Harlon when she told him. "And stop looking so happy. I didn't say I'm going to have it, did I? I just said I was pregnant. I might not have it. We have to talk about this."

They were out in the yard. Angela was inside, practicing walking up and down the stairs in the heels she was wearing in the Sweetheart Pageant. The boys were shooting hoops by the garage. The sun was shining. It was a gorgeous day at the very beginning of February, a Saturday morning, a week before Jo Nell's thirty-seventh birthday.

"Please have it," Harlon said. "I'll do anything you want. I'll get a second job. I want you to, baby. I can't help if it makes me happy."

"I don't know," she said. "Let me think about it."

"Don't think too long," he said. "Don't keep me in suspense."

* * *

She went in the house and started cleaning up the breakfast dishes and thinking. She thought about having her body ruined again after all the miles she had put in on the exercycle at the Washington Regional Medical Center for Exercise. She thought about the stretch marks and the broken veins and the danger of delivery and the chance it could have something wrong with it and how old she was and how much trouble it was to take care of a baby and leave it at day-care so she could work and then it would be sick all the time and have ear infections.

Then it would stand up and walk and start saying things and wanting things and tearing things up and running away at the mall or the grocery store and yelling for candy in the checkout line.

Harlon came into the kitchen and started putting dishes in the dishwasher.

"Something might be wrong with it," she said, without turning to him. "I'm old to have a baby. I'd have to have an amniocentesis. If anything's wrong with it, I'm getting an abortion. I'm not bringing a cripple into the world for me to nurse."

"That's fine with me. Anything you want to do is okay with me."

"If I went down tomorrow morning and got an abortion that wouldn't be all right with you, would it?"

"I don't want you to but I wouldn't stop you." He sat down at the kitchen table, thinking what a pussy he had become. He wanted to get up and pick her up and tell her what to do but he knew that didn't work with Jo Nell. He sighed a deep, long, terrible sigh. She thought it was about having a son.

"You think it will be a boy. You want another boy, don't you?"

"I don't want you to get an abortion until you find out if it's all right. Then you can if something's wrong with it."

"Will you be mad at me if I do?" She put down the brush she was using on the egg pan and sat down across from him. "Tell the truth, Harlon."

"I might be for a while. I can't help my feelings, Jo Nell. I like our children. I wish we had fourteen or fifteen like my grandmother did and I could support all of them and you'd never have to lift a finger. I want you to be happy. That's the main thing."

Harlon started crying. He hadn't cried in so long he barely knew how to do it but he was so smart he knew it was the best idea he had had in months. An employee he was trying to fire had cried the week before and he had ended up keeping her on. He remembered crying when his mother wanted to take away his bicycle and she let him keep it even after she caught him riding it on the highway. So he just kept on crying and Jo Nell came around the table and sat on his lap and said she'd have the baby if it was all right.

Jo Nell decided to ask the new woman obstetrician to do the amnio. The new doctor was the daughter of a nurse on the floor and everybody was very excited about having her back in Fayetteville to practice.

"I can't take a chance on having a baby that's got something wrong with it," Jo Nell told the woman. "I'm not the type to take care of a baby unless it's okay. I'm not sure I want to have it at all."

"Then we'll do the test." The doctor smiled. Jo Nell reminded her of her mother. Women who worked in delivery had to get tough to survive.

"I can't take a chance. I have three kids already."

"We can't do an amnio until fourteen weeks. I could do a chorionic villus now or we can wait a month."

"Now. I need to know right away."

So the test was done and Jo Nell tried to put it out of her mind until the results came back. Not that it was possible to forget being pregnant when she felt like throwing up every morning, not to mention Harlon telling her she was beautiful and doing half the housework and smiling all the time.

Jo Nell was waiting for the test results when Donald Semmes called her again. He called her at the hospital at the end of the eleven to seven o'clock shift.

"I'm pregnant," she told him. "So that might make you feel better about how mean I was to you last month."

"You don't want to be?"

"I don't know what I want but in a few hours I'll know if it's a boy or a girl and if it's okay. I had a chorionic villus procedure. Do you know what that is? It's like an amniocentesis, but you can do it sooner."

"I don't know much about that stuff. Carlie and I never were able to have children. That's one reason we broke up. Well, I have some news for you."

"What's that?"

"I lost fourteen pounds. I'm on Sugar Busters. And I joined a health club and I'm working out five times a week. You'll be surprised when you see me."

"I'm not going to see you. Get that straight, Donald. Harlon said he'd kill you if you came in a room with me. He was an All-State guard in Fort Smith. I wouldn't think that was a joke if I was you."

Jo Nell was standing by the nurse's station on the second floor. She was wearing a blue-and-white-striped uniform with a starched white apron and she had on new white hose and her favorite inch-and-a-half white nurse's shoes. She didn't always doll up this much for work but this day was special since she was going to hear the test results. She sucked in her still flat stomach and held up her head and did exactly what she would have done if Donald Semmes had been two feet away instead of down in Little Rock calling on a cell phone.

"I'll never forget you" was all he answered to her threats. "It's because of you I'm on this diet."

"Get over that," she answered. "I'm hanging up." She hung up the phone and walked over to the nurses' station to read the charts. She was deep into the patient in 313 when the new obstetrician appeared and called her into an office.

"You have a healthy boy in there," she said. "So are you going to have it?"

"What the hell," Jo Nell answered. "I've been reading Darwin. It's like, the way I feel this year, if something wants to be born, let it be born. I'm going to name him Charles Darwin Jennings, after this great thinker." She giggled and slid her five feet, ten inches into the leather chair facing the doctor's desk. "I guess I might as well go crazy one last time. But then I'm having my tubes tied."

"Do you mind if I say something," the doctor asked.

"Of course not. Go ahead."

"I just want to say I think you are one of the most beautiful women I've ever seen in my life. I would be disappointed if you didn't want to reproduce yourself. Beauty has survival value, you know. I think your friend Charles Darwin would agree with that. Though we don't know why, we know it's true."

"Well, I'm not having this baby because of the way it might look. It's just to, well, I don't know why. I'm in the mood to do it, to tell the truth."

"I hope I have the honor of delivering him." Doctor Kirshner stood up and Jo Nell stood up and they smiled at each other. "Since I was the first to see him, albeit on paper."

That afternoon the planet Jupiter began an orbit that would take it very near to Venus if viewed from the central United States on the planet Earth.

In Little Rock, Donald Semmes sweated on a StairMaster. Out at the mall Harlon Jennings demanded a raise and got one. At Ramey Junior High Angela started being nice to everyone since she had found out the student body voted for the sweethearts this year instead of adult judges, at Washington Regional Medical Center Doctor Jane Kirshner rethought her plan not to reproduce herself, and up in heaven the stars looked down on all this wonder without a single thought or anyone to think one. Only on Earth was anybody watching. Only on Earth did anybody make a decision or change an atom's course or give a damn.

BARE RUINED CHOIRS,
WHERE LATE
THE SWEET BIRDS SANG

DAKOTA HAD DECIDED to stop being selfish and go down to the coast and mix it up with her family. Spread out along the Mississippi and Louisiana Gulf Coast she had three sons and five current or ex daughters-in-law, seven grandchildren, and two ex-husbands. Not to mention aunts, uncles, cousins, and two grandchildren in utero, sex unknown in both cases as that was the new style, based on the premise that not to know was not to care. The new sin in childbearing was caring if it was a girl or a boy. In a culture addicted to denial it seemed a logical next step and Dakota pretended to go along with it and never said, "Please find out, I want to know." There were a lot of things she never said to her sons and current and ex daughters-in-law and she was proud of that. At one time she bought a wall calendar and put gold stars on it every time she kept herself from saying "Clean up this house." After all, just because she was full of free-floating anxiety and had to clean up everything in the world didn't mean she had to foist her neurosis onto her progeny.

Well, now she was going down there to warm herself at the fire of her gene pool and practice keeping her mouth shut and take her oldest granddaughters to the mall and pit her immune system against the collected cold and flu viruses of the public school system and stick her nose into her children's lives as far as possible without saying anything that could hurt anyone's feelings. "Do no harm" was her motto where her children were concerned. "Om, mani, padme, hung," she chanted as she slept in the uncomfortable beds in her children's houses. Do no harm, be glad they are alive, count your blessings, only love them.

It was time to make the trip and besides, it was snowing in Kansas City, Kansas, and no one was coming in Dakota's shop to buy dresses. Christmas had been good. Dakota had made almost twenty thousand dollars selling party dresses and figure-flattering suits to wealthy women who wanted service above selection. Dakota loved her customers. She worked assiduously, flying to Houston and Dallas and Los Angeles and New York City to buy clothes that were guaranteed to flatter and to please. She had been the first to bring Donna Karan and Votre Nom and Ballinger Gold to the neighborhood and wasn't ashamed to buy Anne Klein II and DKNY, including the jewelry. Her dream was to send women out into the world looking good, believing in themselves, and being comfortable. That wasn't hard to do. It just took work.

Dakota McAfee was willing to work. What she found hard to do was to take a vacation. If you could call driving sixteen hours to the coast to see her children — without trying to change them — a vacation. "It's a spiritual discipline," her best friend, Shelby, told her.

"We should be going to New York to see plays," Dakota replied. "But we never do. You go to Fayetteville to take care of your mother and I go to the coast to cook for people."

"We could be watching ballet," Shelby agreed. "Remember that plan we made to go to New York for two weeks and see every ballet troupe in town. I still want to do that someday."

"We will," Dakota answered. "It will happen, Shelby."

"But not this year. We love our families. We have to take care of them."

Shelby had danced professionally when she was young and had been a show girl in Las Vegas for twenty-seven weeks one golden summer and fall. She still had the best body in Kansas City. Fifty-four years old and she could still walk into a restaurant and turn heads. She got all her clothes at Dakota's shop. Occasionally she paid full price, but most of the time she bought sale things Dakota put aside for her.

"You're my family up here," Dakota said. "You're the sister I never had."

On Monday, February the tenth, Dakota left Kansas City. She went down to the store at eight to check on every last thing before she turned her business over to the salesladies for two weeks. She walked around the four rooms and the cosmetic nook and the shoe corner thinking and hoping for the best. Retail was a tough racket. Well, I am tough, she told herself. Tough and flexible with *plenty* of moves.

She pulled a pair of white silk pants and a white wool blazer off the sales rack and took them to the cash register and put them into a hanging bag. She left a note saying she had the items and then she left. She didn't want to be there when her girls came in. They would think she had no confidence in them. She went out to her van and hung the new outfit with her other clothes and got behind the wheel and started driving.

She was going down the state of Missouri into Tennessee and then to Mississippi and on down to the coast. She had a little house in Ocean Springs, Mississippi, where some of her grandchildren lived. She had bought the place so she would have a place to sleep that was clean and free of cats. All of her grandchildren had cats. Dakota liked cats but she didn't want them sleeping on her bed or sitting in her suitcase if she left it open.

She was planning on arriving at her house by Tuesday night. One of her sons was coming from Switzerland to introduce his new German wife to his children. "It could be an emotional land mine," Dakota had told Shelby. "I have to be there to pick up the pieces if anybody breaks."

"Don't get too involved," Shelby advised. "You can't fix everything. Everything can't be fixed. You didn't create the situation. Don't feel guilty. They are tougher than you know. You're the one who will get hurt." It was all the stuff they always told each other when they were going to encounter their children.

"It doesn't matter about me," Dakota answered. "I can recover if I'm hurt. The young are sensitive. They have to be protected."

At least they aren't coming until Saturday, she told herself as she drove. I'll have three days to prepare the children.

She had a plan. Be very nice to the German daughter-in-law. Love her if it's possible. If not, appreciate the fact that she's made William happy. Be careful not to slight his ex-wife, Janet, who is the mother of my grandchildren. Go out of my way to be close to her this trip. Love them all. Be there if anybody needs me. Keep my mouth shut. My sons are men. I do not understand them because no woman can ever understand the needs and drives of men. William needed another wife. Now he has one and we have to save the children from the fallout.

What do men want? No woman will ever know. Women want white silk slacks and makeup and chunky Donna Karan watches and good bodies to show off at the beach. They want the world to be beautiful and clean. They want music and romance and a chance at civilization. Men want those things too. But mainly they want to get laid. They keep on wanting *desperately* to get laid even after it is no longer possible. What a terrible burden they bear. I must love my sons. And their wives and ex-wives and children. It's not hard to do. It just takes work and I love work.

Enmity must not arise during this meeting. "Let there be peace on earth and let it begin with me." Dakota turned onto the big six-lane highway and adjusted the rearview mirror and set the cruise control at seventy-five. No point in killing herself. All she had to do was drive at a nice pace and try to make it to the Delta before dark.

In the tiny little river town of Arden, Mississippi, a brilliant old lady lay dying. Her name was Louise Winchester Biggs and she was the younger sister of Dakota's grandmother, Heebe. When Dakota was a child she had gone many times to stay in Miss Louise's house and visit her Winchester cousins. Miss Louise's house was the most wonderful place Dakota had ever been in her life, before and since the summer visits. In the first place, every room was lined with bookshelves full of books. In the second place, the house sat on an acre of land in the very center of town, and from it Dakota and her cousin Taylor could walk out to the drugstore or the grocery or down to the car dealership to look at the new Pontiacs or just stroll around and see what there was to see. They could get into Miss Louise's Buick, which she allowed them to drive as soon as they could reach the pedals, and drive to the levee and walk up on it to look at the river.

They could sit in the porch swings and read the books and nobody ever came and found them and said, Do this, do that, do the other thing, because they were guests in Miss Louise's house and a guest could do no wrong.

At noon the cook would put fried chicken and cornbread and sliced tomatoes and green beans and spinach on the table and Miss Louise would come out with her hair pulled neatly back into a bun and her ironed shirtwaist dresses held at the top button with a pair of Air Force wings and they would drink tea with lemon and sugar and eat if they were hungry and talk about things. Miss Louise never talked about herself. If her corns hurt and she was having to wear house shoes all day, if the rains would not come and water the cotton fields, if she missed her dead husband or the son she lost in the war, you would never know it at her table.

"What are you girls finding to do?" she would begin. "I think you should have a party."

They did have parties. They had bridge parties in the afternoons and Coca-Cola parties in the mornings and dances in the living room at night. For a town of two thousand souls it was surprising how many people were the right age to come to parties given by two twelve- and then thirteen- and then fourteen-year-old girls. Those were the ages Dakota had been when she would ride the train to Cleveland, Mississippi, and be met and driven to Arden to visit Miss Louise.

"Your father was born in this room," Miss Louise told her every summer, taking her into a front bedroom where her grandmother had lain in childbirth. "It was a long night, but when the sun rose he appeared."

In 1987 a town library had been built on half of Miss Louise's lot. She had given the land to the city and had derived much pleasure from watching the building go up and later from the sight of people going in and out all day carrying books. Some of the books from Miss Louise's bookshelves were there. The rest would go when she died and her house would be turned into a children's annex for the library. There were no Winchesters or Biggses left in Arden now. They had all gone to live in Memphis and Jackson and Connecticut and New York City. Only Miss Louise was left, but she had not been lonely as her life came to a close. She was still right there where she had been since she was eighteen years old and entered her house as a bride. Her children had been born there and Dakota's father, because her sister had been visiting when her labor began.

Miss Louise was not afraid to die. She believed her maker was watching over her. She did not believe it was his fault that she had lost half her sight and hearing and now was losing her ability to even get up and walk across a room. He was a fallible God who was doing all he could to help her. He was waiting for her in the heaven where her parents and her husband waited with her son. It was not death Miss Louise dreaded, now that she had decided she was dying. It was the long trip Taylor was going to have to make to come and watch her die. It was the phone calling that would start and people spending all their money flying in from all over the place and having to rent cars in Greenville and drive to Arden to see an old lady who was too sick to get up and tie her hair back and powder her nose. I will have to have those teeth in the whole time, she decided, and wear the hearing aids and cheer them up. I'll call Taylor tomorrow, but not today.

Miss Louise had almost gone back to sleep when Mr. George Monroe the Third stopped by on his daily walk to see how she was doing. His family had sold insurance to the Biggs family for three generations. At one time the Monroe home was across the street from the Biggs place. All his life he had gone in and out of the Biggs house without knocking and he did not knock now. He found the cook, Eileen, asleep with her head on the kitchen table. Eileen was seventy-five herself. She should have retired years ago, but she thought she could keep going as long as Miss Louise needed her.

George didn't want to wake Eileen, so he tiptoed out of the kitchen and into Miss Louise's room. "How are you, darling girl?" he asked. "Is there anything you need?"

"I'm dying, George," she answered. "I suppose we need to call Taylor and tell her."

"Oh, no," he said.

"I know. They'll be calling long distance all over the place and making people interrupt their lives. They'll all start coming here and there's nothing to eat. Someone will have to call the grocery store and have them deliver some things."

George pulled a chair up beside the bed. He took Miss Louise's hand in his. "There was always good food at this house. The best food in Arden and plenty of Coca-Cola." He held her hand. He was crying now. There seemed to be no reason not to cry.

*   *   *

George got Taylor on the phone just as Dakota was pulling into a filling station in Poplar Bluff, Missouri, to stretch her legs and decide what route to take and where to spend the night. She had made the trip many times and had at least three separate routes with many shortcuts and secret roads. Lately she had been staying on the interstates, however, having lost her sense of adventure where traveling was concerned.

She had even acquired a car phone for highway emergencies. After she bought it she decided it was a waste of money, but she had signed a twelve-month contract so she had to keep it. She had three more months to go on the contract or it would not have been in the car on this trip.

She used it now. She wanted to call ahead and make sure there was a motel room waiting somewhere. She had been driving eight hours since she left Kansas City. She had gone past the point of being bored and was just cruising now.

The motels she liked to use on the far side of Memphis were all full. There was some sort of fishing rodeo in the Delta and a Boy Scout convention.

She put the phone away and went into the filling station to pay for her gasoline and get a bottle of orange juice. It was four in the afternoon. She had to make some decisions. She couldn't just drive through Memphis without a place to stay. I could call Taylor, she decided. Except I look so terrible. It will scare her to death to see me without makeup and my hair like this.

She went back to her car and got behind the wheel and started driving again. She was drinking the orange juice slowly, feeling it bring up her blood sugar level, enjoying thinking about the fabulous and orderly processes of the human body. You fed it, you gave it sleep, you tried to stay calm, you did your work, you tried to believe your children knew what they were doing, things worked out. For now, a sixteen-hour drive and eight hours were already done. It's the price I pay for freedom, she reminded herself. Years ago she had gone to Kansas City to get away from her family and its self-inflicted problems. Little by little she had been sucked back in as her sons settled down and got married and had babies. Now she was sucked back in fifty percent of the time. The other fifty percent she lived in the Mission Hills section of Kansas City, Kansas, and dressed the professional women and doctors' and lawyers' wives and even a woman psychiatrist who came in four times a year to outfit herself for work. Doctor Jekyll and Mr. Hyde, Dakota was always thinking. Split personality, separate lives. In Mission Hills she had a two-hundred-thousand-dollar house with four bedrooms and twelve closets and a yard with flower gardens. In Ocean Springs she lived in a little condominium she could vacuum in thirty minutes.

"I love my shop," she said when her children would chide her for living so far away. "I have to make a living. I have expensive tastes."

She was fifty miles down the road from Poplar Bluff when she pulled her address book out of the side pocket of the door and looked up Taylor's number in Memphis and dialed it.

"Taylor," she said, when her cousin answered. "Is that you?"

"Did someone call you?" Taylor asked. "I can't believe news travels this fast."

"About what? I was just driving to Memphis and called to see if I could spend the night with you."

"Grandmomma's dying. I thought someone called you. Where are you right now?"

"Eighty miles from Memphis. Are you going down there? Do you want to wait for me? I'll go with you. How critical is it? Who says she's dying?"

"George Monroe called ten minutes before you did. No doctor's seen her. She told him she was dying. She's never said that before. I've never heard her speak of her own dying."

"Do you want to wait for me?" Dakota revved up the motor and went past the cruise control. A buzzer began humming.

"Yes. If you hurry."

"Wait a minute. I have to take off the cruise control. Okay. There. All right, tell me very carefully what exits to take off Highway 65. I don't have to write it down. Just remind me."

Taylor carefully went over the exits and turns to get to her house. Dakota memorized them, at the same time taking the van up to eighty-six miles an hour and staying there.

"This breaks my heart," she said to her cousin. "We'll have lost them all when she is gone. 'Bare ruined choirs, where late the sweet birds sang.' I guess I read that at her house like I did every book I ever loved when I was young."

"George said her main worry was there wasn't any food in the house. She had him call the grocery store to deliver before he could call me."

"That's just like her."

"I'm going to pack a bag and wait for you. Where were you going, Dakota?"

"Down to the coast to help William introduce his new wife to his children. They aren't coming until Saturday. That can definitely wait."

"His new wife?"

"You don't want to know. She's German, well, Bavarian really. He met her in Switzerland. She sounds nice on the phone. Really fine English. It's not her fault. Okay, hang up. I'm on my way."

Taylor was the godmother of Dakota's son William, who was on his way to the United States to try to put the two sides of his life together.

I guess he learned that from me, Dakota mused as she drove. Where else do they learn anything? But it wasn't my fault their daddy died and even if he had lived that's no guarantee they would have been less wild. Charles was never a calming influence that I noticed. He might have made things worse. Dakota harbored a deep resentment toward her dead husband. He had been killed in a motorcycle accident on a two-lane road outside of Covington, Louisiana. He had been duck hunting with his law partner and had climbed aboard the partner's Harley-Davidson after having a beer and two Bloody Marys for breakfast. Then he was dead, leaving Dakota with five hundred thousand dollars' worth of insurance, three sons under ten, and a leftover life to lead.

No point in thinking about Charles, she decided. He was a glorious thing and the boys are glorious because of him. That's why women breed with men like him. Well, I can't believe Miss Louise is dying and something brought me here to be with her. I want to be with her and tell her that I love her.

It is hard to drive eighty-six miles an hour in a Toyota van while crying, so Dakota slowed down to seventy. She had just settled into her new speed when she passed not one, but two Missouri highway patrolmen trying to guard their state boundaries and finish up their quotas for the day.

When she stopped crying, Dakota drank the rest of the orange juice and pulled a couple of pieces of salt-rising bread out of a sack on the passenger seat floor. It was very special bread she had bought at a

Jewish bakery to take to the coast for a treat, but now she ate it without chewing it. She had been planning on stopping at five to eat but now that was gone. She drove as fast as she dared, thinking of mornings at Miss Louise's house and the toast dripping with butter. She would dip the beautiful curved spoon down into the dish of jelly and watch the jelly run on top of the butter until it found an edge. When she had watched it all she wanted she would take a silver butter knife and push the jelly down into the butter and then she would take a bite. If Miss Louise was at the table, Dakota would chew each bite fifteen times with her loveliest manners and rearrange her napkin on her lap and ask politely about the weather or if she should go into the dining room and pick out some napkins for the bridge party planned for the afternoon. "Taylor will be sleeping late," Miss Louise might say. "She always sleeps late when she's out of school." As if Dakota didn't know her cousin never got up until someone woke her. Now Miss Louise will sleep, Dakota decided. And she will wake in heaven. I believe she will. I will concentrate on that until I see her.

But instead she started thinking about George Monroe and how hot his hands had been when they danced three times at the dance they had in Miss Louise's living room the night before she was leaving to go home the last summer she came to Arden.

"I'll see you next summer," George had said, putting his face down into Dakota's hair, which smelled of shampoo and hair spray and Aphrodisia perfume.

Only there had been no next year because Dakota's father had bought a construction business in Metarie, Louisiana, and she had to move again and begin again for the sixth time in ten years, and make friends again, and get elected cheerleader again in a school full of strangers.

There was no longer enough time to go to Arden, Mississippi, and spend weeks with her father's family.

The first time they danced, George Monroe had been so shy he had just dragged her around the living room floor. But the second and the third time he stopped being afraid and told her about his life at the University of Virginia, where he had just spent his seventeenth year. His parents had sent him to college early because he was so smart there was nothing left for him to do at Arden High School. He told Dakota about breaking his wrist playing rugby and about the English teacher who had them read William Faulkner and write essays about it. "It isn't what they say it is, Dakota. You ought to read it. It's just like being here, where we live. It's so beautiful and the sentences are pages long, as if his brain can barely contain all it knows and wants to tell."

"He's a traitor to the South." It was all she knew about Faulkner, and Dakota was not in the habit of having to admit she had not read an author. She had been reading all her life. It was her great pride.

"No, he's not. They just tell you that because they don't understand what he's doing. I'm going up to Oxford and meet him before I go back to school. I've already written to him and asked if I can come."

Dakota was silent then. Just because George was shy about dancing didn't take away the cachet he had from going to the University of Virginia and being introduced to authors no one Dakota knew had ever dared to read. George was growing in her estimation until he took up the whole room where the young people of Arden and Shaw and Benoit were dancing and eating cheese straws and celery stuffed with pimento cheese and biscuits with sliced ham.

*   *   *

Taylor had called her daughters in Memphis and her son in New York City and told them to stand by. "Dakota's here and going with me," she told them. "And your daddy's coming down tomorrow. He's in Nashville at a meeting. So I'm all right. Just tell everyone to keep in touch until I see what's going on."

"What do you think is happening?" her son asked. He was an editor at *Newsweek*. He was used to digging out the truth.

"She told George Monroe she was dying. So she might be. I've never known her to say that before."

"Then I'm coming," her son said. "I want to see her. I love her too much to take a chance."

"Good," Taylor answered. "Leave a message on this phone and I'll meet your plane. You have to fly to Cleveland or Greenville. You know that, don't you?"

"I'll rent a car. I'll feel better if I have my own transportation."

"George Monroe said she said this is what would happen."

"What?"

"Everyone would start flying places and renting cars."

"Well, she's right. I'll be there late tonight or tomorrow."

Taylor went to stand in the living room and think about what she had forgotten to do. All around her were gifts her grandmother had given her, an antique vase from China, a brass lamp, a shelf of books by Pearl Buck and Daniel Defoe and Miguel Cervantes and William Wordsworth and Aristotle and Plato and Immanuel Kant and all the Bobbsey Twins and William Green Hill books. In a corner was a rosewood secretary Miss Louise had sent to Memphis on a cotton truck when Taylor first was married. On a table was a silver vase that came down the Ohio and Mississippi rivers when Miss Louise's ancestors came to Mississippi a hundred years before.

I love her the most of anyone in the world, Taylor decided. I loved her and my father more than I loved my mother. How could I have helped it? Daddy and Grandmother could read my mind. They let me go. They never scolded me or told me I was wrong or ever did a thing but worship me from the minute I was born. We should worship one another. What else do we have in the world that really matters?

The doorbell was ringing. It was Dakota. They fell into each other's arms and cried and then they went into the living room and sat together on the sofa.

"Do you remember how we used to have such perfect manners around her?" Dakota said. "I thought about that when I was driving. She never asked us to. She never said a word, but when I was at her table I had these precious, perfect manners. I used to chew my food so slowly, as if I was a doll and everything was a tea party. There will never be manners like that again when her generation dies. It was a play. The play of civilization, and we had starring roles when she looked at us. She used to look at me as if I was the most important person in the world, as if she couldn't believe her luck at having a twelve-year-old girl like me at her dinner table."

"She set an example," Taylor said. "Come on. Let's get going. I want to get there."

"Do you want to go in my van?"

"If it's all right. Bob took our good car to the airport when he flew to Nashville this morning. I can drive if you're tired."

"I'm not tired. I'm on a roll. I slowed down at the Missouri border because I was crying and just as I stopped going ninety I passed two patrol cars. I take that as a sign."

"I don't know how you can hold that motorcycle accident against Charles the way you drive."

"Only a cousin would say that to me. I'm going to stop holding it against him. It was how I bore it. It was the only defense I had. Well, come on, let's get going. Where's your bag?"

They drove out of Memphis and got on Highway 61 and followed it to Shelby. Then they turned back west and took 32 to Perthshire, then the famous, old Highway 1 to Gunnison and Waxhaw and Arden.

A young nurse had come in to help Eileen. Between them they had cleaned up Miss Louise and brushed her teeth and put them in her mouth and curled her hair with a curling iron and propped her up against her pillows. Eileen found a pink silk bed jacket in a dresser and carefully got it on Miss Louise's arms and tied the ribbons in two bows.

"I look like a fool," Miss Louise said. "Trying to pretend I'm not dying. What did that boy bring from the grocery store, Eileen? Give Josephine some dinner. It's way past dinnertime."

"We want you to eat," Josephine insisted. "Just a few spoons of soup and some of the Ensure."

"I can't drink that anymore. I don't like it. Give me the soup then. I'll try to drink that and have a cracker. Then we'll have to go through this whole rigmarole with the teeth again."

"Your granddaughter's on her way," Eileen said. "Taylor is coming. Her cousin Dakota is with her, that lives up in Kansas and has the dress shop."

"Then I'll drink the Ensure if you bring it with a straw. I guess it's supposed to be good for me." Miss Louise took a long breath. She wasn't sure how long dying was going to take or if it would be something she could have some say about.

"Doctor Shackelford is coming too," Josephine put in. "He ought to be here in a minute."

"He was already here," Miss Louise said. "How many times is he coming?" Josephine grabbed the Ensure, opened it, popped in a straw, and got her to drink a few sips before she fell back asleep.

Taylor's son, Chris Marks, caught an eight o'clock flight from La Guardia to Memphis. At the exact time he was boarding the plane his two sisters decided to drive on down. "You can't tell," the older one kept saying. "We'd regret it all our life."

"Chris is going," the younger one replied. "He'll need us there."

"I'm going for Grandmother," her sister added. "The rest of them can take care of themselves." The older sister was named Abigail. She had inherited the selfish gene that Dakota McAfee thought was her Achilles' heel where family matters were concerned. But it wasn't a weakness. It was a strength. Abigail Marks knew that even if Dakota McAfee didn't. The younger sister, Augusta, didn't have the gene. She was always getting pushed around by life and other people. She pretended to think she made her own decisions, but secretly she knew she was not in charge.

Dakota drove up the shell road to Miss Louise's house and parked behind the five-car wooden garage. There was a tree beside the garage where Miss Louise's husband had hanged himself when he got tired of having cancer. Miss Louise believed the cancer had been caused by the pesticides they put on the cotton, but George Monroe had done a study of such deaths in the Delta and believed they were caused by the stress of farming. "You don't see the women dying, do you?" he always asked. "The field hands and the women don't get cancer. The ones who get cancer are the planters. They're the ones who borrow the money and have to pay it back no matter what the skies bring."

He had been collecting data and doing research on the subject for ten years. He was in touch with scientists at the University of Virginia and had received a grant to finish the project. Since his wife had died of cancer, ruining part of his theory, he had devoted himself with fierce energy to the project. If it was the pesticides, he'd find out. If it was stress, he'd find out.

"What good will it do to know?" people asked.

"It's always good to know," he answered. "The more information we have, the better we can protect the people who are left."

"I better leave the office early and go on over to Miss Biggs's house," he told his secretary. "Her family will start getting here before too long. Do you think I should call someplace and have them send flowers?"

"You could. I'll call Greenbrook's and see what they have. If they have some tulips that would cheer people up. You want me to send tulips? I could go get them and bring them over if they don't have a delivery this late."

"All right," George said. "Thank you very much, India. That will be very nice of you." He straightened his tie and walked on out of his office and got into his car and drove the three blocks to Miss Louise's house. It was the time of year when old people died, he decided. The time when he had lost his father and his mother, the time when they had lost old Mr. Allen and Miss Cary Hotchkiss and all the wonderful old men and women of Arden, Mississippi. The old people were dying and the town was dying too. There was no use for river towns in 1999, unless you built casinos at the landings and bused people in to fleece them. George hated casinos. He believed the ice storms of 1993 had been a punishment to the Delta for letting them come in.

This beautiful old civilization was built with slave labor, he was thinking, and now will end with gambling and death from stress and pesticides. All civilizations end, all good things lose their purpose and vitality. Why did I stay so long? I guess someone had to be here for the burials. My beloved wife, Sherry, dead at forty-five and no children and all my cousins gone to the cities.

He parked in Miss Louise's garage and got out and went into the house. Walking through the garage he passed a painted sign Taylor and Dakota had made to advertise a play they put on in 1959. It was a play based on *Gone With the Wind*, the opening scenes before the Civil War began. He had played Scarlett's father, Taylor had played Scarlett, and Dakota had played Scarlett's sister Suellen. The real purpose of the play had been to let Taylor, Dakota, and two of their friends wear the hoop skirts and crinolines they had found in Clara Delaney's attic. They were dresses girls had worn to formal dances at Ole Miss. George and two other boys had made the props and set up the stage in Miss Louise's backyard. Dakota had made the signs they put up around town to invite an audience. "Three Scenes from *Gone With the Wind*," the signs read. "For the benefit of the Girl Scouts of Bolivar County. Bring Your Own Chairs. Seven O'clock at Night, July 12, 1959. In Front of William Biggs House on Oak Street. *Everyone Invited.* In the Garage in Case of Rain."

Dakota had been the wildest and most energetic girl who had ever come to visit Arden. She had gotten up every morning at dawn and had ice cream for breakfast and never stopped thinking of things to do. The first time George had really noticed her was after the play. There had been a party and he had taken a friend who was visiting him from Jackson. "Who's the dish in pink?" the friend had asked. "Look at the knockers on her."

So George had stopped looking at Taylor, who was the acknowledged beauty of the town, and looked at Dakota instead.

"She's a cousin visiting from Alabama," he answered, and kept on looking at her and a week later danced with her three times. Then she was gone, never to return, and he finished his years in Virginia and came home to live.

He stopped before the sign, surprised at how the lettering had held up all these years. Then he went in the house through the back door and got ready to attend another dying.

Except Miss Louise was not going to die just yet. Doctor Jimmy Shackelford was not going to let her die. He was sitting by her bed feeding her the fourth of four prednisone tablets he had in his hand. When he had gotten her to swallow them he gave her two Advil and a capsule of tetracycline. There had been a study published the week before that he had been following for months. It proposed to prove that heart disease was at least partly a bacterial infection. He was going to cover all the bases with Miss Louise. He was going to keep her from dying if she would let him. He was not old enough to have made his peace with his patients dying. He knew she would never let him send her to Greenville to the hospital but there were things he could do right there. "Drink the rest of this Ensure, Miss Louise," he begged. "I want you to drink it for me."

"Since you ask so sweetly, I will try." She smiled into his handsome face, searching his features for his father, who had boarded in their house when he first came to Arden to practice. Now this darling boy was here in his place and she didn't want to disappoint him or be difficult.

She drank the tasteless fluid through the straw, batting her blue eyes at him as she drank.

"Don't get in the way if the Lord is ready to have me with him," she said, very quietly so he could barely hear her.

"Hogwash," Jimmy answered. "The Lord can't have what we still need."

Miss Louise started laughing and was still smiling widely when George came in the room and right behind him her precious Taylor and Dakota Clark McAfee looking exactly like her mother had at her age.

The room filled with light and laughter and people talking. Old death skulked out to the back hall and took a seat by the unused butter churn. This was not going to be his night after all. Too many lively, living people had come crowding in and taken the field.

After Miss Louise went to sleep for the night, George and Dakota and Taylor went to sit on the front porch swings in their coats and talk about old times. In a while Taylor went to bed and left the other two alone. "What is Jimmy Shackelford doing to her?" Dakota asked. "I don't know about giving her all those pills. If she's dying, let her die. I don't want him dragging out her suffering. She's not going to live much longer anyway. God, there's no way to know what to do about this, is there?"

"At least I'm seeing you," he answered. "I've thought about you all my life, you know. Missed opportunities and all of that."

"You ought to come up to Kansas City and visit me. Lots of good things are there. Ball games, plays from New York, the opera. Come up and visit me. You could come down to the coast but all I do down there is mess around with my children. They wouldn't like me having a man around. My sons have never been able to deal with that so I just never confront them with it."

"You always were so wise."

"I was not wise. I was the craziest little girl in the Western world."

"No. You were wise. You knew how to live life to the fullest. I bet you still know how."

"Maybe I was. Maybe I do." She was sitting very close to him and she did not object when he pulled her closer and kept his arm around her as she put her head upon his chest. It was a strange sensation, after so much denial, to just rest against a man for a while.

A car pulled up in the yard. It was Taylor's children, Abigail and Augusta and their brother, Chris. They had picked him up at the airport on their way. It was one o'clock in the morning when they arrived, and Dakota and George were still cuddled up on the swing with blankets around them, not talking anymore about a single thing.

They all went into the house and a sleepy Taylor got out of bed and led her children to the beds she had made up for them and lit the space heaters in the rooms and bathrooms and tucked them in as though they were children. Before they went to sleep they tiptoed one by one into their great-grandmother's room and kissed her forehead and Augusta, who was a Christian, said a little prayer and Abigail and Chris said things that resembled prayers so closely they might as well have been prayers. Let her be at peace, Chris said. Let her know she lives in us, Abigail begged. Then they went into their beds and Augusta asked Jesus to be kind while Chris and Abigail cursed the human condition and its end.

*   *   *

In the morning Jimmy Shackelford came back and gave Miss Louise three prednisone and two more Advil and another capsule of tetracycline but he was not hopeful anymore. Old death had come into her bed at night and taken her back into his camp.

Miss Louise talked to her great-grandchildren after Jimmy Shackelford left and she didn't have to take any more pills to make him happy. Then she talked to Dakota and told her she looked like her mother. Then she asked Taylor if she wanted any more of the furniture. Then she told Eileen to get her pearl earrings and pearls out of her jewelry box so she could give them to Abigail and Augusta.

"You already gave them to them, Grandmother," Taylor said. "You sent them the last time I was here. Don't you remember that?"

"I don't know." Miss Louise lay back against the pillows. "You all go on and have some breakfast now. I need to have Eileen work on my teeth and do my hair."

"We could do it," Dakota said. "Let us do it for you."

"No. You go look through the books and see if there's anything you want. The rest are for the library. Some of them are too old now to be good for anything."

When Dakota and Taylor left the room Miss Louise was glad they were gone. She had been having a dream about a summer morning when she was with her grandmother. They were taking the feathers from a gray hat and putting them on a blue one to match a dress she was taking off to school in the fall. Her grandmother's hands were so beautiful, with veins like blue rivers as she stitched the blue velvet band onto the blue wool cloche and pushed the borrowed feathers down into the band. Miss Louise would wear the hat all winter at the school they sent her to in Kentucky, where she had read many of the books that surrounded her still. The books were singing to her now, and somewhere her grandmother's sewing machine was humming and humming, smocking dresses and turning bolts of cotton into petticoats and ruffles and long bags to hold the cotton when they picked it in the fall, in the old times, in the times when no one was dying.

Only Eileen was near when she stopped her old, labored breathing and entered the dream entirely and went to rest in the heaven that is reserved for those who can believe it exists.

Then the activity began. In Munich, Germany, a woman packed a suitcase for a seventeen-year-old boy who was Miss Louise's great-great-grandson. His father was coming from Berlin to take him to the funeral. At a time when the father had been blacklisted by every other member of the family, Miss Louise had sent him checks and letters. Later, he had lived with her for two years while he quit drinking. He was one of the first people Taylor had called when she knew her grandmother was dying.

In Virginia, two college students were on their way to the Richmond airport. On the island of St. Croix, an engineer and his Chinese wife were begging American Airlines to let them get on the eleven thirty plane. In Nashville, Tennessee, a woman architect and an apartment manager and a graphic artist were driving in separate cars to catch the same plane.

A lawyer and a potter and a third-year medical student were driving from New Orleans. A land surveyor in Pascagoula was on his way. Plus, housewives, a registered nurse, and the editor of the Natchez newspaper. A woman in Denmark tried to catch a plane but she was six months pregnant, had had pernicious nausea the whole time, and her physician would not let her fly.

Plus, a retired heart surgeon, a neonatal pediatric surgeon, and more people, all very, truly sad, all saying to themselves, this was it, there is nothing anyone could do.

Miss Louise's worst fears had come true. People were interrupting their lives to come and see her dead. Not that Taylor would let them keep the coffin open. All they'd get to see was a steel box and each other. Do not put a photograph of me at the funeral parlor or in the church, she had meant to say to Taylor. She had noticed lately at funerals that people were putting photographs of the dead person on top of the coffin, as though people in Arden, Mississippi, had turned into illiterate peasants in Mexico or South America.

Fortunately, it never occurred to Taylor to put a photograph of Miss Louise near the coffin. Miss Louise could rest in peace about that.

George Monroe's cousin Cameron came from Greenville to play the organ. He played Buxtehude and then Bach and three beautiful songs that had been Miss Louise's favorites. "I Come to the Garden Alone," "The Church's One Foundation," and "Like a Bridge over Troubled Waters."

First there was the coffin viewing in the church annex, then the funeral in the chapel, then a five-mile trip out into a cotton field where the Biggs family cemetery sat on a ridge surrounded by sycamore trees. They put her into the earth beside her husband with her son to her right, beneath the huge marble stone Taylor's husband had paid for out of love for his wife's family.

After the funeral everyone stayed at Miss Louise's house until the next morning. George Monroe got drunk for the third time in his life and slept fully clothed on Dakota's bed. Augusta got drunk and told her brother and sister they had ruined her life by teasing her and telling her she was unworthy. Taylor slept in her grandmother's bed and pressed her head far down into the pillow. Her husband, Bob, lay beside her and planned a trip to Hawaii to cheer her up.

Eileen went home to her own children. She was surprised when the lawyer came driving up the next day to tell her Miss Louise had left her a large sum of money.

Chris Marks got up at dawn and went for a six-mile run around the town his ancestors had built. What in the hell am I doing in New York City? he kept thinking. I'm getting out of there if it's the last thing I ever do. I'm coming home.

"So do you want to drive down to the coast with me and meet the German wife?" Dakota asked, after George had apologized six times for getting drunk and sleeping on her bed.

"Yes, I do," he answered. "I'll go home and pack a bag."

They left Arden just at dark and drove to Jackson and checked into the Courtyard by Marriott.

"Do you want to call anyone we know?" George asked, when they had settled into their adjoining rooms. They had opened the doors between the rooms and were sitting on the bed in Dakota's room being embarrassed and trying to decide what to do next.

"We could call your brother Cal. His wife, Lura, was a good friend of mine and Taylor's." Dakota sat back against the pillows and pulled her legs up onto the bed. She was an extremely agile and flexible woman for fifty-four, partly as a result of her nervous energy and partly from running around with her best friend, Shelby, for fifteen years and doing exercise tapes in Shelby's living room. I wonder how much flexibility is left in George Monroe, she started wondering. I could stand him up and see if he will bend. I bet he'll bend, she decided. He's just nervous about being in this motel room with me.

"Cal's in Chicago at a meeting of cosmologists. He was excited about being asked to go. He still teaches physics but he publishes papers on astrophysics. He's our star, Dakota. You never really knew him, did you?"

"He was at Princeton when I used to come to Arden. I don't think I ever saw him except once at a wedding. He's tall, isn't he? Even taller than you are."

"Yes. We don't know where the height came from." George stood up. "I think we should go eat dinner. I know a place called Nick's that's good. Are you hungry?"

"Sure." She smiled at him. He was definitely unbending. She would too. "I'm hungry too and I'm tired of trying to decide if we ought to take off our clothes and try our psyches against the gods of sex and love. What if you think I'm old? What if we can't do it? Then we still have to drive all the way to the coast. What do you think? Should we risk it?"

"We might as well." He sat back down on the bed and put his hands very gently on her arms. "I made love to Sherry every night for years, Dakota. I'm not worried about if I can make love to you. I'm just afraid I'll do it and then you'll disappear."

"I'd only be in Kansas City," she answered. "You can drive, can't you?" Then she kissed him, very sweetly and gently and then a lot better than that. "Come on, let's go out to dinner and then we'll come back here and see if there's anything left in me but talk. I've spent most of my life not making love, George. I'm not a practiced Aphrodite by a long stretch."

But when he went into the other room to freshen up before they left she took out the sexiest pair of underpants she had with her and put them on and then took off her traveling clothes and put on the white silk pants and jacket she had brought into the hotel thinking she might wear it. It was the first time she had dressed up since she'd left Kansas City. She went into the bathroom and put on mascara and pale lavender eye shadow and pink lipstick and bigger earrings. It's all right, she decided. It's not like I'm going out to dinner with some stranger.

Things work out in the world. They worked out fairly well for Dakota and George that night. Touching someone you have *always liked* is never a bad idea. What can go wrong when two people really trust each other?

Dakota had talked on the phone to her children only once during the days of Miss Louise's death and funeral. There had been too much to do. She had called the caretaker and had him open her condominium for her son and his bride and she had called her ex-daughter-in-law and asked her to take care of details until she got there. Then she had concentrated on Arden.

"I don't know what we'll find when we get there," she told George several times. "But at least no one we love will be dying."

"I'm ready," he answered. "Whatever happens I will help."

Twice or three times during the week she had been traveling Dakota had noticed a beautiful alignment of planets in the late afternoon and early evening sky. Jupiter and Venus moving closer and closer together, until, by the night she and George arrived at the coast, they were hanging like bells in the sky. Venus on top and Jupiter climbing the sky to meet her.

"I'm going to pretend those stars are why things are falling into place this week," she told George. "And without help from me down here."

Things were falling into place in Ocean Springs. By the time Dakota and George arrived at her condominium, the children had all been introduced to the wife and they were all packing to go to New Orleans to see Mardi Gras parades.

"She's so pretty," the oldest granddaughter whispered to Dakota. "And she brought us presents from Switzerland."

"Dad's going to have us over there to visit in the summer," the oldest grandson said. "We're going to climb in the Swiss Alps."

"Come to Mardi Gras with us, Momma," Dakota's son said. "You and George follow us over there."

"Maybe we'll come tomorrow," she answered. "We're pretty tired. We've just been to a really sad funeral."

"I know, Momma." Her oldest son pulled her against his body and seemed to be truly compassionate and sad. But he was so happy with his new wife and the fact that his children had forgiven him for getting remarried that he couldn't hold on to the sadness long. "I remember Miss Louise," he added. "You took us there a long time ago. There was a swimming pool made of stones with moss all around it."

"The Arden Country Club," George and Dakota said together.

"Somewhere we went and had bacon sandwiches. Well, we've got to get going if we're going to see Bacchus. Are you sure you don't want to go along? We could all go in your van."

"Not today," Dakota said. "I just came down to make sure everybody was all right."

She watched them leave, her hopeful oldest son and his hopeful wife and his children, who had decided to forgive everyone in sight since they were on their way to Mardi Gras with money in their pockets and a father who definitely loved them, after all.

"They didn't need me," she said and turned to George.

"Well, I sure do," he answered. "Could we try that thing again where you pretend I'm an Arabian king with a harem?"

After the funeral in Arden, Jimmy Shackelford, M.D., was so mad he was mean to people all day. He hated death so much. He couldn't believe it could defeat him. After four years at the University of Mississippi and four years at medical school and three years as a resident in Boston and two years of practice and *people still died while he was caring for them.*

It made him so mad he almost felt like calling up that bitch Sally Cafery in Jackson and asking the two-timing whore to marry him.

POSTSCRIPT

In February of 2001 the new children's annex of the Arden, Mississippi, Library was opened with great fanfare. It was called the Louise Winchester Biggs Children's Library and Taylor and her daughters, Abigail and Augusta, came down from Memphis and George Monroe cut the ribbon, since he had given twenty thousand dollars to the renovation of the house, and the lieutenant governor came and several leaders of the black community and everyone spoke of progress and said people should still learn to read even if they did have television.

Jimmy Shackelford's new wife, Sally, had a reception afterward at the old Shackelford place, which she was redecorating and rebuilding. She was five months pregnant and really didn't feel like interrupting her carpenters and plumbers for a day, but Jimmy had insisted, so she gave in. She made the mistake of serving sherry, so the crowd stayed until three in the afternoon and messed up half the sanded floors that hadn't been sealed yet.

*   *   *

George e-mailed Dakota a report on the opening and the reception and she sent him back a photograph of a pair of bikini underpants. He was killing himself driving up to Kansas every other weekend. As soon as he saw the underpants he knew he was going to drive up there again. I don't know what's wrong with me, he kept telling himself as he tried to do his work. I think I'm going crazy.

"How'd he like the underpants?" Dakota's best friend, Shelby, asked when they had lunch the next day.

"He's coming Friday afternoon." Dakota laughed. "I don't know what's wrong with me, Shelby. I must be going crazy."

THE BIG CLEANUP

IT WAS FOUR DAYS AFTER CHRISTMAS and Miss Crystal was cleaning out all the drawers in the house. First she caught a cold from her grandson, King Mallison the Third, age six, then a cold spell came in from the north and the doctor told her to stay inside and not play any tennis until she was better. So she was listening to Beethoven's symphonies and cleaning out the drawers while she waited for the amoxicillin to kill the germs in her nose and throat and ears.

Unfortunately, cleaning out the drawers was turning out to be a depressing way to spend the day. All the memories of when her son, King, was growing dope, memories of her own drunken nights before she got on Antabuse and learned to do yoga instead of drinking toddies, all the poets who used to hang out in the den when Francis Alter was alive, all the antiwar people who used to come and go arguing with the lawyers from Mr. Manny's law firm, all the parties and fried chicken and houseplants and gifts of jewelry, all the writers from Nebraska who used to come and stay, all the old friends of Mr. Manny's from Yale, all the fun and life the house had sheltered, was there in the drawers of the presses and chifforobes and wardrobes and secretaries. All the old dog

collars from four generations of sheepdogs who had lived in the base-
ment and the kitchen and the backyard, all the drunken sailboat and
diving adventures, all the photography adventures, all the boxes of
slides from the Virgin Islands and the Cayman Islands and Iceland and
Denmark and Norway and England and Ireland and Scotland and
France and Italy and Wales.

It made Miss Crystal feel terrible to think it was all over and done
with, the children raised, Crystal Anne at the University of Alabama,
King and Jessie and the children living in Atlanta and only coming
home for a few days twice a year.

"I'm old, Traceleen," she told me when she got me on the phone. "I
was too busy to notice it was happening. Now it's here. Don't you want
to come in tomorrow and help me throw this stuff away? I might melt
in tears without company."

"You just need to get out of the house. A few sets of tennis would
change your attitude."

"I can't. I promised Philip I'd stay inside for three days while the
pills work. He said I might have walking pneumonia if I didn't."

"All right. I was thinking about coming in anyway. I'm about sick of
my relatives, to tell the truth. My cousin Sally is here from Chicago and
all she does is complain about New Orleans. She says we are living in a
fool's paradise down here. She said our black mayor really isn't black and
that the river is going to break through and drown us any day because of
global warming. I've had to listen to that every night."

"You've never mentioned a cousin in Chicago."

"And I won't say any more now. I have made a resolution ahead of
the New Year. I will not talk about anyone behind their back. If they
aren't in the room, I do not discuss them."

"That's a very advanced concept. Where did you get that idea?"

"From a Buddhist text our preacher is having us read in our Comparative Religion group."

"I wish I could do it. I think I'll try. Anyway, when can you come in, do you think?"

"I'll be there by ten thirty. Wait until I get there to open any more drawers."

"I'll try to stop. You won't believe the memories that are in there."

I couldn't help thinking about a poem Miss Crystal wrote one time based on this dream she had. This was when Mr. Alter was alive and would come and visit us and inspire poetry in everyone in town. It was about dreaming there were all these rooms in the house that she had forgotten were there. In each room were chests of drawers and each drawer was full of treasures, diamonds and rubies and pearls, rare books and old letters full of untold secrets and forgotten wisdom.

Her psychiatrist told her it was about all the unfulfilled pages of her life, all the possibilities we all pass by, the talents we never use, the doors we never open.

Of course, in real life we are doing everything we can to give each minute "sixty seconds' worth of distance run." That from a poem we learned in seventh grade.

So the next morning I walked down to the corner of Jackson and Saint Charles and caught the streetcar and rode down to Loyola and got off and walked across the campus to Story Street. When I'm on the campus I always start thinking about the education I interrupted in nineteen seventy-eight, after Miss Crystal insisted on sending me to college. I went part-time for nine months, then summer came and I never went back. I don't know why I didn't want to do any more study. I don't think about it much, but sometimes I walk across the campus and remember myself being a student and the day the philosophy professor told us about Bishop Berkeley and his theories.

I came to the conclusion that it doesn't matter if the tree makes a noise when it falls. All that matters is getting young girls onto birth control pills and stopping them from having babies. Everyone has their main concerns. That is mine. As you know, I am a youth counselor at my church and give it many hours each week. I do not need to feel guilty about interrupting my formal education to go back to my real life.

"You've got me thinking about the past," I told Miss Crystal, as soon as I got in the door and hung up my coat. "There's nothing to be learned from old times. We have to keep on moving to the future. Where is all this mess you've found?"

She had it piled up on the breakfast room table. Signs from when we had the antiwar protest. The photograph of us with our aprons and brooms sweeping up the broken glass in front of the Tulane auditorium after the protest turned into a riot. Miss Crystal and I had been dressed as housewives to make the protest look broad based. Then, when the children broke the windows, we just started sweeping up. A photographer from the *Times-Picayune* had taken our picture and it went out across the country and was in a thousand papers the next morning.

Miss Crystal was on the best-dressed list when she lived in Jackson, Mississippi. Now here she was, being famous in a short cotton housedress.

"We looked pretty good," she said, studying the picture. I looked over her shoulder.

"We surely do. Look how pretty your legs look. We were wrong to be upset when this was in the paper. This is a very flattering photograph of us both."

"Let's don't throw it away," she said. "Get a box out of the storage closet and we'll put things we need to keep in that."

"We could put it in a frame and put it on the wall," I suggested. "We should be proud of what we did at Tulane. It was the lives of young men we were saving. Remember my cousin Franklin had just been drafted when we signed up to help in the marches."

"Good idea." So we left all the stuff on the table and went in the living room and took a framed photograph of a wedding party out of its frame and put our picture in instead. It looked wonderful, that old scrap of newspaper framed in a golden frame and sitting on the piano with the other pictures.

After that we set to work in earnest. I was just hauling my second garbage bag full of memories out to the trash cans when the phone rang and Miss Crystal answered it and it was my niece, Andria, calling from the television station to say she was being sent to Saint Louis to cover the pope's visit in a few weeks

Andria started pleading with me. "Will you let me leave my shelties at your house for three days? I could leave them at the vet's but they get so unhappy there. You don't have to let them inside. If you'll just keep them in your yard."

"Oh, Andria, don't do that to me. They tore up all my flower beds the last time I took care of them. I'm proud of you for getting to see the pope, but don't make me take care of your dogs."

"Say no," Miss Crystal is whispering. "You don't have to take care of her stupid dogs."

"I don't have anyone else to turn to," Andria is saying, so I answered, "Call me back tonight. Let me think about it."

"I will do anything for my niece, Andria, but taking care of her dogs is not in it," I said. I was pulling old sweaters out of a drawer and folding them on the bed. We were making two piles, one for the Catholic Church Honduran Mission and one for the Salvation Army. We had made a pact to throw away everything in the house that had not been used in the last two years. With exceptions to be made, of course, for anything with great sentimental value or that we thought King the Third might someday want. "I kept my daddy's old Auburn letter sweater until I was in my forties," Miss Crystal said. "I wish I had it now that he is dead. God only knows what happened to that sweater. I don't know why that man could never say he loved me. Be sure and tell Andria that you love her, Traceleen. Even if you don't take care of the dogs and I sure don't blame you for that, you must always let her know that you care."

"I told her not to get that second dog," I said. "One dog was bad enough, but at least you could let it in the house."

"We don't have to do everything they think up for us to do." Miss Crystal was vacillating over a skiing sweater from up in Colorado. She pulled it over her head and went in the bathroom to look at herself in the mirror. Miss Crystal is still a very good-looking woman for her age, but she is no longer able to wear a sweater with a picture of trees in snow across the front.

"It's not a very flattering color, is it?" she asked.

"No. But they sure won't get much use of it in Honduras."

"I'm going to keep it. It won't hurt to keep one drawer full of things I like remembering. So how would you feel about going to

Atlanta with me to take care of King and Madison Amelie? We could drive up through Nashville and you could see your sister and I could see my nieces."

"I can't plan that far ahead. I don't travel well anymore. You know that. I get my bowels all mixed up. I might. I'm not saying I won't do it but I can't decide today."

Miss Crystal added a pair of practically new blue jeans to the pile for Honduras, then she stepped back and looked at what we had accomplished. She was still wearing the sweater and from the side she looked much older than fifty-three. I couldn't help thinking maybe the pact she had made with her psychiatrist to never get a face-lift had not been such a good idea after all. Those thin blond women seem to fade so fast once they start fading.

"My hair is getting thin," she said, returning my look. "I have told you before and I tell you again, if we give in to vanity about such things, we are too dumb to be allowed to vote."

"It might be a good idea to get it a little shorter and have a perm," I suggested. "That way the back would be fluffed up."

"Get the boxes I put in the hall. Let's pack this stuff up and deliver it. I'm dumping the other two drawers in on top. King has not touched a thing in this room in seven years. I do not have to keep this place as a shrine."

I went out into the hall and brought in two more packing boxes. Then I went into the kitchen and made a fresh pot of P.J.'s French vanilla coffee. While it was brewing I couldn't help taking a look in the huge old mirror over the dining room table. My own hair was not looking very good lately either. White coming all along the temples and little strands curling up from the bun I had only half bothered to make before I left my house.

Miss Crystal came in the dining room while I was looking at myself. She started smiling. "We need a touch-up, Traceleen. When we get rid of these clothes, let's go down and spend the afternoon at the new day spa over by the dance school on Maple Street. I've got two hundred dollars my mother gave me for Christmas. Why she sent me money as old as we both are I do not know but she did and I bet it would really make her happy if she thought we spent it on our nails and hair."

I looked down at my fingernails. They had chipped red polish from some I had put on a week before Christmas.

Miss Crystal looked at her own. Then she started laughing the old crazy laugh I have not seen on her in several years. I started laughing too. What were we doing standing in the dining room five days after Christmas looking so dismal and old and used? There was a life to be led somewhere in the world and neither of us was the sort to give up yet.

Half an hour later we were driving down Claiborne Avenue in Miss Crystal's BMW sedan on our way to deliver half the contents of the house to Catholic Charities and the Salvation Army. Then we were on our way to Maple Street to be made over. We had put a mean message on the answering machine. "This phone accepts praise, blessings, and good news. Please rethink all requests for financial aid, baby- and dog-sitting, or change of telephone services."

After we delivered the boxes we went through the drive-in window of the Saint Charles Avenue McDonald's and got some biscuits and scrambled eggs. Neither of us had had any breakfast.

"I'll feel guilty if I don't go to Atlanta and take care of the children," Miss Crystal said, wiping eggs daintily from her lips with a paper napkin. "How can I say no to Jessie? Jessie is my heart and soul. The daughter-in-law I dreamed of having."

"If it's June the children could come here," I suggested. "That way we could nurse them without having to sleep in strange beds and have our bowels confused."

"Anything that messes up the lower intestine can't be a good idea," she answered. "I heard Walker Percy say that at Tulane when they asked him why he wouldn't travel and do parties for his books. He was a physician, so I guess he knew."

"I read that book of his about the hurricane hitting Covington. I couldn't figure out why his characters were so closemouthed about everything they did. All of them were so full of secrets. No wonder they couldn't figure out what to do."

"That's why men are so unhappy. They don't talk enough. They carry all their troubles around in dark little sacks in their head."

"Well, not your brother, Phelan." One of the things we had thrown away that morning was a hunting magazine with Phelan on the cover and an article about the rhinoceros he killed being the second largest ever killed in the world. We have had a lot of trouble with Crystal's brother, Phelan, but I'll say one thing for him. He knows how to be happy. I have seen him open a bottle of red wine at breakfast when it wasn't even Mardi Gras. And he is not an alcoholic, like Crystal became when she was drinking. It is interesting to study Phelan. I have been doing it for years. For one thing he has ten children by a number of different women. It is easy to say that's a bad idea in the modern world, but nature is not interested in ideas. It only wants men to reproduce their genes.

"Phelan," Crystal repeated. "He's been awfully quiet. I wonder if he's spent all of Grandmother's money yet." She was referring to the insurance scam Phelan had created in North Carolina a few years before. He had made his grandmother's last years a happy time. While he was there he had put most of her money in his bank account plus about two hundred thousand dollars he collected from her health insurance providers. It is always hard to get mad at Phelan for the things he does. Some of it is so close to things all of us would like to do in retaliation for the corporate greed that has covered the United States like a cloud. Crystal and I have both become very cynical about things like health insurance companies and even some of our doctors. I went in last month to have a corn removed from my big toe and the doctor told me I had to have surgery on my feet. This is where being cynical pays off. "There is nothing wrong with my feet," I told him. "All I want is the corn off."

Back to the fifth day after Christmas and how Crystal and I got our makeovers at the day spa.

It is called Rejuvenate and it has only been in operation about three months. It's squeezed in right between the dance studio and a shop that sells Mexican imports. I guess it could have been a house at one time but all the interior has been changed so much you can't tell.

The first thing they did was put us in hot tubs to soak in water with seaweed and sea salt. Then we were given a massage, then a pedicure while our hair was being soaked in something that felt like Vaseline but was said to contain ginseng and vitamin E.

Next we had scalp and neck massage, then manicures, then we were shampooed and delivered to the hairdressers. Crystal was already in her chair when I came in wearing a baby blue terry cloth robe and was seated beside her. "Anything will be better than this pitiful little hair with holes showing on the back of my head."

"Cut mine and straighten it," I said. "My niece, Andria, says black women should not straighten their hair, but if Crystal is curling hers surely I have a right to straighten mine."

I closed my eyes. I sat back in the chair. I was letting a young man I had never met before take my hair and do with it what he liked. It will grow out, I told myself and let the day run its course.

You would not believe how good Crystal looked when we left the place. I don't want to brag about myself but I will say this. If you had met me in the morning on the streetcar you would not have known it was the same woman.

"This was a perfect day for this," I said, as we came out on the street. "I'm going to write your momma a note and tell her how much we enjoyed spending her Christmas money. Tonight I have to make a presentation to the elders in my church about getting more money for the after-school program for latchkey children. This hairdo, not to mention the makeup, will carry the day." We had been made up by the Aveda expert when our hair was done. We had let her pluck our eyebrows and put enough mascara on us to sink a battleship.

"I'll drop you off at home," she answered. "Then I'm going downtown and drag Manny out of his office and take him out to dinner in the Quarter."

"Put on a skirt and some high heels," I advised. "Men still fall for that no matter how the world keeps changing."

"This has been a breakthrough day," she said. "Instead of being used, morning, night, and noon, we have broken out into the larger world and opened our horizons." She drove at her usual breakneck speed over to Magazine and down Austerlitz to my new duplex I got last summer with some help from Andria's boyfriend, Charles Light, who is a real estate agent. He sold my old place for twenty thousand dollars more than I thought it was worth and set me up in this duplex where I rent the other side to two Chinese students who are as quiet as mice. How could I ever despair or get depressed when in my own life I know that progress is being made. If it happened for me, it can happen for any good person who works hard, doesn't drink whiskey or take dope, and just keeps believing in the future. That is the theme of my talks to the young people whom I counsel.

The next morning we had a visitor we had not expected. I had hardly taken off my coat when the doorbell rang and it was Manny's cousin, Shelly Horowitz, from New York City, who has come to the south to do research for a book she is writing about Huey Long. She has taken a position teaching history at a college near here, which shall remain nameless, in order to make a living while she does her research. We have had her over many times to dinner and both Crystal and I think she is a fascinating person and full of ideas that put things in new perspectives. She is a fan of Huey Long and thinks he has been served badly by his biographers. It is her mission to right that wrong.

Well, here she was in tears, standing on the doorstep in a long, brown dress. The first thing I thought was: We need to send her to the spa.

"I can't go on," she was crying into Crystal's arms. We took her inside and put her on the living room sofa, one of us on each side. "The wife of the chancellor collects Beanie Babies. He shut down the university press. Now he's talking about closing the philosophy department. I knew it was going to be a change. I didn't expect it to be Yale, but, my God, I can't talk to those people. The students all believe in God. I have a classroom full of Bible-thumping Baptists. Plus, they said they had a house fixed up for me to live in when I came back from Christmas. I had been living in the apartment they keep for visiting lecturers. So I got back in that hard freeze last Monday and they had moved all my things into a shack. It's a shack. A hut. The place they had planned on fell through so they moved me into a hovel owned by the chancellor's personal trainer. The heat didn't work for two days. I went to a motel. Then when I moved back in the water pipes broke. I can't live there another day. It's the worst place I've ever been in my life."

"It's the world Governor Long knew," I answered. "I guess this is a test to show you the poverty he knew."

"She collects Beanie Babies," Shelly kept weeping. "And she keeps trying to talk to me about *Cats*. She's seen *Cats* five times. She thinks it's a shame T. S. Eliot never saw it. I'll get ulcers if I have to go to another dinner party and have that woman at my table. She's stalking me. She asks to be seated by me. I can't go on. I can't stay another week, much less a semester."

"I'm going to put you in the guest room to get some sleep," Crystal said. "First, we're going to feed you, then I want you to get some sleep."

"There's this new day spa in the neighborhood that would be good for you," I suggested. "After you get rested we might just take you over there."

"Three hundred and twenty-six Beanie Babies," Shelly moaned. "They are building a new chancellor's residence for this fool. I bet they will have to build shelves in the living room for her collection. He doesn't read. He brags about it. He's on-line. He sends e-mail. He won't give the history department enough money to receive periodicals and he only gave us three thousand dollars for speakers for the whole semester and they are building him a two-million-dollar residence to house the Beanie Babies. God, your hair looks great, Traceleen. What did you do to it since I last saw you? I really like the cut."

"What about mine?" Crystal asked.

"Yours too. It's shorter, isn't it?"

"It's falling out," Crystal said. "I'm in denial over it."

"They have this special program at the beauty parlor part of the spa," I said, noticing how long Shelly's hair had become, much too long for a woman almost forty. "If you cut as much as six inches of hair you can have a free haircut and setting if you donate your hair for kids in chemotherapy. They are making wigs for the ones who get bald."

"First we are going to feed you." Crystal stood up and shook her curls from side to side, fluffing them with her fingers. "You don't have to go back to that place. You can quit anytime you want to quit."

We moved into the kitchen and I made some poached eggs on toast and warmed up some orange muffins while Crystal set Shelly a place at the table. She was still ranting on about the house they put her in but she had stopped crying and was beginning to seem more like herself. She is a graduate of Vassar College and we all knew she was going to have a hard time in her new job. I had heard Manny say he was surprised she lasted a semester.

"There were fleas!" she was saying now. "My Skye terrier was covered with them. He's never had a flea in his life. He got sick from the stuff the vet used to kill them. So I called the exterminator and told them to go out and bomb the house. Then I called a mattress company and told them to deliver a new bed and then I got in the car and started driving. I won't stay in that house another night."

"Of course not," I answered, putting the eggs down in front of her. "Where's Julius now? You didn't leave him there? With the exterminator coming?"

"He's in the car in a kennel. I'm going to go stay at a motel so I can take care of him. He's still throwing up half of what he eats."

"Give me the car key," I said. "I'll bring him in." So I went out to the front of the house and opened Shelly's Lincoln Navigator she leased to come to the South and got the dog out of his kennel and carried him in. He is a precious little dog so smart he almost talks to you. I had developed a fondness for him when Shelly stayed here for a week on her way to her new college. He must have remembered me because he put his head down into the crook of my arm and let me carry him in.

Shelly had wolfed down the poached eggs and half a muffin and now she and Crystal were going down the hall to the guest room. I followed with Julius. When we had Shelly settled in the bed underneath the linen sheets and with the beautiful French blanket cover on top of the electric blanket, I set the dog on a chair beside the bed and decided if a creature that smart tore up the room we would just have to deal with it. "Put him in the bathroom," Shelly said. "He won't mind. He can smell me. He knows I'm near."

"If you're sure," Crystal said. "He can stay in here."

"I'd feel better if he was in the bathroom. Just turn out the lights so he can get some rest."

I picked up Julius and took him into the adjoining bathroom and patted him several times and left him. He barked once, then seemed to settle down. Crystal was standing by the bed. Shelly had sunk down into the pillows. She was calming down. Once again Crystal and I had turned chaos into Zen. Many people have laughed at us for our many years of yoga training and Zen Buddhist retreats, but the strength that has given us had paid off for many people who come within our circle of attention.

We left the room and tiptoed back into the kitchen. "I might make a cake," I suggested. "Shelly looks like she's lost ten pounds."

"Could it be true about the Beanie Babies?" Miss Crystal giggled. "The wife of the university chancellor?"

"Why would you be surprised by that? We know people in power are just ordinary people who have been put into positions that make them forget they are ordinary. Remember the march at Tulane? Where was the president of the university that night? Not lying on the grass with those of us who were pretending to be the dead of Vietnam. The person I respect most in New Orleans is old Doctor Finley, who left his wife and came and lay on the grass with us. Right down on the grass in his good suit with his wife standing over him like she might faint. It is my main memory of the march until the windows started breaking."

"That was twenty-five years ago, or more. I wonder if we could meet such a challenge if it came again. Sometimes I wish one would come. Life's become too easy, Traceleen. Where are the bells and whistles? Well, if you're making a cake, I'll get out a chicken and fry it."

We set to work cooking. It was the first task I'd had that put my manicure in jeopardy so I found some rubber gloves and wore them. I noticed Crystal had hers on too. Just because we have been pressed back into service so soon after our makeover doesn't mean we can't try to maintain the good it did.

"If we have the children here in June it might be nice to teach them how to cook," Crystal was saying. She was beating the eggs to dip the chicken in. "They live on fast foods and things they put in the microwave. I can't change that, but we can introduce them to real food while they're here."

"Andria doesn't even cook in her microwave," I added. "If you can't eat it in the car I don't think she knows it exists. You should see her refrigerator. It is completely empty except for Gatorade and leftover Chinese takeout food. She thinks food is the enemy of her life. She thinks grocery stores should be sued along with the cigarette companies, for causing people to get fat. She wants to sue potato chip factories."

"What did you decide to do about her dogs?"

"I'm keeping them, but only on the weekdays. On the weekends her boyfriend is coming to get them and take them to his place. I'm trying to strike a balance. I am the only person who ever loved Andria. I can't desert her just because she's selfish. That's one thing I've learned counseling young people. Everyone has to have one person who loves you even when you act like a child. Just get on first, Mark and I used to tell her when she was a child. We'll knock you in."

"Well, she is going to see the pope. I guess you have to make sure she has peace of mind while she's gone."

"I'm going to get some of those little fences at Lowe's House Supplies and put them up around my flower beds. They dug up the tulip bulbs the last time I kept them."

"You-all knocked her in. Now she's on television every night and going to see the pope. And we had our glory too, finding that newspaper clipping reminded me of that." Crystal paused, with a piece of thigh held dripping above the egg batter. "Remember how wet the grass was that night? When we got up off the ground there were impressions of our bodies in the grass. The little red sundress you were wearing was plastered to your body in the back. Your derriere was outlined perfectly. Also, grass was sticking to Doctor Finley's pants. Then a great roar went up from inside the auditorium. *Hell, no, we won't go. One, two, three, four, we don't want your fucking war.* We started yelling too and Doctor Finley was yelling with us. Then the noise kept getting louder and louder and the students inside broke out of the doors and that's when the windows broke. We had our signs on brooms for the housewife motif and you picked them up and we moved to the side because the children were all running and the police were moving in. We stood behind some azalea bushes and when the police had cleared the area you went right over and started sweeping up the glass. It was the most magnificent thing. So I started sweeping too and Doctor Finley was picking up the pieces and putting them in a pile by a column. We participated in the world back then, Traceleen. We were players. We took the field when our culture needed us. We have nothing to regret. I'm proud of my wrinkles. It reminds me I was there when it counted."

I looked away and when I turned my face back to her she was crying. I went to her and put my arm around her shoulders and let her cry.

"I'm so glad I found that photograph," she said. "I'm so glad I was reminded. We are the same stuff we were then, just wiser and more cautious. We still have work to do. We aren't finished yet."

"Starting with Manny's cousin Shelly," I added. "Tomorrow morning we'll take her to the spa. No wonder she's having such a bad time at that college. Wearing long brown dresses may be all right in New York City but it won't get you any action in the South."

Shelly was still sleeping when Manny came home from work. He came in the kitchen and started eating fried chicken while we told him the story. "We're going to have dinner when Shelly wakes up," Crystal said. "Don't spoil your appetite."

"One chicken breast. Then I'll take a walk while we wait."

"We'll eat at seven whether she's awake or not," Crystal said. "Traceleen has to get home sometime tonight."

"I'm in no hurry," I answered. "As long as someone drives me so I don't have to ride the streetcar in the dark."

It has always been the oddest thing to me to have the days of winter be so short. I love the long, hot days of summer. I never want the sun to go away. I think I am probably one of those people who might get depressed if they lived in Denmark because all I do in January and February is count the days until March 21, the vernal equinox, which is also my darling Andria's birthday.

Manny changed into his tennis shoes and went out the back door to take his walk. Once or twice a year he gets on a program to exercise but it never lasts long. He used to have to practice football every afternoon when he was a young man and run around a track in the heat whether he wanted to or not and he cannot learn to think of it as fun. Miss Crystal, on the other hand, loves to exercise and will run around the park seven times or even more if she runs into anyone she likes.

I was just putting the finishing touches on the dining room table when Shelly came out from her room. She had changed into some white slacks and a pink cashmere sweater and looked like a different person. Now if we could just get her to cut off some of that hair and get a stylish hairdo she might begin to feel better about things.

Manny came back from his walk and embraced his cousin and we all got to listen to the stories about the college again.

"The chancellor keeps a Bible on his desk," she said. "He puts his hand on it when he wants to make a point. He uses the Bible for a prop. He is the most unattractive man I have ever met. He wears black suits. The chancellor who was there when I signed my contract was a darling man, a lover of the arts, an historian himself. Then during the summer he was fired and this man was put in charge. I think I have a suit, don't you, Manny. I mean, if I quit, I think I can argue that I signed up to be under the direction of an historian, not a Bible thumper."

"What can I do to help?" Manny asked. "Just name it, Shell, I will do it."

"Dinner is ready," Miss Crystal announced. "Let's go in. Shelly, you sit there at the end where we can look at you. Traceleen, take the seat by Manny and I will get the mashed potatoes and join you." I used to refuse to eat at the table with my employers and often I still do, but if it is late and I have stayed to help with dinner, they have convinced me it makes them nervous to have me pretend to be a servant after all these years. I was raised to be a servant down in Boutte and so it took us all some adjusting, but Manny explained to me that in Israel no one is allowed to act like a servant, and on the basis of that I sit with them. The main reason I don't care to do it often is that diabetes runs in my family, and I cannot eat half the things I cook without feeling guilty. I have been tested many times and so far am all right but I still watch my diet.

While we were having dessert the phone rang, and I went into the kitchen to answer it as I wasn't having cake. It was my niece, Andria, with big news. She and her boyfriend, Charles Light, were getting married on Saturday. "Why so soon?" was all I could say. "We can't have a wedding with only three days' notice."

"We're going to have to," Andria said and started laughing. "I'm pregnant, Auntie Traceleen. We just did the test. We did two different kinds. We are so excited."

"Oh, no," I answered.

"Don't sound like that. We're thrilled. We haven't done anything for months to prevent it. We were really getting worried. Haven't you noticed I had a worried look?"

"No, I hadn't."

"Come over here as soon as you leave there. We're having champagne. We want you here with us. Charles's parents are on their way."

"It might be an hour. I have to finish here."

I went back into the dining room and announced the news. "Well, you'd better get over there and start celebrating with them," Manny said. "Get your coat. I'll take you now."

So in the end we all went to say hello and congratulate the wedding pair and the parents-to-be. "I don't see why they couldn't have gotten married while they waited for the pregnancy," I couldn't help saying. "I don't understand that thinking."

"Taxes," Shelly Horowitz suggested. "It's the marriage penalty. Why pay it until you have to?"

"It's a good thing I'm a deacon in my church," I muttered. "Reverend Brown does not like this sort of thing. I'm fighting with him now over use of the gym we're building. Now I have to ask for favors or we'll have to have the wedding at home."

"Have it at home," Crystal advised. "Don't spend your political capital on something that will be happy one way or the other."

So there went our Friday morning yoga class with Miss Lane Marismo. We have it with two other ladies in Crystal's living room. They went on and had it without us but Shelly joined them and said later it was the yoga that gave her strength to go back to work and get ready for her second semester on alien ground. Also, she is planning on taking yoga there, but I am getting ahead of my story.

Just when Crystal and I had decided our best days were over, it seems we were being called back into action every time the phone rang. While I was spending two days getting ready for Andria's wedding, Crystal was on the phone with Jessie making arrangements for baby-sitting during King and Jessie's trip to Greece. "There's one slight glitch," Jessie said the third time they talked. "It seems I'm a week late, Crystal. Don't let Dad know, but there's a chance I might be pregnant. Of course, that might cancel all our plans."

"Oh, no," Crystal said. She told me later that was all she could ever think to say when young women blithely declare they are pregnant. As if there is nothing to worry about, nothing to fear, no problems to be foreseen.

"That's how the young people are," I told her. "The joy and greatness of them is that they do not fear the future. We have gestational diabetes in our family. Andria weighed thirteen pounds when she was born. There's a good chance Andria will develop it with this baby. But I'm not saying anything. As long as she has a good obstetrician and is checked every month."

"Does she know about it?" Crystal asked.

"I will tell her, of course. I mean, remind her, but not this week. Not until a month has passed. They don't borrow trouble, the young, why should we lend it to them?"

The wedding was a beautiful affair, if I do say so myself. We had it in the small chapel of the church and Crystal's gay friend, Billy Farley, came over and did the flowers, which were banks of white roses falling down onto the floor and sprays of fragrant tuberoses and lilies. Crystal and Manny gave the flowers to Andria for a wedding present. Shelly Horowitz came with them to the ceremony, dressed up in one of Crystal's dresses and with her hair done up on her head and pearls roped in it.

At the reception Shelly danced with all the men. I was surprised at how well she dances for an historian. She was very popular with the men and met a professor from the University of New Orleans who is also very interested in Huey Long. He is a Creole from an old family here. Crystal says she thinks Shelly got a crush on him so I told her to tell her to beware. The Creoles from New Orleans are very haughty people and usually only marry within their group.

Update: It has been almost a month since I had time to add to this. So much has been going on I can barely get my teeth flossed, much less write in my diary. Andria's baby is due in September, which means she must have been about five days pregnant when they did the drugstore tests. The television station has hired a consultant to dress her so she can go on being on the air up to the very day she delivers. That seems to be the style now in broadcasting. Andria has talked on the phone to a woman who broadcasts the weather on the national weather station and she has offered to e-mail designs for the clothes she wore.

I would like it if Andria thought about the baby more and what she is going to wear on television less, but it is not up to me.

Jessie Hand Mallison is too much the other way. She calls up Crystal at nine o'clock every morning to talk about how she is preparing King Three and Madison Amelie for the new baby coming into their lives.

"I don't want them to ever hate each other," she keeps saying, but

Crystal tells her, "You were an only child. You don't know how much children enjoy sibling rivalry. My fights with Phelan are the most vivid memories that I have. My plots against him, my joy when he was off at camp, my jealousy. You can't stop the river of life, Jessie. If you are going to have a houseful of children, you must get ready for some strife."

"It's how you teach them," Jessie insists. "If you explain and listen and get them to talk about their feelings, there is no reason for children to fight."

So the trip to Greece is off. Unlike Andria, who thinks her pregnancy will attract the pope and make it more likely she will get close to him and maybe even get an interview.

Plus she and Charles are going to Toronto, Canada, for a week in March and who do you think is going to keep the dogs?

"Why are you going to Canada in the winter?" I asked.

"To see the Shakespeare theater."

"They have a perfectly good one in Montgomery, Alabama, where your father lives," I suggested. "I don't approve of flying all over the world on airplanes when you are pregnant."

So our lives are going on. Shelly is back at her school. She has added Plato and Kant and Schopenhauer and Bertrand Russell to her history course as a slap in the face to the chancellor she dislikes. She has been giving interviews to newspapers in the area about how philosophy is the basis for Western civilization. Also, the professor from UNO she met at Andria's wedding has been up twice to visit her. They are planning a trip to China together in the summer.

"Remember my dream about the rooms full of treasure," Crystal said to me this morning. "Our life is opening up like that. Around Christmas I would have told you I thought life was getting smaller and smaller, shrinking like old people do, but I'm not all that old yet. It was just a slow time of the year, the dark old slow time Christmas is supposed to distract us from but never does."

"See, that's how getting old does you," I added. "When you're young you just have winter and then spring comes and so what. Long days in summer, short days in winter and the only thing that matters is romance, romance, romance. If we could get some romance back into our lives we might not pay so much attention to the ebb and flow of things."

"There's a sale at Victoria's Secret. Thirty percent off of already discounted items."

"Mark could use some cheering up. He thinks he's losing the power of his gonads."

"Let's go. This house is clean enough. Let's go see what we can find to wake up the men."

So we went out to the big mall by the airport and went into the Victoria's Secret and fitted ourselves with some bright red underwear that was not on sale and then I bought a pair of green lace panties and a brassiere and Crystal bought a pair of fluffy white panties that looked like a chicken but I didn't tell her that. After we finished our shopping we drove over to the day spa and got our hair done again. I think we have turned into Philistines. We were not doing all of this for our husbands.

It scared Mark to death when he saw that little set of panties and brassiere spread out on my side of the bed when he came in from work.

"What's going on here, Traceleen?" he demanded. "What does all this mean?"

Crystal got a similar reaction from Manny. She said first he was scared to death of the furry white panties, then he had a drink and rose to the occasion and the next day he bought her an emerald ring. Mark didn't buy me any jewelry but he did take down the little rickety fences I'd put up around my flower beds and replaced them with some that had posts. Unless those shelties die I suppose we are going to go on having them for guests now and then.

Crystal and I have made New Year's resolutions in February. We have pledged to live our lives to the fullest while we wait to be called back into action in the lives of the young. "After all," she said, "Doctor Finley was older than we are now when he left the dignitaries going into the hall and came and lay on the grass with us."

Shelly sent us a nice letter with some clippings of the interviews she's been giving and a quotation she said made her think of Crystal and of me.

"To be alive becomes the fundamental luck each ordinary, compromising day manages to bury."

We are taking that as a compliment and have upped our yoga sessions to four times a week from now until spring.

ABOUT THE AUTHOR

BORN IN MISSISSIPPI, Ellen Gilchrist is the author of sixteen previous books, including the short story collection *Victory Over Japan*, which won the National Book Award in 1985. She lives in Fayetteville, Arkansas, and Ocean Springs, Mississippi.

Also by Ellen Gilchrist

The Courts of Love

Stories

"Some of the most indelibly etched characters in contemporary fiction. . . . This is the first book I've read in years that I found myself consciously *not* wanting to finish, wanting it to last forever."

—Hart Williams, *Washington Post Book World*

Rhoda

A Life in Stories

"Rhoda's feisty, sexy, and devastatingly acute sensibilities make her one of the most engaging and surprisingly lovable characters in modern fiction."

—Robert Olen Butler

Victory Over Japan

Stories

"Gilchrist's writing is funny, wise, and wonderful. There are plenty of small, goofy victories for us to cheer at in this book. That's the good news for all of us who wish these stories could go on and on."

— *USA Today*

Available in paperback wherever books are sold

Also by Ellen Gilchrist

Collected Stories

"Every story is crisp, biting, and deceptively simple. . . . Ellen Gilchrist deserves to be celebrated among the first rank of American writers."
— Joan Mellen, *Baltimore Sun*

Flights of Angels

Stories

"Readers will find the penetrating intellect, deep compassion, and dark sense of humor that mark Gilchrist's best work and place it among the best writing coming out of the South—or anywhere else, for that matter—today."
—Ron Carter, *Richmond Times-Dispatch*

Sarah Conley

A Novel

"A joyous book. . . . Stunningly Gilchrist from start to finish with all the quirky philosophy, the wonderful romantic fantasies, and, best of all, a new and vibrant heroine who understands what it means to be mature."
— Mary A. McCay, *New Orleans Times-Picayune*

Available in paperback wherever books are sold

Look for Ellen Gilchrist's new collection of stories

I, Rhoda Manning, Go Hunting with My Daddy

Available in hardcover in August 2002

Little, Brown and Company